Planning for LOVE

ELLEN BUTLER
Author of *Heart of Design*

Crimson Romance
New York   London   Toronto   Sydney   New Delhi

CRIMSON
ROMANCE

Crimson Romance
An Imprint of Simon & Schuster, Inc.
1230 Avenue of the Americas
New York, NY 10020

ISBN 978-1-4405-8366-7
ISBN 978-1-4405-8367-4 (ebook)

To Mom, the ultimate planner.

Acknowledgments

Thanks to my husband; his support allows me to pursue my writing career. I'd also like to thank my girlfriends; they dredged their memories to provide me some hilarious "bad date" stories. A special thanks goes out to Becky, who inspired the Taco Bell date.

Many people ask how I research my stories. Luckily, in this day and age, there is nothing better than the Internet, where you can pretty much find the answer to any question. For online medical research, the Mayo Clinic website, WebMD were invaluable. Additionally, both my mother and mother-in-law shared their experiences with Mohs surgery providing me a more personal viewpoint of the procedure. Finally, thanks to the rest of my family for all their positive encouragement.

Chapter One

The incessant ring of the phone interrupted my brief commune with the now-lukewarm latte. My hand jerked, and the creamy mixture sloshed over the side, spilling onto my black pants. I knew today would be busy, but it wasn't yet nine and this was the fifth time the phone had interrupted me.

Damn. I pulled a tissue out of the box on my desk and wiped at the stain, hoping it wouldn't be visible when it dried, because I didn't have time for a trip back to the house to change. The phone continued its insistent ring as I shuffled a pile of papers aside in search of my headset. Obviously, this morning wasn't going as I'd originally planned. I located the little black earpiece buried under a pile of menus, hooked it on, and pressed the answer button on my desk phone.

"Go for Poppy," I answered while at the same time pulling up an email from tonight's restaurant manager.

"It's Cody."

"Where are you? Are you coming in to the office today, or going directly to the venue?" I typed a quick response to the restaurant manager's question while Cody spoke.

"I'm on my way into the office right now. I got an email this morning from the M.O.B. of the Moscowitz wedding, and they don't want the white, horse-drawn carriage. They're asking if it can be painted apricot to match the orchids in the bride's bouquet. She's even gone to the paint store and picked up swatches. I didn't want to respond until I got your thoughts on it."

"That woman is off her rocker. They can't afford that; they're going to have to mortgage their house by the time this wedding is done. I'm sorry you have to deal with her."

"No problem. It's nothing I can't handle, and she won't be the last. But what do you think I should do? Head this scheme off at the pass, or …?"

I sighed. "No. You have to at least ask the question. Call Sandra at Classic Carriages and see if they'll accommodate the request. Have her give you an estimate on the cost to paint the apricot and repaint the carriage back to white. Inflate it by twenty percent because it always costs more than anticipated, and then tell the M.O.B what the price would be for her latest notion. Make sure to cc the F.O.B. I have a feeling once Mr. Moscowitz sees the bottom line, he'll put an end to it, but if they're willing to pay, we'll make it happen."

The other line rang.

"I've got another call. Let's touch base at ten to make sure everything is set for the parties tonight."

"Ten it is."

I hung up on Cody, my second in command, and pressed the blinking light to my other line.

"Go for Poppy."

"Go for Poppy? What the hell is *that*? I think this town is getting to you. You sound like a snooty, high-powered agent or something." My best friend, Sophie Hartland, laughed at me through the phone lines.

I brought up another email, an invoice. "Hey, Soph. My phone's been ringing off the hook this morning. Cody and I both have Valentine's parties tonight, and everyone seems to be having meltdowns over inconsequential details. What's up?"

"I said yes,"

I forwarded the email to Rachel, my bookkeeper, approving the invoice and directing her to pay it. "Yes to what, doll? Did you score a new hotshot client?" I asked in a distracted voice.

"I said yes, to Ian."

My fingers froze over the keyboard, and I sucked in a breath. "Are you saying what I think you're saying?"

"Yes!" She let out a very un-Sophie-like squeal.

"Omigod, omigod!" I jumped out of my chair and let out a un-Poppy-like squeal. The headset ripped off my head and fell to the floor. I snatched the handset from the cradle. "You're going to be Mrs. Ian O'Connor."

"I know. Can you believe it?"

"It's about time. You've been torturing that poor man since Thanksgiving. I still don't understand what took you so long to say yes."

"C'mon, Poppy, I told you I didn't want to jump into another marriage and have it end up like the first. If Ian and I are getting married, I'm going in eyes open. I'm not a young, twenty-something any more. I'm thirty. I need to make decisions like a thirty-year-old."

Sophie was an interior designer. We met more than six years ago at a party I was running; she moved a few things around on a tablescape, added some of the hostess's collection of crystal balls, and an "eh" table setting turned into a "wowee." I hired her on the spot to design private, themed parties. But with her own design company taking off, she had less and less time to give to my party planning business.

"Sure, sure. So have you picked a date yet?"

Sophie's laughter floated through the lines. "We haven't gotten that far. I just got off the phone with Ian a few minutes ago. I'm driving over to a client's house as we speak. You're the first on my speed dial."

"Wait a minute, you said yes to Ian over the phone?"

"I told you he's been asking me at all sorts of odd times. So, if he's going to pop the question over the phone, that's how he'll get his answer. I promised to swing by the set during lunch."

"I hope you're planning something nice for dinner tonight."

"You bet I am. It'll be served in a red teddy with whipped cream and a cherry on top."

I hooted. "Ooh, la, la. Naughty, naughty."

"What about you and Rich? Any plans? Or are you working?"

"I'm running a Valentine's gig in Beverly Hills, but we're planning a late-night rendezvous. As a matter of fact, I'm heading over to his place around lunchtime to drop off some champagne and caviar."

"Nice."

"So, does he have a ring?" I asked.

"Knowing Ian's persistence for the past few months, I would say it's not out of the realm of possibility." Sophie let out another breezy laugh "I don't really know."

"Well, I'm going to have my hands full planning such a high-profile wedding."

"About that …"

"Don't tell me you're planning your own wedding, Sophia Hartland. That bird won't fly."

"No, I'm not planning it. But, neither are you."

It felt like a punch to the gut. I couldn't believe my best friend didn't want me to plan her wedding. I plopped down in my chair. "What?"

"Cody's planning it, because you're going to be in it. You're going to be my maid of honor."

My breath whooshed out. "Aw, Sophie. That's … that's …. I don't know what to say." My throat clenched, and I coughed to clear away the sentimentality.

"Say, yes, you goof."

"But what about your sister?"

"She got to be my maid of honor the first time around. She'll be a bridesmaid this time. She's a single mom now, and she won't have time to do all the maid of honor stuff. Besides, you earned the position. After all, it was you who introduced me to Ian,"

Ian played Ryder McKay on the cop show *L.A. Heat*. At one of my swanky birthday parties for a Hollywood director, Ian commented on the retro theme Sophie had designed, and I offered to introduce him. Not long after that, Ian hired Sophie to redesign his own home, top to bottom. He doggedly pursued her, and eventually she gave in to the steamy chemistry they shared. At Thanksgiving he popped the question, but she turned him down and instead offered a compromise. She moved into his place, and as Soph would say, "they'd been living in sin" ever since.

"So, are you in?" she asked.

"Of course."

"Good, that's settled. You can plan the engagement party."

"Just tell me when and where."

"I'll get back to you."

My cell phone rang.

"And that's my cue," Sophie said. "We'll talk later. You have a lip-smacking good night with Richard."

"Thanks. You, too, and congrats, girlfriend. That's the best news I've heard all day. You and Ian will make beautiful children."

"Hey, hey, one thing at a time." She hung up, laughing.

• • •

My pearl-gray Lexus SUV rolled to a stop in front of Rich's ultramodern two-story home. I keyed into the house, entering the chrome and white, vaulted foyer and met silence.

Hmm, Rich must have forgotten to set the burglar alarm this morning.

The red flats I wore quietly slapped against the black marble floors in the kitchen where I placed a Trader Joe bag on the quartz countertop. I opened the fridge and unloaded the sack. A bottle of champagne slid onto the bottom shelf, caviar and Brie above it, and lastly, strawberries and whipped cream on the top shelf. The stainless steel fridge closed with a whisper-soft click. As I folded the paper bag, my eyes lit on Richard's keys lying on the breakfast bar. I put the bag aside and picked up the keys. They dangled between my thumb and forefinger, and I stared at the Infiniti emblem on the ring.

He's here.

My eyes traveled to the ceiling. The keys dropped back onto the counter with a clink. Something—call it woman's intuition—kept me from hollering out his name. Instead, I noiselessly climbed the stairs and proceeded to the back of the house where Rich's mammoth master bedroom lay.

The door was shut, and as I approached, a feminine giggle met my ears. "Ooh, lookee here. That's a big weapon you're packin', cowboy."

"Well climb on up there, girl, 'cause it's cocked and ready to fire." Rich's smooth voice responded.

A breath hissed between my teeth. Muffled moans and titters intermingled with the bed's creaking. My hand rested on the doorknob, and I debated whether I should enter. Deciding I didn't need to torture myself by seeing what was going on behind that door, I turned on my heel and stalked down the hall. I sailed past the guest room, paused, and backed up to stare at the brand-new comforter and goose down pillows I'd purchased from Sophie last week to freshen up the space for an upcoming visit from Rich's brother. Fury flashed, and my feet moved of their own volition to the bed, where I yanked off the comforter and pillows. Gathering the fluffy mass into my arms, I tossed it over my shoulder, and stalked down the stairs.

Step, step. *How did this happen to me?* Step. Step. *No good, cheating sonofabitch!* Step, step, step. *If he thinks he'll get away with this, he's got another think coming.*

Unfortunately, midway through the internal tirade, the little Jiminy Cricket sitting on my shoulder reminded me this wasn't the first time I'd been cheated on, and I paused at the last two steps. I had a habit of collecting "bad boys" with commitment issues. The last fool who'd cheated on me found himself locked out of our hotel room in Hawaii, all his crap in a plastic dry cleaning bag sitting by the door at four in the morning. I shook my head to erase the memory. Right now wasn't the time to think about the past. Not when confronted with the present treachery.

I threw the mess of bedding by the front door and stared down at it. Contrary to what people might think, my anger didn't match my fiery red hair. Instead of flashing, screaming rage, I tended to bank my ire into cold, tundra-like fury. Moreover, when it came to cheating bastards, I refused to turn into a lump of crying mess … well, not until after extracting a bit of payback. My brain ticked away, forming and subsequently discarding revenge schemes until I realized one was staring me in the face; something I remembered from a movie. I scooped up the goose down pillows and tiptoed to the kitchen, although considering the howls and yehaws I'd heard coming from the bedroom, there was little need for stealth.

Fifteen minutes later, the comforter, champagne, and other assorted odds and ends I'd brought to the house were keeping company in the front seat of my car. The trap was set. Plastic wrap attached with Scotch Tape to two steel pillars zigzagged across the kitchen entryway. It dripped with honey and two kinds of syrup, the cheap, sticky kind from the grocery store that came in a plastic bottle shaped like a cabin. Richard, the bastard, loved that stuff. I'd slashed open the two pillows and denuded them of their feathers. Their white fluffiness created a small mountain on a side table I'd pulled up just for the occasion. A big box fan that Rich normally kept in the garage sat behind the pile of feathers.

I lit a rolled piece of paper, climbed atop the counter, and waved it below the fire alarm. It took about thirty seconds before the screeching pierced the relative quiet. I dropped the burning paper into the stainless steel sink—after all, I didn't want to burn the man's house down—and placed myself next to the fan.

I wonder if he'll put on a pair of pants. It didn't take long to answer my question.

My slimy, cheating *ex*-boyfriend, buck naked and still sporting a woody at half-mast, stumbled into the coated plastic wrap, which detached from its tenuous Scotch-Taped hold and wrapped around him. He pulled the plastic off and his eyes lit on me in shock and confusion.

"Poppy?" He called over the shrill alarm. "What the hell?"

I squinted and allowed a wicked smile to cross my features. With a gentle flick, the fan turned to high. It succeeded much better than expected. A big clump of feathers moved, en masse, to land on his sticky torso and nether regions. The rest of the feathers blew in a willy-nilly whirlwind and attached to his face, shoulders, and legs.

"Damn it!" he shouted, spitting feathers out of his mouth.

I couldn't help myself; I held up my cell and snapped a photo. The ringing of the house phone added to the cacophony of noise.

I shot past him and tore up the stairs, knowing I had a very short window of opportunity to get my things and make a clean getaway. A naked bimbo with enormous, cartoon-like breasts screeched and pulled the sheet up to her neck. She couldn't have been more than twenty-one, if that. I ignored her and went directly to the bathroom, searching for my favorite silver drop earrings. Luckily, they sat on the shelf where I'd left them two days ago. A few pieces of my clothing rested, neatly folded, in a drawer in the big walk-in closet. I dumped the trash out of the wastebasket, stuffed everything into it, and zipped out, ignoring the screeching blonde on my way.

Back at the kitchen, Rich plucked at feathers surrounding his nose and mouth while yelling at the security company over the noise into the phone. He sneezed, and a giggle bubbled up my throat. I had already retrieved my own house key from his key ring, but I took a moment to remove his from mine and chuck it onto the marble floor by his feet. We both watched as it slid past him underneath the refrigerator. Using my middle finger, I blew him a kiss, flipped my red curls over my shoulder, flung open the front door, and strutted triumphantly to the car.

The smile of satisfaction remained glued to my face well into the evening as I went about my duties, making sure the Valentine's Day party flowed successfully into the night. I ignored the repeated calls from Rich and laughed every time his feathered photo popped up on my phone when he called.

It wasn't until driving home at 2:00 a.m. in my silent car that the pain of betrayal caught up. Visions of happy Valentine's couples dancing and kissing ran through my head, and my sweet revenge on scum-sucking Richard left a hollowness in my gut. Earlier in the day, I had desperately wanted to call Sophie to crow about the successful retribution; now I wanted to cry on her shoulder as it hit me that my status, once again, had returned to singlehood. I held off contacting her, because I didn't want to rain on her engagement parade with the sordid tale of Rich's cheating.

Unchecked tears slid down my cheeks as I keyed into the house. My head whirled with painful "what if" emotions, and I knew I had to talk to someone. Sophie was out, and it would be too late to call Cody or anyone else for that matter, so I fired up my laptop.

To: Adam from Hawaii
From: Poppy Reagan
Subject: Cheating Bastards

Adam,

I know it's been awhile since we've communicated. I'm sorry. It's been a bad day. Remember that guy I'd been dating, hereinafter to be referred to as Detestable Richard? I found Detestable Richard in bed today with a young blonde with huge boobs. Don't worry, I took my revenge; see attached photo.

Perhaps you're not the right person to be telling this to, but I'm at a low point. It's the middle of the night, all my girlfriends are asleep or having wild gorilla sex, and it's just hit me that the man I've been sleeping with cheated on me on Valentine's Day. Valentine's Day, for crying out loud! Who *does* that? What is wrong with men? How do I attract bastards like Detestable Richard? You're a man—are all men pre-programmed to cheat? Or is it just to cheat on me?

A plastic surgeon passed me his card tonight. Maybe I should go in for a consult to enhance my bust. Perhaps cantaloupes for breasts keep the cheaters away. You're a man, you've seen the goods, tell me the truth. I know I'm skinny. Do I need to get a boob job?

Okay, enough blathering and feeling sorry for myself. How's it going with the schoolteacher? Still all flowers and candy? Did you do something romantic for V-day? The way to a woman's heart is to listen and always compliment her, and don't friggin' cheat! Don't forget, Adam. Don't be a cheater! It's bad! Very, very bad! Now I'm going to drown my sorrows in a bottle of Scotch.

Thanks for listening to me whine.

Your loser friend,

Poppy

• • •

Adam had five minutes before his first patient, which gave him just enough time to check his private email account and maybe clear out some of the spam. He logged in and scanned the subject lines. Delete. Delete. Delete. His mouse paused at an email from a woman. No, not just any woman, a magnificent woman with a smile that could light up Broadway, pearlescent skin that glowed in the moonlight, and the most glorious red hair he'd ever wrapped his hands around.

He'd happily played her rebound guy, and his vacation in Hawaii had turned into an unforgettable, passionate, fun-loving week. Afterward, he reluctantly returned to his life in Ohio. However, to his pleasure, Poppy started a fiery electronic flirtation. The attraction he'd felt during their trip in Hawaii was still in full gear, and he encouraged her to come out for a visit. But to his regret, only a few weeks after their tryst, Poppy began dating a new guy, a schmucky casting something-or-other. As her relationship with this guy grew more serious, Adam backed off and eventually turned his sights elsewhere. Their sexy flirtation tapered off and turned friendly.

With mixed emotions, he opened the email and skimmed its contents. He immediately saw through the sarcasm and humor and could tell she was hurting more than she admitted. His gut clenched at this asshole's perfidy. Honestly, he had no idea what a good thing he had going with Poppy. From her initial emails, Adam had feared that Detestable Richard was a shady character. Maybe it was his prejudice against the Hollywood scene, or perhaps it was the fact her best friend warned her about this guy and she'd ignored it. Ultimately, Rich's cheating didn't come as a shock to Adam.

Oh, good Lord! Implants? What was she thinking? Implants would seriously mar her stunning, athletic figure. Her breasts, though small, fit her body to perfection, and they were so incredibly sensitive, he remembered with a smile. Implants could ruin those lovely, rosy nipples. *I have to tell her to put a stop to that crackbrained idea.*

His curiosity piqued, Adam clicked on the picture icon attached to the email. Patients in the neighboring exam rooms probably heard his uproarious laugh, and he tried to tone it down a notch. The photo showed a guy who looked like a half-plucked chicken-man, and he was *pissed. Damn, that woman is creative. I hope to never get on her bad side.*

The phone at his elbow rang. "Good morning, Georgia."

"Morning to you, too, Dr. Patterson. Something funny?"

"Just a joke a friend sent to me."

"Your first appointment has arrived."

"Thank you. Have the nurse take him back and check the vitals. I'll be with him in a minute."

Adam typed a quick email back to Poppy. He hoped it would cheer her up. As he signed out of his Yahoo account, his mind began turning over ideas. Could he get Poppy back into his life on a more permanent basis and not be seen as the "rebound guy" this time around?

Adam pushed back against his chair and stretched his arms over head. It had been almost a month since he and Sarah had broken up. Sarah had given him an ultimatum to get engaged because her biological clock was ticking. He wanted to continue dating a few more months to expand their relationship and revisit the conversation at a later date. They fought, and Sarah refused to wait. A week after she dumped him, Adam heard she was dating a tax accountant.

Ouch, that hurt.

Now things might be looking up.

As Adam walked down the hall to his first patient, his mind worked on a plan to get his California honey on a plane out to Ohio to reignite their fiery flirtation.

Chapter Two

"Oh, Poppy. I am *so* sorry, hon." Sophie's sympathetic, but laughing voice said over the phone lines the next day.

"Well, *c'est la vie*." I flicked my hand airily as I sat at the red light, pretending the infidelity didn't hurt as much as it did.

"You give new meaning to the phrase tar and feather. Remind me to never get on your bad side. Detestable Richard is a big turd."

"Yes, he is. If I'm honest with myself, you and Ian did warn me."

"Yeah, but ... we thought he'd changed. Ian told me Rich had never dated a woman this long, and he seemed really into you. It's been what? Three months?"

"Almost four. And as we both know, a zebra doesn't change his stripes."

"What the hell was he thinking?" She sniffed angrily. "You're gorgeous, smart, successful ... What kind of man cheats on a woman like that?"

"Apparently, a number of men," I muttered as traffic rolled forward.

Sophie sucked in a breath. "Angel doesn't count."

"Angel wasn't the only one. Did I tell you the bimbo was barely twenty, with no wrinkles, and huge boobs?"

"Poppy! Your beauty is far more striking than that of some unformed twenty-year-old. It's disgusting, really. And huge boobs are waaay overrated."

"Thanks, girlfriend. You're a real balm to my battered ego."

"Listen, Ian's having some guys over on Sunday to watch the Lakers game. Why don't you come, too, and I'll invite my sister?

It'll help balance out the testosterone. You're not working, are you?"

"No, we don't have any events for Sunday." I paused. "You're not trying to set me up already?"

"*Hell no.* One of the guys is gay, one is married, and the other is in a relationship. Let's be girly. We'll retreat to the bedroom and give each other manicures, read trashy magazines, and watch *Say Yes to the Dress.*"

"Okay. You're on. What time?" I turned right onto Burbank Boulevard and coasted to a stop behind traffic.

"Everyone's coming over around two."

"Okay. Do you ..." I paused, hesitant to voice what nagged at me.

"Do I what, Poppy?"

"What is wrong with me, Soph? Do you think I attract cheaters? Is there a sign across my forehead, saying 'it's okay to cheat on me'?"

Sophie sucked wind and didn't respond immediately.

"Sophie?"

"Well ... do you want the truth?"

"No, lie to me." I snorted. "Of course, I want the truth. Give it to me straight." I pushed back against the seat, bracing myself.

"Okay, here's the thing. There are lots of men who would fall all over themselves to date you and treat you like a queen. You know, normal guys, with normal jobs. But for some reason you seem to choose to date the bad boys. The ones with a reputation, or fuckwits, as Ian would say, with commitment issues. It's not just the guys, Poppy. It's the choices you make. I've seen you date a good guy—you know, a really nice guy who would worship at your feet. Remember Tim? But after one or two dates, you dropped him and moved on to the exciting but emotionally unavailable."

I scanned through my "relationships" over the years, flicking through faces from past failures like flipping through an old-fashioned Rolodex.

"Poppy? Are you still there?"

"Yes."

"I'm sorry, I shouldn't have said anything. Crap. Ignore what I said. What the hell do I know? My first husband cheated on me with his assistant." She sighed. "So unoriginal."

She was right. On the other hand, Sophie had learned from her mistake. She'd taken it slow, and even though her sexual instincts told her to jump in bed with Ian from the start, she put on the brakes and waited. They developed a friendship as a result. Ian stopped seeing her as his next conquest and subsequently fell utterly in love with her. He'd gnaw off his right toe before he'd cheat on her.

"No … I think you may have a point. You've said out loud something that's been nagging at me."

"No, no, forget what I said. It was out of line. I'm sorry. Are you mad at me? Will you still come on Sunday?"

"No, I'm not mad. I'll see you at two on Sunday."

"Hooray! Later, girl." She hung up.

I pulled into the parking lot of my office on Burbank Boulevard in North Hollywood and stared at the frosted storefront window. Tasteful lavender and green lettering etched across the glass: Poppy's Party Planning—Weddings, Parties, Special Events. The engine silenced, but I didn't get out of the car. Instead, my fingers reached for my phone and I scrolled through the last four months of photos. Rich in the parking lot of a concert. Rich and me in formal wear for New Year's Eve. Rich and me with our heads smashed together doing duck lips. Rich doing a tequila shot. My thumbs deleted each photo that popped up. Within ten minutes, all images from our relationship, except for the "chicken suit," were erased.

I halted at the image of another man. A man I met a few weeks before Rich. A man I sent a crazy, blubbering, email to last night.

I stared at the utter joy reflected in my face. My smile was so wide it created crow's feet and scrunched my nose, and even on the tiny cell phone image you could see the sparkle in my green eyes. Doctor Adam Patterson stood next to me, his arm looped across my shoulder, wearing a pair of Groucho Marx glasses with nose and mustache attached. He was a few inches taller than me, his wet, sandy brown hair stood on end, and his lithe swimmer's body looked yummy in the red board shorts he wore. The loony grin he sported actually made my heart jump, and I put a hand to my chest.

We met during the second half of my Hawaiian vacation, after I kicked Angel—the loser who slept with the surf instructor—out of the hotel room. Adam plunked down on the empty pool lounger next to me, fed me a cheesy line about how my milky white skin would make the moon weep—or some such nonsense—and bought me a drink. We spent six idyllic days splashing in the ocean, snorkeling, playing water volleyball at the resort, and drinking mai tais. On the second evening, I invited him to my room for cocktails. It was an unforgettably sweet, yet sizzling, night of sex. The magical night left my inner spirit singing with pleasure and was a boon to my sagging, cheated-on confidence. The sex only got better the rest of the week as we explored each other's bodies. The last day of the trip we spent almost all day in bed, only leaving the room, sore but sated, around four in the afternoon.

Then … the vacation fling was over. Adam flew home to Ohio where he was a practicing dermatologist, and I returned to California. We exchanged phone numbers and emails, and friended each other on Facebook. At first, we sent dirty texts to each other, laughing at who could make up the craziest places to do the nasty. Then the emails started. We shared history. He told me about breaking the news to a twenty-five-year-old patient that her melanoma had returned. I revealed more to him about my erratic childhood than I had to anyone else. Even Sophie didn't know the full story about my unstable youth.

Our communication morphed from rebound beach fling into friendship. Every so often it crossed my mind that things might be different if Adam and I didn't live two time zones apart.

I tapped the email icon on my phone.

To: Poppy Reagan
From: Adam from Hawaii
Subject: Your Breasts Are Perfect

Dear Poppy,

    I only have a moment, so I'll be succinct. Detestable Richard is an asshat. DO NOT get breast implants. As a doctor, I can confirm your slim body and flawless skin is perfect! Don't mess with it. We'll talk more later.

    Adam, Admirer of Your Breasts

Smirking, I tapped my fingers against the steering wheel. My heart and mindset perked up; Adam could always raise my spirits.

To: Adam from Hawaii
From: Poppy Reagan
Subject: Admirer of Breasts

Adam, Thanks. You made my day.

I spent the rest of the week analyzing the dating choices I'd made in my life. A psychiatrist would have a field day with my dysfunctional background and immediately point to my flawed upbringing. Mom never married my own father, and truth be told, never knew much about him. The sordid tale of my conception included a rock and roll band, a party where drugs flowed freely, various sexual partners, etc. She told me it was the drummer. However, when I was twenty-five, after six months of private detective services, an inconclusive DNA test, and almost ten grand, I came to the conclusion my biological father was likely some unnamed groupie. I gave up on the daddy hunt and resolved myself to the fact I would never know.

Mom and I spoke a few times a month. I moved out of the house during husband number three, an auto mechanic and inveterate gambler with a penchant for the ponies. He had two monstrous boys who visited once a month. There were no half-siblings, but stepsiblings littered the country. Most of them had passed in and out of my life so quickly I couldn't even remember all their names.

Were my relationship issues really abandonment issues? Did I purposely choose men who would let me down? If I were honest with myself, every one of them had hurt me with their betrayals, but I wasn't utterly devastated by any of them. Even Rich, whose cheating cut the deepest by far, damaged my ego more than my heart.

Was I the one afraid of a true commitment from a good man? Did I have the capacity to give my heart to another?

By the time Sunday arrived, I'd moved past self-analysis and decided in order to fix this bad habit of mine, I had to play to my strengths. Finding the right man would take planning. Therefore, I devised a plan, and with Sophie's help, I'd set it in motion.

• • •

Waving at the little security camera, I followed a white convertible up Ian's drive and parked behind it. I recognized the short, dark-haired man who stepped out of the car as one of the hair stylists from Ian's show.

"Hello, Julio," I called.

He turned and waited for me to catch up. "Well, hello, gorgeous."

I leaned down so Julio and I could give each other the requisite air kiss.

He fingered my hair as we stood back. "Tsk, such fabulous color, but these split ends. My dear, you must let me cut it."

I shook my head. "Julio, I've heard what you charge for a style. I'm a working girl; I simply can't afford you." In truth, Julio had been trying to talk me into cutting my hair to chin length, and I feared he would do exactly that if I allowed his scissors anywhere near my head.

"I'll give you twenty percent off. Just so I can get ahold of those tresses."

I laughed. "I can't even imagine what my Donna would say. She'd think I'd cheated on her, and I'd never hear the end of it. No, I'm sorry, Julio. My answer is the same as last time."

"Well, you can't blame me for trying." He rang the bell.

The door popped open, and my curvy, chestnut-haired best friend stood on the other side wearing jeans, flip-flops, and a purple, long-sleeved T-shirt. I knew Sophie envied my willowy, size-four frame and felt self-conscious about her pin-up girl curves. She never believed me when I bemoaned my lack of feminine curves. I suppose the grass is always greener …

"Yes! Reinforcements." She grabbed my hand and hauled me through the door, giving me a bear hug. "Holly couldn't make it."

"What am I? Chopped liver?" Julio whined.

"Hello, Julio." Sophie hooked a thumb over her shoulder. "The boys are out back standing around the grill, scratching themselves, and talking nerd about Superman versus Batman." She rolled her eyes.

"And what are you two planning?" He walked into the foyer.

Sophie closed the door behind him. "We're doing estrogen things."

"Discussing my dating life," I added.

"No men," she added. "Even ones of your persuasion."

Julio tilted his head and put a hand to hip. "Very well, if that's the case, I'll take you up on the wine and go play with the boys. Besides, the game starts in half an hour, and I don't want to miss out on the betting. Last time we got together, I won 500 clams off those suckers." He gave an unrepentant grin.

We followed Sophie into the large, modern kitchen, where she poured each of us a glass of Malbec. I sat down at the breakfast bar. After thanking Sophie, Julio slipped out the sliding glass door to join the rest of the men. The pregame show quietly droned on the TV in the background.

Sophie raised her wine, and as she brought the glass to her mouth I noticed a flash of sparkle.

"Hold up. Is that a ring I see?" I snapped my fingers and held my palm out.

Sophie's grin spread from ear to ear as she placed her left hand in mine. I estimated the princess cut, pink diamond at two to three carats; it was surrounded by white diamonds and set in platinum. "It's stunning. Simply stunning." I looked up at her shining blue eyes. "Did you two pick it out, or did he already have it?"

"He had it. He said he'd been sitting on it since Christmas. It came in a little blue Tiffany's box." My normally staid friend danced gleefully in a circle, snapping her fingers like castanets.

"He has exquisite taste."

"Yes, he does." Sophie agreed. "So what do you want to do first? Manis and pedis? Are you hungry? Do you want to eat?"

The back door slid open, and I turned on my stool. Ian stepped into the room.

"Luv, we're ready for the kebabs."

His accent pronounced it key-baabs. My girlfriend's eyes shined love, and a little bit of lust, at her gorgeous, six-foot, dark-haired, blue-eyed fiancé.

"Coming right up," she answered, and turned to pull a platter of shrimp and vegetable kebabs out of the fridge.

"Hello, Poppy."

"Hi, Ian." I gave a finger wave. "Nice ring. You did good."

Ian blushed, and his beautiful white teeth flashed. "I heard about Richard. Would you like me to kick the wanker's arse?"

I gave a wan smile and shook my head. "No, thank you. I've already gotten my revenge."

His eyebrows rose in confusion. "You didn't tell him?" I asked.

She shrugged. "I didn't know if it was confidential."

"Not at all." I replied. By this time, Ian had crossed the room and stood at the end of the counter while Sophie put the finishing touches on the seafood. I thumbed through my iPhone's icons, stopping at the tarred and feathered Richard, and slid it down the counter to Ian.

He scooped it up and took a gander. "It's bloody brilliant, and nothing less than he deserves." Ian's lovely Irish accent rolled out with his mirth. "I've got to show the fellows." Ian loped across the great room with my phone in hand, and out the back door. "Mates, you've got to see this." The back door slid closed.

I turned and met Sophie's gaze. We stared wide-eyed for a moment, then muffled baritone-deep laughter filtered through the closed door. I broke first with a hissing snicker, and Sophie joined me with her own merry giggles.

"I'll take this out and retrieve your phone. You'd better stay here, or they'll hammer you with questions, and I don't want them interfering with our girl time."

I sipped the earthy wine and watched Sophie's thick ponytail bob as she carried the platter out back. When she returned, we put together a tray with the wine, some veggies with dip, a sack of chips, and two frozen Snickers bars. I followed Sophie upstairs into the enormous, Tuscan-inspired bedroom she'd decorated and now shared with Ian. She placed the tray in the center of the coffee table.

"Have a seat. I'll go get the nail polish."

I snatched a chip and plopped down on the comfy, cream love seat, while Sophie disappeared into the master bath.

"Where's Sirius?" I asked.

"He's out back with the boys." Sophie's voice echoed out of the bathroom. "That dog's no dummy. Whenever Ian grills, Sirius plunks his butt right at his feet and waits for a snack to drop. Which invariably happens. I haven't figured out if Ian does it on purpose, or if he's just a messy griller." She came out carrying a caddy full of polish, files, and clippers, placed it next to the tray, and dunked a carrot into the dip before sitting next to me on the couch. "Okay, dish. Tell me all about dickhead. Did he break your heart? Do you need a shoulder to cry on? You don't have to keep your strong face on in front of me. *Wait.*" She crunched into the carrot, popped up again, and strode across the room to grab a tissue box off the bedside table. Returning, she placed it on the couch between us, and sat on one leg facing me, her eyes wide and sympathetic. "Okay. Go."

I sighed. "Okay, yes, what Richard did hurt me. And, yes, I think he's an utter jackass for shitting on me. But over the past few days, I've had time to reflect, and I thought about what you said ... my other relationships, my mom and her love life ..."

"Uh, oh."

"I've come to a few conclusions." I took up a celery stick and brandished it. "First, you were right. I do choose guys who aren't right for me. I mean, look at Angel." I rolled my eyes, and crunched down. "What was I thinking?"

"Um ..." Sophie's eyes grew wide.

"Don't answer that."

"Well he was kinda cute, in that bad boy biker kind of way."

"But, then there was Matt, the musician, Nolan, the frat boy, Naveen, the painter who was eight years younger. The list goes on."

Sophie nodded her head.

"I mean, I'm going to be thirty-four in a few months. What the hell am I doing with my life? I don't think I've ever truly given my heart to a guy. Am I even capable of loving?"

"Of course you are." Sophie plunked her wine glass down with a jarring clink. "C'mon, Poppy. Don't be so hard on yourself. You're a warm-hearted person."

"I don't know …"

"Don't be silly. *I know it* by the way you treat your friends. Good heavens, when I think about how you helped me out when I was at my lowest point after Michael." She shook her head. "What you've been doing with your life is building a successful company. You've been pouring your heart and soul into those brides and all the parties you plan. Romantic relationships have been secondary to your work. But I'm sure once the right guy comes along, it'll hit you. Smack." She smacked my forehead with the heel of her hand. "You'll get that punch to the gut and know he's the one, and work won't be your first consideration anymore."

I didn't want to tell Sophie that after all my self-analysis, I was afraid that gut-clenching lightning bolt may have come and gone. Sophie knew about my Hawaiian fling, but not about our communication afterward or the way I was strangely drawn to Adam, even while I dated Detestable Richard. I wondered if he felt the same way but dismissed the thought immediately. It didn't matter; he lived 2,000 miles away, and the last I'd heard, was dating a schoolteacher. I'd never seen her, but I imagined a petite brunette with a heart-shaped face. Also, our sexual relationship had morphed into a friendship, and I was hesitant to reintroduce the sex back into it.

"Right." I patted her hand. "However, I'm not in my twenties anymore. This body and face won't look like this forever. I'm getting more wrinkles by the day."

"No you're not." Sophie sat back. "You have perfect skin, and you're going to look fantastic ten, twenty years from now. It's in your genes. Look at your mom. She's still beautiful, and she's what? Fifty? Sixty?"

She was fifty-nine and was indeed still beautiful, but I didn't want to go down similar roads as my mother who, Lord love her, was currently living in Kenya with husband number four, a tea exporter. I swished my hand, like flicking away an annoying gnat. "I'm not my mother, and I'm not getting any younger. Now is the time to get serious about my love life, and I've decided on a plan."

"Uh-oh. Poppy's got a plan."

"That's right. Planning is my forte."

"Are we talking accountant? Lawyer? Actor? Will there be stalking involved?"

"No actors!" I snorted. "Sorry, Sophie. Ian's awesome, but he's a one of a kind, and I couldn't put up with the tabloid crap that follows them around."

Sophie cringed. She'd had a few run-ins with the paparazzi, and she wasn't a fan.

"Besides, I work on so many parties for those in the movie and television industry, I don't want to come home to it."

"You're right about the press." She bit into a chip. "Does this mean we're done with 2:00 a.m. drive-bys of your latest Hollywood infatuation?"

My face burned, and my eyes darted away from hers. There had been a few times when I'd found out where the latest crush lived, and we'd driven by his home at odd hours, changing to a coffee shop where he'd been spotted in hopes of catching a glimpse. "Yes. My stalking days are over. Besides, I haven't stalked anyone in

28

over nine months. After the scary middle-of-the-night, flat-tire incident I kind of gave up on them." I shrugged.

"Good, I'm glad to hear it." She patted my hand. "So what's your plan?"

"Starting today, with your help, I'll be joining Match.com, and I'm going to go on as many dates as I can fit into my schedule. Second, I'm going to ask one of my awesome girlfriends to invite a bunch of single guys to the next party she throws." I tilted my head and gave Sophie the puppy dog eyes.

"Sure, as long as you plan the catering, I'm on board. How many singles exactly need inviting?"

"As many as you can get. And ask married people to bring a single guy with them."

"And what type of mate do you have your sights set on?"

"First and foremost, he has to be a professional, have a mortgage, be at least my height, and reasonably close in age."

"How close?"

"No younger than thirty, no older than forty."

"Okay, that's a ten-year span. I can work with that. Can they be divorced?"

"Yes, but no kids."

"Hmm."

"I know, I know. Humor me. There's got to be divorced guys out there without kids. Right? You were divorced with no kids."

"Yes, but I'm not sure I'm the norm. When do you want this party?"

"I don't know. I figured we'd start with the Match.com project first."

"Hmm. I have an idea. Ian wanted me to talk to you about putting together a party to celebrate the engagement. I'll be sure to invite lots of unattached males for you to shop."

"Won't they mostly be Ian's industry friends?"

"Some. But I know people, too, and not all of Ian's friends are work friends."

"I don't know. Won't Ian want to invite Rich? After all, they were roommates back in New York."

She frowned and her eyebrows crunched up. "Over my dead body. That man will *not* be welcome in this house as long as I'm living in it. Trust me. Ian merely tolerated Rich in deference to our friendship. His Irish Catholic gene runs deep, and he frowns on cheaters. He wasn't kidding when he asked if you wanted him to go kick Rich's ass." Sophie's eyes shone as she talked about Ian.

"Okay, we'll use your engagement party. When do you want to host it?"

"I'm not sure. I'll talk with Ian and send you a couple of dates."

"That'll be fine."

"Now, we have so much to do. I'll get my laptop so we can get you signed up and get your love life rolling."

Chapter Three

Sophie sat on the bed across from me, reading glasses on and her laptop open to the Match.com website. Her fingers flew across the keyboard as she entered in answers.

"Drinker?"

"Yes, of course."

"Moderate, social, regular?"

"Oh, Lord. Do they really ask that? Let's say social. If you answer moderate or regular everyone will think I'm a lush."

Sophie nodded and continued to type information while mumbling under her breath. "Non-smoker, single, no kids. What type of degree do you hold?"

"Bachelor's in hotel and restaurant management."

Click, click went the keyboard. "Okay, we've entered everything. Now we need a photo. What have you got?" She looked up from the screen.

I grimaced. There were dozens of candid shots in my phone. Many of them goofy selfies taken at arms length with my head smashed against someone else's. Then there were my professional photos I'd had taken for my brochures and website, but I worried they would look too stiff and formal.

"We can always crop a headshot out of a photo. Why don't you give me your phone, and you can scroll through mine. I'm sure I've got some shots of you." She leaned over to the bedside table and tossed her iPhone next to my knee.

A blend of male voices shouting at the television drifted through the open door. Ian and company must have come inside to watch the game. I climbed off the bed, closed the bedroom door, and retrieved my phone from the coffee table, tossing it next to Sophie's. She scooped it up and thumbed through the apps. I took hers and opened the photo gallery. My eggplant nail polish flashed as I organized the pictures into a grid pattern. There were photos of Ian, her friends and family, before and after shots of clients' homes, and photos of various decorating items. Most of the photos of me were in groups or included at least one other person. There were a few with Rich, which I bypassed immediately. I'd leave them to Sophie to delete.

"This is it." Sophie broke the silence.

"Which one?"

She turned the phone to show a shot of me wearing a blue bikini with a white gauzy cover-up. I wore a dazzling smile, and my head was slightly tilted toward Adam, who took up the other half of the photo; he wore green swim trunks, his arm was slung over my shoulder, and he held up a beer.

"You must be out of your mind. I'm not putting a bikini shot online."

"No, no. We're going to crop it to just the head." She pushed the laptop off her legs and crawled around to sit next to me. "Look, your red hair is flowing over your shoulder, your smile is perfect, and your eyes are practically sparkling off the shot. It must have been all that ocean air." She elbowed me and wiggled her eyebrows. "Or maybe it was the sex. That dentist sure is a cutie. It's too bad he lives out … where did you say he was from?"

"Dermatologist, from Ohio," I responded in a distracted tone. Sophie was right. I looked good—healthy and happy.

"That's right. Here," she took the phone out of my hand and began tapping on it. "I'll email the photo to my laptop so I can crop it and see how it looks."

Her computer dinged as she handed the phone back to me. She brought up her email and clicked to expand the shot fully onto the page. Sophie whistled a catcall.

"Wow, it looks even better full size. Are you sure you don't want any of your swimsuit in the shot? Guys'll be lining up around the block to get a date."

"No bikini. Just see what you can do with the head."

Sophie monkeyed around with the photo program, cropping the shot in a few different ways. We settled on a headshot that came down just above the bust line, and she uploaded it to the profile.

"Now we get to put in your preferences on guys. I guess this helps to filter the candidates. Okay, age preferences we already know. Do you have a height range?"

"How about five eight to six two?"

"Okey doke."

We spent the next few minutes inputting my preferences regarding religion, schooling, kids, smoking, drinking … the list went on and on. I had no idea there were so many filters. I had Sophie mark kids and smoking as deal breakers. I don't care how many Altoids a guy sucked down to cover it up, kissing a smoker was like kissing an ashtray. Near the end, the form asked for a little paragraph telling prospective dates about myself.

"Here, I'll let you write this up." Sophie pushed her reading glasses atop her head and passed the computer over to me.

I drummed my fingers on the bedspread for a few minutes before inspiration hit.

My professional life keeps me busy, but in my downtime I enjoy boating, yoga, and beach volleyball. Evening activities include getting together with friends to enjoy good food and wine or seeing outdoor concerts. I don't like the three S's—snakes, spiders, and scorpions. A fellow who dates me will be expected to dispose of, in whatever fashion he deems appropriate, any of the creatures listed above that happen to invade my personal space.

When I finished I passed the computer back to Sophie.

She pulled the glasses back down to her nose and read the passage. "I didn't know you enjoyed boating."

I shrugged. "What's not to love? Breeze blowing, water spraying as the boat cuts through the waves. I thought it might bring a different clientele."

She chewed her lip. "Not a bad plan. I like the part about the spiders and stuff." Her shoulders shuddered, and she made a disgusted noise in the back of her throat. "I found what I swear was a black widow in the bathroom last week. Although Ian says it wasn't. I don't care what it was—I didn't stick around to classify it; I ran out screaming like a banshee. Ian thought there was a burglar in the house. A good man will kill a spider for you even if it's not poisonous," she said seriously.

I nodded, mashing my lips together in an effort not to laugh, but a snicker snuck out.

"It wasn't funny." Sophie glared.

"You're right." I wiped the smirk off my face. "There is nothing funny about spiders."

She sniffed and gave a small half-grin. "Okay, it was kind of funny, because I'd just gotten out of the shower and the towel fell off. So, I was racing around the house naked and dripping wet, screaming at the top of my lungs, with Sirius barking and chasing me. Ian laughed his ass off once he understood what I was freaking out about."

I couldn't hold in my snort anymore. Sophie shoved me, and I flopped to my side, giggling at her antics.

After we finished the questionnaire, Sophie and I reviewed some of the possible candidates.

"No, yes, no, no, maybe, yes, yes, no." I checked off the boxes.

"Hey wait a minute." Sophie pointed at one of the candidates. "What's wrong with him?"

"No baldies."

"He's not a baldy; he obviously shaves his head. He looks kind of hot."

"Shaved head usually means the hair is on the way out."

"So, what? It just means he's accepted his lot in life and is embracing it. Look, he's got a nice-shaped head. What does his profile say?"

"Oh, all right. I'll leave baldy in. Okay?" I clicked a check into the box.

After ten more minutes of debate we logged out.

"What about eHarmony? I think you should spread out and get on more than one site."

I sighed. "Really. You think?"

"Absolutely." Sophie grabbed the laptop and began clicking away.

I got off the bed, retrieved one of the Snickers bars, tore open the package with my teeth, and took a big gulp of wine before biting into the chocolaty goodness.

"Oh, look, they're running a special: free communication for the next five days."

"It must be kismet." I sighed. I was still having trouble grasping the fact that my dating life had been reduced to Internet sites. "Let's get started."

Forty-five minutes later, I had profiles set up at Match.com and eHarmony. Sophie closed the laptop with a triumphant flourish, tossed her glasses on the bed, and scooped up her wineglass from the tray.

"Now can we paint our nails and watch *Say Yes to the Dress?*" She swallowed the last bit of wine.

"*Absolutely*. Let's talk wedding, my soon-to-be-married friend." I leaned in to give her shoulders a squeeze.

"Maybe your Mr. Right is finding your profile online as we speak." She grinned.

I didn't want to burst her bubble of excitement, even though I had my doubts. "Maybe so."

• • •

To: Adam from Hawaii
From: Poppy Reagan
Subject: Back in the saddle

Adam, I'm taking a new approach to my dating life. I'm joining various online dating sites and am determined to be more open-minded. Sophie seems to think I choose the wrong men. Maybe she's right, so I'm allowing a computer logarithm to choose for me. Is it a sad commentary when I allow a computer to take over my dating life? Am I nuts? Here's the link. You can check out my profile.

Poppy

Damn it! Adam couldn't believe it. Just as he'd been devising ways to get her out to Ohio and pick up where they'd left off in Hawaii, she'd jumped back into the dating pool like a kissing fish searching for its mate.

He clicked on the link she'd provided. The photo she'd put on her profile was stunning; her smile leapt off the page. Poppy never took a bad photo, and he knew because he had more than a dozen stored on his phone from their time in Hawaii.

He'd planned to give her a few weeks to get over her break up with Detestable Richard before moving into action. But now this … online dating? Seriously, this was her new plan? He knew the TV commercials portrayed online dating as happy-happy, lovey-dovey, you'll-find-your-mate type of thing. However, he wasn't so sure that stalkers and serial killers weren't hanging out there to find desperate and unsuspecting women. Now, with this new wrench in the works, he'd have to shorten his timeline and come up with some way to get face time with her.

To: Poppy Reagan
From: Adam from Hawaii
Subject: Computers are no substitute

Poppy, I know online dating is all the rage, but really, I fail to see how this is going work for a girl like you. What's wrong with the men in California? Honestly, I'm concerned with the type of men you'll meet online. How do you know there aren't psycho killers surfing these sites looking for their next victim? Maybe you should move east. Come visit me in Ohio. We could pick up where we left off in Hawaii. You can show me more of your hula moves.

Adam
P.S. I didn't know you were into boating.

Poppy must have been online, because his chat window popped up with her response.

Poppy Reagan: Tsk, tsk, Adam! You shouldn't say things like that! What would your girlfriend think if she saw that email? Delete this thread immediately! Also, I plan to take precautions and meet all my dates at public places, so don't worry about me.
P.S. Who doesn't like boats? A cocktail, swimsuit, and a sunny day are all you need.
Adam Patterson: Sarah and I are no longer seeing each other. You should take one of your girlfriends on dates to make sure you're safe. P.S. You forgot about fishing. I have a boat, and it's for fishing. Although you're welcome to bring your swimsuit and cocktails on board anytime.

Poppy Reagan: Oh no! So sorry, sweetie. Why didn't you say something? You poor thing. Are you heartbroken? Call me tonight if you need to talk. Also, no need for a chaperone. Sophie or Cody will be on cell phone standby. One button away in case of a disastrous date.

P.S. Once you get over the heartbreak, join Match.com. Everyone's doing it.

P.P.S. What's the name of your boat?

Adam Patterson: Forget it. I'm not heartbroken, and I'm not joining a computer-dating site.

P.S. The boat's name is *Siren's Song*. I didn't name it. Come for a visit, and I'll take you out.

He waited for a response from this volley, but after a moment her chat icon showed that she'd signed off. He checked his watch and realized it was six o'clock California time. She'd probably left for a party.

Adam ground his teeth at her breezy lack of concern for her own safety. Yeah, meeting in public spots was fairly safe. Maybe having your friends on speed dial would help, too, but—come on. A savvy psychopath could easily get around those things. Walk her to her car and get her license plate. Steal her cell when she wasn't looking.

He rubbed his eyes and sighed. He was being paranoid. The reality: he was jealous and didn't want her dating other men. He wanted to go back to what they had in Hawaii, and then some. He knew it would be even better since he wouldn't just be the "rebound guy;" after all, they'd developed a friendship.

Chapter Four

"And immediately after Campbell says, 'you may kiss the bride,' we leap out the door and kiss midair."

"Um hmm." I nodded gravely at the enthusiastic, wide-eyed couple sitting across from my desk. Erika, the bride, leaned forward grinning at me, one hand tucked into her fiancé's and the other gripped around a purple, three-ring binder. Her knee bounced the binder up and down, like Tigger from *Winnie-the-Pooh*. "And you want to land where?"

"The drop zone is near Malibu." Neil stroked his scrubby goatee.

" Hmm. So … you want me to set up the reception on the ground? Or arrange for the jump itself?"

"Oh, no. Just the reception. Neil and I will set up all the skydiving business. After all, there will only be about half a dozen of our attendants jumping. Everyone else will be waiting on the ground for us. Oh, and you can jump too, if you want," Erika said.

I made an effort not to roll my eyes as I declined the "opportunity" to join their insanity. I'd been in the planning business for ten years, and I'd even heard about the skydiving weddings. This was the first time I'd been asked to organize a reception around it. Most of all, this was the first time I'd heard of half a dozen attendants foolish enough to jump as well. *I suppose when your job is stunt work and your life revolves around the adrenaline rush, when it comes to your wedding, you either jump out of an airplane or go home.*

The rest of the meeting carried on normally. An hour later, I ushered the pair out of the office with promises to email sample menus.

My watch read half past six. I shut down and locked up before optimistically heading out for my first computer date.

A chilly breeze swept down the street, and I pulled my sweater tighter as I walked the block to the restaurant. I'd had time to change into a pair of casual slacks and a green top that highlighted my eyes. I also decided to pull my hair into a low ponytail, a more conservative look for a date with an accountant.

My date suggested the restaurant, a generic American-style grill. A large group of approximately fifteen people crowded in the entryway, and I waited patiently as the hostess and another waitress scrambled off to set up a table large enough to accommodate the assembly. Finally, she returned and the cluster shuffled off. When my path cleared, I walked past the hostess station into the bar area where I was supposed to meet my date. My eyes searched for a man matching the image from the computer.

"Poppy?"

"Yes." I answered, turning to find a man who vaguely—very vaguely—resembled the photo on the website. The picture must have been close to ten years old. At least fifteen to twenty extra pounds had added jowls and a fleshy wattle beneath his chin. I had a feeling the daily gym visits he claimed in his profile were more like a nice thought than a reality. In the picture, his hair had been thick and swept to the side; now it was clipped short and thin enough that it exposed his pink scalp.

"Are you Lyle?" Normally, I would have ended things immediately; however, Lyle fit a good number of my requirements: non-smoker, professional, social drinker, and no kids. I stuck my hand out and allowed my lips to form a polite smile, determined not to be deterred by the looks.

He gave a cool but firm handshake. "Lyle Ballnich. You're ten minutes late."

My eyes widened at the remark, and the smile dropped. "Yes, unfortunately there was a large group that came in just before me, and it took a while for the hostess to sort them out."

"That's okay then. I have a table over here." He turned and walked over to a small two-seater table and pulled out one of the stools.

That's okay then? I chewed the inside of my lip to keep silent as I climbed onto the stool, hung my purse on a wall hook, and laid my phone on the table. Lyle walked around and heaved himself onto the stool across from me. I took a breath and made an effort to put myself into a positive mindset; after all, some people are particular about punctuality.

A waitress approached, pad in hand. "What can I start you folks out with?" She gave us a perky grin.

I opened my mouth to answer, but Lyle cut me off.

"I'll have a Miller Lite, draft. And can you make sure the glass is clean? I'll have to send it back if it's dirty."

"Certainly, sir." The waitress made a note on her pad, and turned to me.

"I'll have a California Cabernet if you've got one."

"We sure do." She wrote down my order. "Can I get you an appetizer?"

Once again Lyle piped up. "I'd like a plate of potato skins; make sure they aren't burned. And make sure the chef doesn't put any of those green onion thingies on it; they give me gas. And can you also bring extra sour cream? I hate when they cheap out on the sour cream."

My positive mindset turned south.

The waitress nodded, taking notes as Lyle outlined his nitpicky needs, and then she turned to me, wide-eyed, perky grin vanished. "Anything for you?"

"No, thank you. Just the wine." I gave an apologetic smile.

After she left, I turned my gaze to the socially inept bean counter across the table. I'd met scads of people from all walks of life through my work, and Lyle was not ranking high on the personality like-o-meter.

"You look just like your photo. Very pretty. Although I'm not usually attracted to redheads."

"Thank you." I said. I didn't return the "compliment." Lyle *did not* look like his photo, and even though he wore a well-cut, dark suit with a tailored white shirt, I couldn't honestly say he looked handsome. On a scale of one to ten, old Lyle was a four—five would be pushing it. "I understand you're an accountant?"

"Financial planner and CPA, that's me, graduated cum laude from University of Oregon." I zoned out while he babbled on about his qualifications. While he spoke, he unrolled his fork and knife from the black, cloth napkin and rubbed the tines of the fork and the knife-edge with it, inspecting as he went. "With bonuses, I made a seven-figure salary last year, and I'm due to make even more this year. Our busy season has started, you know. After all, taxes are just around the corner."

I nodded but didn't think he even noticed as he carried on the one-sided conversation.

"I drive a Mercedes E-Class. Bought it last year with my bonus money. It's a sweet ride." The fork and knife were placed perfectly perpendicular to the table's edge. He laid the napkin in his lap. "What do you drive?"

"A Lexus."

"That's a good car, a good car. Not as good as the Mercedes, but Lexus has produced safe vehicles."

One of my eyebrows flew up.

Lyle pulled the decorative handkerchief out of his suit pocket, removed his wire-rimmed glasses and proceeded to clean them with the same intensity as the knife and fork. "I had a Lexus ES about four years ago. Nice, but I like the Mercedes better." Old Lyle was off on his next one-sided conversation tangent.

His blathering was thankfully interrupted by our waitress. To my relief, she placed a glass of red wine in front of me, which I picked up and immediately downed half of in one gulp. As I was sucking the booze, she laid a frosty glass of beer, a plate of fatty potato skins, sans the scallions, and a rather large bowl of sour cream in front of Lyle.

"Can I get you folks anything else?"

Lyle slipped his glasses on, picked up the beer, held it close to the pendant light hanging above the table, and examined the mug, deliberately turning it left and right, then left again.

The waitress and I dropped our mouths, both mesmerized and appalled by his inspection. Listening and observing Lyle was like watching a house burn down—you knew you should step away, only the fire was so hypnotic you remained to see its destruction. I couldn't seem to force myself out of the chair and to walk away. I can only conclude curiosity addled my brain.

"Uh … no. I think that … will be all," I stammered.

We locked gazes, and she gave me a look that I interpreted to mean, "good luck with that wacko," and escaped.

Lyle slathered on a glob of sour cream, cut a slice of potato, and popped it in his mouth. *I wonder if he'll offer to share.* Not that I wanted anything, but it would have been the polite thing to do.

"So, what is it you said you do?" he asked with his mouth full.

I guess that would be a no. I turned away from the "see" food and took another sip of wine before answering. "I'm an event planner."

"Oh, yeah, that's right. Like you plan parties and stuff?" He made smacking noises as he chomped his food.

"Yes, something like that." I answered faintly, trying to wrap my head around the fact that such a fastidious person had the table manners of a swine.

"Who do you work for?"

"I run my own company."

"Hmph. Any money in that?"

I frowned, looking at the middle distance over his shoulder so I didn't have to watch the repulsive mastication. "I do okay."

"You need an accountant?" Another bite went in.

I wrinkled my nose. "I have one, thanks."

"I'll bet I can get you double your tax returns." He cut another slice. "As a matter of fact, I guarantee it. Change to my firm, and I promise to double your tax returns from last year." He pointed his sour-cream-slathered, potato-filled fork at me.

"I'll think about it." My phone jiggled. I glanced down. A text notification popped up.

"Is that work?" He wielded the knife again. "You should take that if it's work. I don't mind. I know how important clients can be. Right?"

Lyle was so socially inept, he didn't realize he'd given me the perfect out to this hideous date. Even though I could handle social oddballs in my professional life, I had zero interest in dating one, especially one with the table manners of a St. Bernard. I brought up the text.

It was from Sophie.

How's the date going?

"It's my assistant. She's having trouble with a client," I lied. I responded to Sophie.

U can't even imagine.
That good?
No! Bad! I'm getting out. Will call u soon.

I glanced up at my potato-shoveling date and decided it was time to let the building burn down on its own. "I'm sorry to have to cut the date short, but it seems I'll need to go back to the office to deal with this situation." I unhooked my purse and slid off the stool.

"Here," Lyle pulled a card out of his inside pocket, "take my card. I wasn't kidding about the taxes."

I took it out of his hand with two fingers. "Sure, I'll call you," I said and began to stride away.

"Wait."

I paused and looked back over my shoulder.

"What about your wine?"

My brows knit in confusion. I'd finished it. He rubbed his forefinger and thumb together. Realization dawned. *Are you kidding me!*

"Lyle, didn't you say you made seven figures last year?"

His face turned red, and his fingers dropped.

"I think you can swing it." I tilted my head. "Don't you?"

He had the decency to look ashamed.

"Don't call me, I'll call you," was my parting shot as I fled the bar area.

I stalked back to my car and got in, slamming the door. My head flopped against the headrest, and I released a full-blown sigh. Maybe Adam was right. Maybe this Internet dating was a bad idea.

My phone rang, and Sophie's image popped up. "Hi."

"Omigod. Is he still there?" she whispered.

"No, I'm back in my car."

"What happened?"

I proceeded to outline every gory detail of the penny pincher's backhanded compliments and arrogant comments during the hideous, thirty-minute date.

"Omigod, he actually called you back to pay for that measly glass of wine?"

"Yes. I think accountants are off the list."

"No-o. Come on, you can't judge an entire profession by this one guy. After all, your own accountant isn't that bad, is he?"

"*My* accountant is a lovely lesbian named Simone. And you're right, she is not socially inept."

"Maybe it's just guys named Lyle you should stay away from."

"You may be right about that."

"Who's up next on the list?"

"I have another date tomorrow night, but now I'm having second thoughts. Maybe I should cancel and make a new plan. I mean, I can't believe how far off that photo was. It's like false advertising."

"*No.* Don't give up yet. That guy was an anomaly; they've got to get better. You just fished out a bottom feeder with your first cast. Maybe we need to add some more filters. You'll find something better; it just takes persistence. What does tomorrow's guy do for a living?"

"His name is Paul, and it just said executive on his profile."

"Ooh, that sounds promising."

"And we are meeting at Osteria Mozza."

"Well, he's got good taste. Can't go wrong with a free dinner. Right?"

"I suppose." I said unenthusiastically.

"Tell you what. Text me when you arrive. I'll call about fifteen minutes into the date. That way, if you need to make an escape, you can say the call's a work emergency and you need to leave. Otherwise, ignore it and have a great time. How's that for a plan?"

"Déjà vu." I muttered. "Whose insane idea was this anyway?"

Sophie's gurgled laughter came across the line. "Yours!"

•••

Adam put down the medical journal to check his incoming text message.

Poppy: I may be wrong. Don't get on Match.com. Logarithms are not all they're cracked up to be.

Adam: I warned you. Computers are no substitute. Come check out the heartland. What happened?

Poppy: Smarmy accountant with the manners of a PIG!
Adam: Give up yet?
Poppy: Not yet. Sophie convinced me to try again. Lay on, Macduff!
Adam: Sucker.

"Hmm." He rubbed his five o'clock shadow. Maybe this online dating thing was a better idea than he'd originally thought. If she had a few horrific dates, she'd give up and be ready to run right into his arms. But when? He searched his calendar for a time to invite her. With an upcoming conference and the lecture series he'd committed to until the end of the month, he couldn't seem to find a good weekend, and it was driving him crazy.

"Come, on. Think." He groused at the calendar on his phone pulling at his lower lip. Wait a minute; just maybe, they could meet in the middle.

Chapter Five

My feet pounded against the black belt of the treadmill, slowing as the machine automatically decelerated into cool-down mode for the last few minutes of my morning run. The gym was empty except for me, which wasn't that unusual at six thirty. Red digital numbers counted down from ten, and the treadmill came to a halt. I took a long drink of water and was mopping at the sweat running down my neck when my cell phone rang. The country calling code was from Africa.

"Hello, Mom."

"Hello, darling. I'm so glad I caught you." The connection was scratchy, and her voice sounded far away, as if through a tunnel. "I'm coming to town in a few weeks, and I wanted to make arrangements to see you."

"Great. Is Hamisi coming with you?"

"No, I'm coming by myself this time."

My intuition sat up. She'd not traveled to the United States without Hamisi since they'd married four years ago. "Is everything okay?"

"Yes, dear. Everything is fine. Hamisi couldn't get away right now. There are some business meetings coming up over the next few weeks that he must attend. So, I'm coming on my own."

If my mother had been normal, I wouldn't have thought twice about this statement, but her delivery sounded off. Knowing her penchant to give up on a relationship rather than work it out when things got rough, I feared her visit to the States was the start of her next break up.

"Why don't you wait until the meetings are over?"

"No, no, I want to do it now. I'll email you all the details. And by the way, I'll be staying at the Marriott."

"The Marriott? You can stay with me, Mom."

"No, I don't wish to be underfoot since I may stay for a few weeks. I'll see you then."

The crackling line went dead, and I stared disconcertedly at my phone. Something smelled fishy; I wrinkled my nose. Mother's plan to stay more than a week without Hamisi likely meant she was back in my life. Don't get me wrong, I loved my mother, but having Amalina Reagan Mendez Heller Brillhart Kwambai living within a thirty-mile radius for more than a week did not bode well for my peace of mind.

My phone vibrated in my hand, and a ship's bell tolled as a text arrived.

It was from Rose Diaz, one of my upcoming March brides.

Wedding is OFF!!! B/c Chester is a cheating asshole!!

It held an emoticon I'd never seen before, but if I had to guess, it was supposed to represent the body part she'd referred to. The text had been sent to what looked like her entire phone directory.

Key-rist! Cheating must be catching, like a virus. The phone rang. My assistant, Sierra's, number flashed.

"I guess you received the text?"

"Just came in," Sierra replied.

"I'll be in the office in an hour. I need to review the contract and see if they purchased any cancellation insurance. Otherwise, we're going to have a very unhappy M.O.B. and F.O.B. who are out a lot of *dinero*, and I have a feeling it's going to be ugly getting paid."

"See you in an hour, boss. By the way, how did the computer date go last night?"

"Unqualified catastrophe. I don't want to talk about it." I hung up before she could ask more questions.

An hour later, I walked into the office carrying two cappuccinos and a sack of bagels. I wound my way back to Sierra's cubicle. She sat at her desk, wearing a plaid, private school-style miniskirt, with a white button-down blouse. Frankly, I didn't care if she wore pink sweats and stripper shoes to the office. We had an agreement—as long as she did her job efficiently, effectively and wore appropriate clothes for the events we worked, she was free to express her creativity in the office. So far, Sierra had never let me down and had shown she could think quickly on her feet during disastrous situations.

I placed the tray and bag on her desk, and she handed me a copy of the Diaz-Stone wedding contract.

"You were right; they didn't buy the cancellation insurance package, and with the wedding only two weeks away, they're going to be out a lot of money," Sierra said.

"Damn." I sighed, pulled one of the coffees out of the tray, and headed to my office to begin making phone calls.

I contacted the family and ascertained that the wedding was indeed off, due to the fact that the groom had been carrying on a three-month affair with a woman who was now pregnant with their child. After speaking with a barely simmering Mr. Diaz, he assured me all the fees would be paid if he had to pull it out of his daughter's ex-fiancé's ass. Mr. Diaz's threatening voice gave me the heebie-jeebies, and I had a feeling Chester the Cheater would pony up the dough to Daddy Diaz or find himself with a couple of broken kneecaps, or worse, buried underneath Mr. Diaz's next construction project.

Poppy: This sucker is off for Round 2—ding, ding. Wish me luck.
Adam: Don't forget your mace.

Chapter Six

That evening, I made sure to arrive early and park myself at the bar in a seat with an easy view of the front entrance. It was still early, and there were only a few patrons in the restaurant. I wore a scarf and fedora as camouflage. I figured if another false advertisement came in, I'd simply slip out the back exit by the bathrooms.

Twenty minutes later, my phone rang, and I answered without looking at the caller ID. "This is Poppy."

"Hey, it's me. You never texted. Do you need to bolt?" Sophie whispered conspiratorially.

"Apparently, I'm being stood up."

"You mean he's not there yet?" She said in her normal voice.

"Nope."

"Humph. Has he called?"

"He doesn't have my cell, and I just checked email. Zilch."

"Well, he's only fifteen minutes late. Maybe he got caught in traffic."

"Maybe. I've finished my wine, and I'm about ready to bail."

"Give him ten more minutes. I heard there was a bad accident on the 101, and traffic is a mess."

I processed this for a minute and decided to give Paul the benefit of the doubt. "Okay. Call me back in ten."

A few minutes later, a middle-aged brunette, with a cropped bob, wearing a gray business suit and little black glasses, staring down at her phone, walked directly into my line of vision. I leaned to the side to see around her.

The glasses zeroed in on me, and she cleared her throat. "Excuse me, are you Poppy?"

"Yes?" My eyebrows knit. "Have we met?"

"No. My name is Melody Anderson." She held out her hand, and I automatically shook it. "I'm Paul Chapman's executive assistant. I'm sorry to tell you, but his flight was delayed, and he won't be able to make it tonight."

"Ah."

"He didn't have your cell number and asked me to come in person to give you his apologies. He also asked that you go ahead and have dinner; he'll take care of the check."

"Oh, that won't be necessary." My cheeks burned with embarrassment at being stood up and having the message delivered by his executive assistant. I rose and placed a hand on my small clutch.

"No, please, don't leave." Her cool fingers gently covered my wrist. "Paul insists. He feels terrible. He said he'd email you about making arrangements to get together on another night." She removed her hand.

"Well, I'm flattered. That's very kind of him."

She flagged down the bartender, gave him a credit card to run, ordered me a $200 bottle of wine, and explained that I had carte blanche to get whatever I desired.

After she left, I dialed Sophie.

"Did he show?"

"Nope."

"Bastard."

"Not really. Actually, this is quite possibly the nicest non-date I've ever had." I went on to explain my situation.

"What did you say his name was?"

"Paul Chapman. Why?"

"I don't know. That name sounds familiar. Just a sec, let me Google him."

I waited while Sophie searched her computer.

"Ho-ly Moses."

"What? Don't tell me he's some kind of serial killer."

"Nope. He's the founder and president of an Internet tech company."

"Not too shabby."

"He also started a foundation to provide computers and technology to poor, inner-city schools."

"And he's a philanthropist as well." My salad arrived, and I mouthed a thank you.

"Wikipedia says he's thirty-nine, and a picture here shows a nice-looking fellow. A bit of premature graying, but a silver fox nonetheless. I can see why you said yes."

"I wasn't sure I believed the 'he missed his flight' excuse. But, now that you've told me all of this, it does seem possible."

"He's got potential, that's for sure."

"Obviously." I took another sip of wine. My phone buzzed as a text message arrived, but I ignored it.

"I think you ought to accept another date if he contacts you."

The wine slid effortlessly down my throat. "I agree." *If only to enjoy more of his excellent wine choices.*

"You should …" A barking dog interrupted whatever Sophie was about to say. "Sirius, Quiet! Ian's home. I'd better go. We'll talk later. Enjoy your free meal."

"Later." We hung up, and as I forked a piece of kale, I checked my texts.

It was from Adam.

I have a med conference in Denver in two weeks. Meet me there.

I frowned, and my brows crunched together.

My thumbs paused above the screen as my mind churned. Adam and I were both free agents. Denver was a two-hour plane ride over the Rocky Mountains. If I didn't have an event, there was a possibility I could make an overnight maybe on Sunday. I pulled up my calendar to check the dates, and he chimed in, again.

I want to see you. Please.

I chewed my bottom lip. So far, both my computer dates were a bust, and if I were honest with myself, I wanted to see Adam, too. Although I knew it wouldn't go anywhere, we were good together. At least we had been in Hawaii. There was no reason I couldn't enjoy a little fling, see if we could turn some of that beach vacation magic into a mountain retreat magic.

Send the dates. I'll look into it.

My quail arrived, and I slid the phone into my purse in an effort to calm the sudden, giddy thoughts spinning in my brain. *I need to go shopping and get some new lingerie. What is the weather in Denver like this time of year? Did I pack my ski parka under the bed?*

Halfway through the quail, someone tapped my shoulder, and I turned to find Holly, Sophie's younger sister. She wore black jeans and a beautiful, multicolored sweater belted at the waist.

"I thought that was you." She brushed a strand of toffee-colored hair behind her ear.

A grin broke across my face and I hopped off the stool to pull her into an embrace. "Hello, girlfriend. I haven't seen you in ages. How have you been?"

Holding her at arm's length, I searched her face. She looked good. Her cheeks had filled out, and her eyes were no longer hollow and dark from fear and sleepless nights. Back in November, Holly fled her abusive husband while he was on a business trip, and she showed up on Sophie's doorstep with her daughter, Eva. Ian offered them shelter at his place and hired an enormous bodyguard named Ziggy to watch over the pair. Holly's husband, a security specialist for a Las Vegas Casino, tracked her to California, where he was able to bypass Sophie's security system and hold her at gunpoint. Thanks to Sirius and Ian's quick actions Sophie's injuries were limited to an injury from a ricocheted bullet that embedded in her booty.

Holly had taken a job a few months ago as a curator at a local art gallery, and she and Eva now rented Sophie's house in Sherman Oaks. Her soon-to-be ex-husband was doing an eight-year stint in San Quentin.

"A colleague from New York is in town this week, and I took her out for dinner. What are you doing here?"

"I was supposed to be meeting a date, but something came up and he couldn't make it. Are you done? Why don't you and your friend join me?"

"Diana grabbed a cab. She's catching the redeye back to New York." She glanced at her watch. "But, I guess I could stay for a few minutes. Eva's sitter said she could stay on until nine."

The bartender arrived. "Can I get you something to drink?"

"Go ahead and bring another glass. Holly can help me finish the bottle."

The bartender adroitly flipped a glass on the counter, poured the rest of the wine into it, and slid it in front of Holly.

"Thanks." She turned to me. "What should we toast to?"

"Paul Chapman."

Her eyebrows rose in confusion. "Who's Paul Chapman?"

"The gentleman who stood me up and purchased this exquisite wine for us." I clinked her glass.

"By all means, to Paul Chapman." She took a sip. "Mmm, yum."

"Tell me how things are going at the gallery."

"Great. I just scored a wonderful Brâncuşi collection last week. Marcello is over the moon, and can't wait until it arrives."

"How is Eva?"

"She's good, good. She and Annie are like two peas in a pod."

"Who's Annie?"

"Omigod." She grabbed my arm, her eyes wide. "You don't know?"

I made a swirly motion with my free hand. "I'm out of the loop."

"You remember the detective who helped me last year? Sophie's friend?"

"Sure, Detective Sumner. Right?"

"Yeah, his name is Gary. He lives around the corner. Anyway, on New Year's Eve, while he's on duty at a homicide scene, his wife skipped town with some sort of import-export, Euro trash, leaving Annie with a babysitter and a Dear John letter on the mantel."

My jaw dropped. "Good Lord. That's terrible. She just left her daughter like that? What the …? What kind of monster does that?" I thought about the variety of husbands my mother burned through. One thing remained consistent—my mom never, ever left me behind; she always brought me along for the ride.

"Yeah, I think Gary's trying to get her to release all her custody rights, claiming abandonment. I put him in contact with my divorce attorney."

"I should say so! What kind of mother leaves her baby to run off on an adventure?"

"I don't know. Gary's made some cryptic remarks that make me think she's got mental issues, like depression or bi-polar."

"Maybe she went off her meds."

Holly shrugged. "Maybe. Anyway, since our schedules can be erratic, we decided to join forces and share a nanny to watch the two girls. Luckily, we have an awesome nanny, and she's available to stay later if we need her to. Like if Gary gets called onto a case or I've got a potential buyer on the line."

"You're lucky to have each other and that the girls get along so well."

Holly's face softened as if a pleasant thought came to mind. "Annie's a doll. She's like an older sister to Eva. Sometimes she can be bossy, and she'll start directing everyone around. I think it's hysterical, but Gary cracks down on it." She crunched her nose. "He says she'll turn into a tyrant if he allows it, but I don't believe it. Her disposition is far too sweet,"

I sipped the end of my wine and contemplated Holly's demeanor. She'd changed somehow, in a manner I couldn't quite put my finger on. Was it Annie? The new job? Or simply Holly's new life, free from fear?

"So, who's Paul Chapman?" She interrupted my train of thought.

I explained about getting stood up, and put Holly into stitches over my horrid date the night before with Lyle.

"That'll teach you not to date men named Lyle." She guffawed at me.

"You better watch out, or I'm going to put your name on Match.com and see what kind of winners you dredge up."

Her laughter faded. "No. I don't think I'll ever get married again."

Squeezing her hand, I said. "Give it time. Maybe one day." I couldn't envision Holly and her adorable daughter remaining single for too long, but she'd had a rough time, and it would take a special man to get past her fears and defensive walls, so I changed the subject.

About eight thirty, we said our goodbyes in front of the restaurant.

Holly gave me a bear hug, and we walked away in opposite directions. I pulled out my phone to dial Sophie and give her an update. Adam's text with the dates of his medical conference awaited me. The meeting fell during the weekend of the canceled Diaz-Stone wedding.

"Serendipity," I murmured.

• • •

I'll book my ticket tonight.

Adam mentally patted himself on the back after reading Poppy's text. Only a few short weeks until he'd be able to see her, and in Denver, no less, one of his favorite towns to visit.

Can't wait

he texted.

If Poppy was coming, he needed to upgrade his room to a suite.

Ten minutes later the reservationist gave him the bad news. "I'm sorry, sir, we're completely booked, including all the suites."

"Nothing? Even the Presidential Suite?" Adam didn't want to pay the exorbitant amount for the penthouse, but if that's all they had left …

"No, sir. The conference coordinator has that booked up."

Damn. "Okay." He sighed and hung up. Maybe one of his buddies attending the conference had booked a suite, and he could do some wrangling. He wracked his brain. *Who was flashy enough to book a suite?* Only one name came to mind. Smitty. Adam scrolled his contacts and dialed his old friend.

"Walter Smith."

"Smitty, listen, this is Adam—"

"Adam, good to hear from you. What's up, buddy?"

"Are you attending the Denver conference in March?"

"You bet. I saw you're doing a few lectures. I plan to attend just so I can heckle you."

"Thanks, pal. Listen, I'm looking to upgrade my room to a suite. You wouldn't happen to have booked one?"

"I sure did. Why are you looking to upgrade?"

"Well, uh … I've invited this lady to join me."

"A woman! I knew it. Do I know her? What does she look like? Is it Carol from Michigan? You two seemed pretty close last conference."

"No it's not Carol, and there was nothing going on with her last year. It's a woman I met in Hawaii."

"Oh-ho, Hawaii, huh? Did you fetch yourself a hula beach-honey?"

"No, she's from California."

"California? Where? Close to me? Maybe I should call her, and she could stay with me in the suite. I'm free at the moment."

Adam's patience at his friend's ribbing came to a screeching halt. "The *hell* you say!"

"Whoa, whoa, buddy. Just joking. Relax."

There was a pause in the conversation as Adam got a grip on his flash of anger… *Where did that come from?* He took a deep breath and continued, "Anyway, all the suites are booked. If you give yours up to me, I'd owe you one, buddy. You name it."

"You'd owe me one, hmm? This girl must be something if you're scrambling around for a suite."

"She's a classy lady who deserves the best."

"Well if that's the case, you should call and request the presidential suite." Smitty snickered.

"It's booked."

A low whistle pulsated across the phone lines. "Something special indeed."

"Are you willing to let me have it?"

"On one condition—you make good on a promise you made several years ago."

"What's that?"

"Come out to California. Visit my practice and give some consideration to my proposal."

"What proposal?"

"We'll talk about it in Denver."

That was a dubious invitation, but his desperation to make this weekend with Poppy as perfect as possible prevailed over any sort of good sense to dig deeper into Smitty's proposal. "You've got a deal. See you in Denver."

After he hung up, he rubbed his eyes, still confused about the unusual spark of jealousy over Smitty's joking. Rationally, he knew his friend was just pulling his leg, and it'd been an unexpected surprise to realize that Poppy could evoke such a reaction from him. They'd had uncommitted fun in Hawaii. Now that they'd gotten to know each other better over the months, what exactly was he hoping to get out of their visit to Denver?

More.

Now the question remained, how much more?

Chapter Seven

Thursday morning dawned sunny and far too early for my taste. I rolled over and pressed the snooze button on the alarm. A dull ache throbbed in my temples, and I cursed myself for not drinking more water before bed. The wine left me dehydrated. I groaned and draped an arm over my eyes to block out the muted sun drifting through the drapes.

Exercise was out this morning, not because of the hangover, but due to the fact my skydiving couple requested an early morning meeting at a coffee joint in Sherman Oaks to look over the menus and discuss the rental options for tents.

At seven fifteen, I stepped into the coffee shop sans headache, wearing leopard print heels, black slacks, and a rust, V-neck top. My clients sat at a round table in the front window. Three of the four chairs were occupied. Neil and another man stood as I approached.

"Good morning, Neil." We gripped hands.

"Morning." He nodded.

Erika turned and shot me a cheery grin. "Hello! So glad you could meet us this morning."

"No problem." I slid an oversized tote off my shoulder and let it rest on the ground.

"Poppy, I'd like you to meet a friend of ours. Poppy Reagan, this is Campbell White." Erika introduced us.

Immediately, I recognized the name as the officiate of their wedding. I turned my attention to the plane-jumping lunatic and was met with a full on, dimple-peeping smile that I couldn't help but return. He wore a plain green hoodie, worn denims ripped at the knee, and a pair of dark hiking boots. His brown hair was long and thick and rested at his shoulders. There was an earthy sexiness about Campbell.

He held out his hand and I automatically grasped it. "It's nice to meet you."

The grip was firm as his calloused hand wrapped around mine. "I understand you'll be performing the ceremony."

"That's the plan."

"Are you an ordained minister or something?"

"Or something, thanks to the Internet." He released me, and I sat in the open chair. "Can I get you something to drink?"

"That would be great. Coffee, vanilla latte, nonfat milk and one blue packet of sweetener, please. Hold on." I pulled a twenty out my purse and held it up.

He waved the money away. "I'll get this round."

"Thank you." Digging into the depths of my tote, I located a black three-ring binder. "I thought we'd discuss the menu first, if that's okay with you guys, and then discuss the options for invitations. I'd like to get as many of your decisions as I can today, so we can move forward quickly,"

Erika nodded as she sat on her hands with a goofy grin plastered to her face. Her own wedding notebook was on the table to her right.

I flipped open to a menu and turned the notebook toward the couple to explain the different options.

Two heads bent over the menu.

"Nonfat vanilla latte." Campbell held the coffee at eye level.

"Perfect, thanks." The coffee aroma warmed my senses as I peeled the lid off to add the sweetener. Surreptitiously, I watched Campbell as he returned to his seat and shoved up his sweatshirt sleeves. Blue veins stood out on his muscular forearms, roping down to his hands. I noticed the edge of a tattoo peeking out from under his sleeve. A small scar cut his left eyebrow in half. His brown eyes caught mine, and my gaze zipped back to Erika and Neil.

"So what do you think?"

Neil sat back, crossing his arms and looked at his fiancée. "All right, I think it's time you came clean, hon."

My brows knit, and my gaze turned to Erika in confusion.

She sheepishly ducked her head. "He's right. I brought you here under a false pretense."

"I'm sorry?" I braced myself for whatever bad news was coming next.

"Yeah, we've already decided on most everything. I went through all the materials you provided and wrote down what we wanted." She opened her binder, pulled out a handwritten sheet of notebook paper, and passed it over to me.

Bold, loopy handwriting listed everything from caterer, to wedding cake, to invitation style.

"This is fantastic. You may be my favorite clients ever." *This wedding was going to be a snap. Boo-yah! Wait, what was the false pretense?* I put aside the materials. "So, what's the problem?"

Erika was suddenly absorbed with picking at a hangnail and refused to meet my gaze. Neil stared at her bowed head. Apprehension washed over me. My glance swept to Campbell, but he gave a shrug and an innocent look.

"Erika …" Neil's voice held a warning tone. "You need tell her."

"I sense there is something else going on. Is it financial? Because, let me assure you, we can work out a payment plan. Or I can provide similar, but less expensive options."

"No. The money's not a problem." Neil pulled at his goatee. "What my lovely fiancée isn't telling you …"

"Wait." She placed a hand over his mouth. "Okay, okay, *I'll* tell her." Erika removed her hand and turned back to me. "Okay, he's right. We did bring you here for a different reason. You see, when I called the office last night, your secretary told me you'd left for your computer date."

My jaw clenched. *I'm going to strangle Sierra with my bare hands when I get back to the office.*

"Anyway, you're really nice and smart, and Neil thinks you're attractive, so …" Her gaze landed on Campbell. "I thought I'd … setyouupwithCampbell." She spoke so quickly her words ran together, and I wasn't sure I'd understood what she said.

"What?" My mouth dropped.

Everyone but Campbell stared at Erika as she squirmed uncomfortably in her seat. The hairs on the back of my neck stood up, and I sensed Campbell's eyes continue to rest on me.

"She's playing Cupid. She set this meeting up so you and Campbell could meet." Neil frowned.

My gaze traveled from a flushed Erika, to a grimacing Neil, to Campbell who sat back in his chair with his arms crossed, grinning in amusement as he watched the show.

"I see. Um. Did you know about this?" I asked Campbell, fiddling with my necklace.

"Nope." His dimples winked at me. "I found out about ten minutes before you arrived."

"Uh huh. Are you looking for a relationship right now?"

"I wouldn't say I'm actively searching. However, when you walked in the door, I decided to take it under consideration."

"*Campbell.*" Erika reached across her groom and smacked Campbell on the arm. "Be nice. You told me just last week that you were looking for someone new to date."

"Was I sober?"

"That's not funny." She smacked him again.

His gaze returned to Neil. "You'd better get control of your woman."

Neil snorted. "I'll chain her up in the basement until she promises to keep her nose out of other people's love lives."

I sighed. I'd seen this before. Engaged and newlywed couples lived in a fluffy, pink "cloud of love," and all they wanted to do was set up their friends so they could enjoy the "cloud of love." This, however, would be the first time I stood in the crosshairs of the setup.

Erika tsked and crossed her arms. "That's the last time I ever do a favor for you, Campbell White. I don't know what you're complaining about. All I've done is introduce you to a beautiful, intelligent, successful woman." She gestured to me. "I must apologize for him, Poppy. I *thought* he was a good guy and normal human being. *Clearly,* I was mistaken."

Campbell turned an unrepentant grin back to me. "Perhaps I did say something, but I didn't realize she would take it so seriously and become a professional matchmaker."

My eyes bounced back and forth, like watching a tennis match, as the conversation carried on around me.

"You're behaving like a jerk." Erika harrumphed.

His grin finally faded. "She's right. I apologize, Poppy. Let me make it up to you by buying you breakfast."

My brows rose. "Like, *now?*"

"Right now. Yes. Even though it's unexpected, my misguided, but well-meaning friend is indeed correct. I *am* interested in getting to know you better." His head tilted. "One-on-one."

I tapped a finger against my chin, debating the merits of continuing this unexpected date. Campbell didn't exactly meet my requirements. I didn't know what his current profession happened to be, but considering the company he kept, his rugged physique, and willingness to jump out of an airplane, I was pretty sure he didn't have a desk job. To be honest, he seemed to be a bit of a bad boy, similar to a few of my former, failed relationships. However, there was a rugged handsomeness that drew me to him. I had a feeling that if I were ever lost in the middle of the forest, Campbell was the type who would know how to make tree bark stew and get us out by navigating from the alignment of the sun and stars. What the hell? Even though it wasn't part of my "plan," blind dates weren't much different from having a computer hook me up. Besides, it's not as though he was hard on the eyes.

"Okay."

"Good." He released his breath.

"Well, hon. I think your work here is done." Neil rose, and Erika scrambled to gather her notebook, keys, and phone off the table.

Grabbing her sweatshirt off the back of the chair, she leaned down to whisper in my ear. "Give him a chance." She straightened and winked at me.

Neil held out his hand and I gave it a brief shake.

I didn't watch as the two of them exited, but I felt the cool breeze on my back when the door opened and closed. My stiff shoulders relaxed, and I slouched in the chair, regarding the man across from me. He didn't flinch under my scrutiny, and finally I let out a small puff of laughter.

"Well, this is embarrassing."

"What, the blind setup? Or the fact you're sitting across from a total stranger who knows you've been online dating."

"The first. I'm not embarrassed over the online dating. Everyone's doing it."

"I'm not."

"You're behind the times."

"Probably so. I'm not much on technology. My phone is four years old, and I'm told it's considered a dinosaur. So, how have the computer dates been going?"

I stared at the green lip on the coffee cup. "I've just started."

He snorted, "That well?"

I allowed the silence to speak for me.

"Sorry. I'm not usually such a jerk. I'm out of my element."

My lashes swept up. "What *is* your element?"

His eyes narrowed, and his jaw muscles worked. "You like adventure?"

I lifted a shoulder. "Sure. Who doesn't like an adventure?"

"You have anywhere you need to be in the next, say …" he studied his watch, "three hours?"

My curiosity piqued. "Three hours? Not in particular." Considering my breakfast with Erika and Neil wrapped up so quickly, I had time.

He ducked under the table to glance at my crossed legs. "You wouldn't happen to carry a pair of boots or tennis shoes in your car?"

"I have a gym bag. Yoga pants, T-shirt, sweatshirt, shoes, socks." I rattled off, listing each one by finger.

"A well-prepared woman; I love it." He rose and held out his hand. "C'mon, let's get your stuff."

"I need gym gear for a three-hour breakfast?"

"That's right. I promised you breakfast. Wait here."

Campbell sauntered over to the counter and perused the glass case of pastries. He exchanged conversation with the barista behind the counter and pointed to different confections, and I turned back to the table to gather my materials.

"All set." He held the bag aloft.

I rose, shouldering my tote and grasping my coffee like a lifeline.

What the hell am I doing?

It's an adventure; you said you were up for an adventure.

Yes, but I hardly know this guy.

Just go with it.

As my subconscious argued with itself, Campbell held the door for me. "Where's your car?"

"I lucked out. Street parking, around the corner."

"That's me, right there." He indicated a black, four-door jeep with a hard top, big knobby wheels, and splashes of dirt fanned along the sides.

"Okay, why don't you stay here, and I'll drive round the block and follow you."

"No need. Let's get your stuff. I'll drive."

My head moved from side to side. "I don't think so. I'd feel more comfortable if I followed you."

"It's about forty-five minutes away."

"So."

"Fine," he sighed. "We'll take your car."

"Hold up," I placed a hand on his chest. "I'm not getting in a car alone with a stranger."

A light bulb went on. "Ah. I see. Did you read this in a dating handbook? You're right. You shouldn't get into a car with a stranger, except I'm not a stranger. We were introduced through mutual friends."

"First, Erika and Neil, though very nice people, are not my friends. They're clients, and I've only known them a few days. Second, you're much larger and stronger than I am. It wouldn't take much to overpower me, steal my car, and leave me stranded along the side of the road in the middle of nowhere."

"Hey, I offered to drive." He ran his hand through his hair, tucking it behind his ears.

I frowned.

"Okay, okay. I get it. Here's what we're gonna to do. Who's on speed dial on your phone?"

"Why does that matter?"

He rolled his eyes and sighed, "Work with me. Who's on speed dial?"

"Office co-workers, best friends, my mom …"

"Who's expecting to see you soon?"

"That would be either Sierra or Cody."

"Call one of them and tell her you're going to Malibu for an adventure. Then take a photo of me and text it to her. Tell her if she doesn't hear from you in three hours to call the police and turn me in."

"Hmm … it's a thought."

"Here," he reached into his pocket and pulled out a knife, deftly flicking it open.

I sucked in a breath.

He laid the sharp end in his palm and offered the handle to me. "You can hold onto this for security. If I make any false moves, you have my permission to gut me with it."

A passerby eyed the knife and scuttled quickly through a neighboring shop door.

"Oh, for the love of Pete. Put that thing away," I hissed. "We'll do the photo thing. Say cheese." I held up my phone and clicked a photo. "Call Cody." The phone rang twice before she picked up.

"You're up early. How'd the big date go last night?"

"We'll talk about that later. Listen, I'm kind of on another date, and I should be back around noon."

"Another date? Planning them pretty close together, aren't you? What's this one like?"

"It's a long story, but he's kind of cute. I'm texting you his picture. Listen, if you don't hear from me by noon … um … call the police."

Cody's cackling laughter belted out over the lines. "You slay me."

"I try," I said weakly.

"What are you doing until noon?"

"I don't actually know. It's an adventure."

My answer met silence.

"If I don't hear back from you by noon. I'll call the cops."

"I'm sending a photo of his license plate, too." I clicked a photo of the back of the jeep.

"Poppy, are you sure you know what you're doing?"

My eyes flicked up. Dimples peeped at me. Another sigh escaped, "I'll be fine. See you at lunchtime."

Thirty minutes later, we were dodging traffic on the 101 heading west. My gym bag rested on the backseat, our coffees sat next to each other in the cup holders, and the pastries sat in my lap.

"So you think I'm cute?"

"I beg your pardon?" My head swiveled to view his profile.

He downshifted as traffic slowed. "You told your friend you thought I was cute."

"Oh, right. I would say that statement was inaccurate."

"So I'm not cute?"

"No ..." I tilted my head and squinted. The sweatshirt had been tossed in the back, and I could now see the tattoo of an eagle sitting on an anchor and trident. He'd pulled his hair back into a low ponytail, and a scar running from behind his ear to the jawline was now visible. It did nothing to detract from his looks; it simply added to his essence of danger.

I decided to yank his chain a bit. "Nah, I'd say you have this raw animal magnetism about you." My voice dropped an octave to deep and breathy. "I feel as though if we ever hooked up, the sex would be dirty. You know ... passionate ... shirt-ripping gritty ... with some stank on it."

His foot slipped off the brake, and we jerked forward.

My ringing laughter filled the car, and I turned my attention to the bag of pastries. "Mmm ... chocolate croissants, my favorite." I licked my lips.

Sunlight flashed off Campbell's sunglasses as he glanced at me.

I didn't return his look. "You'd better keep your eyes on the road, adventure boy. We wouldn't want to have an accident, now. Would you like one of these pastries?" I held up a croissant.

He cleared his throat and returned to watching the road. "Sure." Bits of crumbs fluttered to his lap as he ate.

"So, Campbell, what do you do for a living? Minister?"

"Nah, I did the online thing two years ago for another wedding. My day job is stuntman, like Neil."

"Sounds exciting. Where did you get your training?"

"The military."

"Really? Let me guess … marine."

He shook his head. "Navy SEAL."

I whistled. "That would explain it. How long were you in?"

"Seventeen years. Explain what?"

"When we met, I had this feeling that if I were ever lost in the woods, you'd be a good guy to have on hand to get me out."

"I'm better in water, but woods or desert, I'll get you out."

"What was it like being a SEAL?"

"Intense. But you train your body to become a lethal weapon, and you form lifelong friendships. What's it like being a party planner?"

"Intense. But when everything works out at the end of the day, you've brought some happiness and joy to someone's life."

His lip curled. "Touché."

The jeep pulled off the two-lane road onto a dirt road that we bounced along until coming to a stop in front of a squat, white, cement block building. Painted on the side was a sizeable mural of a parachutist. The realization why my gym clothes were necessary slammed into me like a garbage truck. My heart sank, and for the first time since leaving the coffee shop, I sincerely regretted getting into Campbell's car.

"Uh. What are we doing here?"

"You said you wanted an adventure."

"And you're idea of an adventure was …?"

"Skydiving. Tandem jump. It's a total rush. You'll love it."

"Why … would I love jumping out of a moving airplane?"

"Trust me." He opened the door and slid out.

I remained seated, gripping the coffee shop bag with white knuckles. Campbell came around to my side of the car and opened the door. I didn't move.

"Poppy."

I continued to stare at the mural.

"Poppy." He slipped his glasses off, and his dark gaze speared me. "Trust me. I wouldn't let a hair on that red head of yours get hurt." He pulled the bag out of my grip and took my balled-up hand. "It's okay. If you don't want to go up, you don't have to. Just come in and find out about it."

I gave in and climbed out of the front seat.

"Good girl."

He held the door open, and I walked into a waiting room area that possessed a dozen hard, plastic chairs. A woman who looked to be in her late fifties sat behind a white counter with chipping paint.

"Hello, Martha." Campbell greeted her.

"Well, hello, hot stuff. Been a while since we've seen you here. You been working?"

"Just finished two days ago. Martha, this is my friend Poppy."

I nodded. "Hello."

"Hello. So you're letting this daredevil take you up?" She clicked her tongue.

I gulped.

"Martha, this is her first time. Let's inspire some confidence."

"Don't you worry, dearie. Campbell's one of the best. You've got nothing to worry about."

"Who's piloting this morning?" Campbell asked.

"I saw Chuck out there about twenty minutes ago. You want me to call him in?"

"Nah. I'll go track him down. Poppy," he turned to me, "the ladies locker room is down the hall, second door on your right. Go ahead and get changed. Make sure to remove all your jewelry.

I'll find you once you're done, and we'll pick out a jumpsuit for you."

Fifteen minutes later, the door to the locker room opened as I finished tying my sneaker. Martha came around the corner holding a wad of pink and purple nylon.

"I thought this one would fit you." She allowed the wad to unravel, revealing a one-piece jumpsuit, similar to something a racecar driver might wear.

My mouth felt cottony, and my knees weakened as I beheld the flimsy material.

"You okay? You look a little pale?"

"Martha, can I be honest with you?" I sat on the wooden bench and dropped my head onto shaky hands. "I don't know what the hell I'm doing here. I'm not even sure I've got the guts to really do this. Campbell asked me if I wanted an adventure, and I said, 'sure.' I had no idea this is what he had planned. I don't think I can do this."

"You poor thing." She sat next to me. "Is that boy bullying you into this?"

"I don't know. Maybe."

"You stay right here." Her work-worn hand patted my thigh. "I'll be back."

I rocked back and forth with the heels of my hands pressed against my eyes.

What the hell am I doing? I can't jump out of plane. This is insane. Who jumps out of a perfectly good plane? Why did I agree to this? Did I agree to this?

My racing mind imagined falling thousands of feet. I tugged and tugged at the red latch, but the parachute refused to deploy. Green grass sped up to meet me. There was a ringing in my ears, and I felt lightheaded. I couldn't seem to get enough air. There wasn't enough air in here. My leaden legs refused to move. *Why can't I stand up to get outside and get some air?*

"Poppy, you're hyperventilating. Put your head between your knees and breathe slowly." Campbell's heavy hand gripped my neck and guided my head downward. "You're okay. You're going to be just fine. You don't have to this. Just breathe deep. Slow it down. That's right. Deep breaths, in and out. In and out."

Eventually, the ringing faded, and I became aware of my surroundings—the hard, wooden bench beneath my rear, the warmth of Campbell's hand on my neck, the cool air blowing down from the vents above. Paint peeled off the lower corner of the sky blue locker in front of me.

"I'm sorry. I said I was up for an adventure, and I thought I was. But I lied. I can't do this." I babbled through my fingers.

"Hey, hey. It's okay. No worries." His hand rubbed against my back as I sat upright. "Here. Drink this."

I took the bottle and drank deeply. The cold water flowed down my throat, its chill cooling all the way down to my stomach. "I'm sorry I didn't say something earlier."

"It's no problem. Better you said something now than thirteen thousand feet up standing at the door."

I continued staring ahead.

"Is it the height? Flying?"

A bark of laughter escaped, and my head turned to meet Campbell's concerned gaze. "It's the jumping out and falling to my death part."

His eyebrows rose. "Ah. Hm. I see. How would you like to take a plane ride? No jumping. Old Chuck will be disappointed if he doesn't get to fly the pretty lady I just promised him."

My lips twisted, "As long as I can stay in the plane."

"Promise." He made a crisscrossing motion against his chest.

Chuck turned out to be a grizzled gentleman in his early sixties with flyaway white hair and a five o'clock shadow. I adored him on sight. He took us up in a four-seat, single-engine, blue-and-white Cessna. Much like Chuck, the interior of the plane had seen better days. Duct tape decorated the seats, and some of the words on the instrument panel had been worn off from use. But, the engine started up immediately and buzzed along like a reliable workhorse. I pointed at dials and buttons on the complicated instrument panel, and Chuck patiently explained what each of them meant.

The late morning sun shimmered and danced along the water as he flew us up the coastline. I'd never flown so low and been able to see the California landscape in this manner. Surfers skidded along the waves, leaving a white trail in their wake, and a pod of dolphins leapt along the water's surface. All too soon, we were bouncing along the short, asphalt runway and slowing to a halt in front of an open hangar.

"So? What did you think?" Campbell had my gym bag slung over his shoulder as we walked off the tarmac.

"It was … an adventure. Thank you for taking me up."

"Maybe next time I can get you to jump."

I grimaced, "Maybe not. But I might consider flying lessons."

"That's better than nothing."

I texted Cody on the drive to Sherman Oaks, assuring her I was alive and well, and that Campbell hadn't stranded me in the middle of nowhere.

When we reached my car, Campbell double-parked, hopped out, and came around to open my door. I tossed the gym bag in the passenger side and turned to face him.

"Thank you, again. I had a fun time."

His eyes stared into mine then drifted down to my mouth. I knew what was coming and did nothing to halt its progress.

The kiss was … let's just say it didn't make my toes curl the way I'd expected. It was nice. Not the dirty, hair-sizzling kiss I'd imagined from adventure boy. I'm not sure why. Perhaps it was me and my new focus on the future.

Campbell ended it and stepped back. "Hmm." He rubbed his chin as we eyed each other. "Shall we try that again?"

I held him off. "Campbell, you're a good guy with a wild adventurous streak that's kind of a turn-on. And honestly, we could try dating, maybe tear up the sheets, but the reality is … this isn't going anywhere. I think we both know that."

He shrugged. "Does it have to go somewhere? Can't we just have fun?"

"I think not. You're looking for the 'right now' girl, which I've been in the past, and I could certainly see slipping into that role with you. But I'm not that girl anymore. I'm looking for more than the 'right now' guy. I'm looking for the 'forever' guy." I tilted my head.

He cleared his throat and nodded. At least he was honest about it.

"Friends?"

I nodded. "Absolutely, friends. After all, I never know when I might need someone with the skills to jump out of an airplane, or navigate me out of the woods."

"Yeah. Keep me in mind in case you ever want to release the wild child inside."

"You'll be the first one I call." I grinned.

He retreated back to the Jeep and gave a "beep, beep" of the horn before driving off. I waited for the heavy rain cloud of disappointment to set in. Nope. I only felt a sense of serenity. For once, I said no to the bad boy. And it was okay.

On my way back to work, I phoned Sophie and told her about the non-skydiving adventure, which turned into a lovely plane ride and ended with the nice, but uninspiring kiss.

"So, no sparks?" Sophie asked.

"It was less sizzle and more like pssst …." I imitated a leaky tire. "I think we could have had fun together, and the sex would have been okay, but it wouldn't have gone anywhere."

"I'm proud of you." Sophie said.

"Gee, thanks, Mom."

"C'mon, I'm being serious. You're keeping your eye on the ball. This Campbell guy sounds exactly like the emotionally unavailable, bad-boy type you normally hook up with. Yet you took a step back, didn't give into the thrill, and made the hard decision to let him go. I think you're on the path to finding Mr. Right."

"Well … thanks, I guess." I appreciated hearing my own assessment voiced out loud. "I've got another computer date tomorrow. So, I'll let you know what time to provide the emergency phone call."

"You're on."

. . .

Adam pushed himself to the wall on the final lap, slapping it with a tired hand. He stood and, in a fluid movement, pulled the goggles and swim cap off, and rubbed the water out of his eyes. It had been almost a week since he'd gotten in a swim, and he knew he'd feel it in his shoulders tomorrow. They were right—getting old sucked. His body would never be in the form it once was in his college days when he was a champion swimmer.

As he dried off by the pool, his phone rattled like a snake. Poppy's name blinked at him.

His heartbeat picked up. Was she calling to cancel? "Hello, stranger. What's up?"

"Hey, darlin', it's good to hear your voice. It seems as though we've only been able to communicate electronically these days."

"You, too. I'm looking forward to Denver."

"Listen, that's why I'm calling."

He tensed. "What's the matter?"

"Nothing. I just need to know if we'll be skiing, because if we are, I'll need to dig my ski gear out of the creepy storage crawlspace, and I'll probably reconsider the amount of shoes I'm mentally packing."

He released a relieved breath of laughter. "Of course you do."

"Hey, this is no laughing matter. Female packing is an art. You boys have it easy. Suit, shirts, pair of shoes, you're done."

"Don't forget the tie."

She snorted. "Right, the tie. You have no idea. We ladies have daytime and evening clothes to pack, matching shoes for each outfit, belts, jewelry, and accessories. Not to mention makeup and hair care products. If you toss in a ski trip, the luggage practically doubles."

Adam's grin grew wider as Poppy listed off all the junk she needed to pack. "Yes, I see your dilemma. Fear not, no skiing this time. So stay out of the spider-ridden crawlspace."

"Good news."

"So what have you been up to? Any more inspiring dates?" He dreaded asking, but curiosity won out.

"Actually, I found myself set up on a blind date this morning. Long story short, my clients arranged it. He took me out to go skydiving."

Adam plopped down on a bench by the pool. "Skydiving? Have you lost your *mind*?"

"Don't have a heart attack. I panicked and talked him out of that idea."

"Jesus. Skydiving?"

"Yup."

"Where do you find these nut jobs?"

"Actually, Campbell was probably the most normal guy I've been on a date with since I started this," she said defensively. "However, as … interesting as the date was, I felt Campbell was one of the emotionally unavailable types and a little too much of a thrill seeker for my current dating goals. So we parted friends. Sophie claims she's proud of me for not succumbing to his good looks and 'keeping my eye on the ball.'"

"I see." Great, now he needed to figure out how to turn her eye on his ball.

"As a matter of fact, I've got another date coming up tomorrow. But don't worry, I'm still planning to have fun at our tryst in Denver. I consider it a little vacation, away from the dating merry-go-round of trying to find my 'forever' fellow. It'll actually be nice to be with someone I know who isn't a blind date or a stranger from the Internet. I can relax."

That's not exactly the news he was hoping for, nor was it the mindset he wanted her to bring to Denver.

"Oh crap," she said before he could respond. "I've gotta run. I've got a bridezilla texting me. See you soon."

Adam ran a frustrated hand down his face. He couldn't believe she was still going on these crazy computer dates to find her "forever guy." So, she viewed their upcoming visit as another vacation fling. She didn't even seem open to the possibility that it might lead to more. He was going to have to figure out a way to change her mind when she arrived. It would be nice if she could get on the same page he was, but he wasn't willing to make any dramatic declarations that might force her to cancel altogether. Until then, he'd have to sit tight and hope her dates continued on their ruinous journey.

Chapter Eight

The burnt orange glow of sun rode low in the sky, and Echo Park foot traffic was scarce as I approached the statue of the Lady of the Lake, her hands up in a submissive gesture. The fountains behind her shot high into the air, water clouds billowing in the breeze. A man in a green jacket splayed across the center bench behind the statue, his blond hair ruffled by the breeze. As I came around the front of the seats, he spotted me and rose.

"Hello, are you John?"

"You must be Poppy. Namaste." He nodded and gave a serene smile.

To my relief, his likeness resembled the online photo. The hair looked a little longer, but the blue eyes were the same, and he sported day-old stubble.

"That's me. Uh, namaste."

We shook hands, and as he indicated the bench, a whiff of something sweet and herbal swept by. I crossed my legs and angled toward him, but he left a fair amount of space between us and reclined into a slouch.

"Here." He pulled a bottle of water from his sweatshirt. "I thought you might be thirsty from walking."

"Thanks. I found a parking spot about a block away." The cap clicked, and I took a few sips. "So, John, your profile said you were in marketing? Tell me about that."

He slid a pair of aviators on and tilted his head back. "Not anymore. Quit my job last week."

My eyes flared wide in surprise. "I see. What are your plans now?"

"I'm becoming a life coach."

I'd heard of this sort of profession and even had some acquaintances swear by their life coach's advice. It just seemed a bit of a divergence from marketing, but who was I to judge? "Okaay … Have you been training for that? Is there some sort of degree or certificate to become a life coach?"

"There's an online course I'm thinking of taking. But, no I don't have a degree. See, I've been in the marketing biz for almost fifteen years, and one day I decided I'd had enough." His words were measured and slow.

Sure, I could see that. "Rat race get to you?"

The serene smile returned. "Have you ever seen footage of the New York Stock Exchange trading floor from the 80s? People yelling, throwing paper around in a frenzy, like shark-infested waters? It's all about competition and knowing your career could go down the toilet with one wrong trade."

I knew what he spoke of and nodded. "Yes, I believe I do."

My phone rang. It was Sophie providing our agreed-upon, rescue phone call. There was something about John; I kind of understood where he was coming from, and I wanted to hear more. "Sorry, let me turn this off." I sent it to voice mail and turned my ringer on vibrate. "You were saying?"

"That's what marketing became to me. The shark-infested waters of the Stock Exchange. For my two-week vacation, I went to an ashram in the Napa Valley. While I was there, I found peace with nature and within myself." He folded his hands across his heart. "As my time drew to a close, I realized I couldn't go back to the insanity of meaningless absurdity. On my last night, I spoke long into the night with Mohir, the yogi. He helped me understand that my life's mission wasn't promoting infantile and futile products that poison our bodies and our society. It's to help people release the insanity poisoning their lives. To focus on what's important and identify their purpose on this Earth. Thus, life coach."

"Life coach." I nodded. John's Dalai Lama-like peace within himself made sense. I understood. Sometimes in the midst of a crisis, I too wondered what all the hubbub was about. Why should we get upset if the flowers didn't perfectly match the bridesmaids' dresses? Perhaps spending time with John, I could learn to channel some of this tranquility into my own life.

He rose and held out his hand. "Shall we walk?"

I fell into step beside him. The herbal scent wafted past again, and I tried to pin down where I'd smelled it before.

"That sounds rather brave. Giving up a concrete income and branching out onto a completely different career path."

"Not at all. Not after the light came to me."

"Um hm. The light?"

"Some might call it the light of God, Allah, Vishnu, or whatever higher being you believe in. I believe a higher being spoke to me, took my hand, and led me in this direction."

"Interesting." Wow, I'd never met a person who'd had such a cerebral, God-like experience. John pulled at my curiosity, and I found myself fascinated to hear more. *Maybe I should research this ashram thing.*

"What about you? You said in your profile that you're a party planner."

"Yes. I help people plan weddings, bar mitzvahs, birthday parties. Celebrations, you know. I help bring joy into people's lives by making their day the best it can be."

"Yet you're playing into the idea that tablecloths and music will create the fairy tale, when really it should be about the joining together of people. The open exchange of ideas. The love families bring together."

"Yes, you're right. I do help with the trimmings, I guess." I chewed my lip. John had a point. Some of my parties were absolutely frivolous. But I loved what I did, and I felt as though I needed to defend myself. "You see, on a wedding day, there is nothing more special as when the bride walks down the aisle … and the groom sees her, in the beautiful dress … and his face transforms from nerves into love. You can't put a price on that. I guess I'm kind of like you—I want to help people experience happiness."

"Admirable, but at what cost? What does it cost you in stress and time and your own familial obligations? Don't you ever want to get off the highway and travel the back roads?"

"Hmm ... I never thought about it. Sure my job can be intense and stressful at times. But that's life." I shrugged.

"I could help you release that stress."

I remained silent.

"We can talk more about this later. I'm starving. How about we grab a bite to eat?"

By this time, we'd walked to the edge of the park and my own stomach made a growly noise. "What did you have in mind?"

"There's a place a few blocks up that I know. Are you comfortable walking?"

I'd worn flats, so walking wasn't a problem. The streetlights of Glendale Boulevard blinked on as we strolled up the busy street.

After about two blocks, John's mellow, striding gait came to a halt. There wasn't much to see. A Taco Bell stood across the street, a drugstore was on our side of the street, there was a church. I didn't see a restaurant.

"Where's this place you know?"

"Right there." He pointed to the Taco Bell and removed his sunglasses.

Is this a joke? "Taco Bell? Seriously?" My brows rose.

"Yes, I'm jonesing for a burrito."

Oh, hell no!

"Are you kidding me? You don't take a woman to Taco Bell on a first date; I don't care what new age revelation you've just had. What are you smokin', pal?" I threw up my hands.

"Well ... I did have a toke of White Widow before you showed up. Why? Do you want some?"

He gave me that slow, serene grin, and I leaned in close, squinting at him. John's pupils were dilated, something I hadn't noticed earlier; and I now realized the herbal odor emanating from him was aroma of marijuana. Christ! He wasn't some sort of enlightened guru; he was a pot-smoking washout.

"That's it. John, good luck with your life coach business. I'm outta here."

I pivoted on my heel and stalked back toward my car.

"Wait. Are you sure?" he called at my back. "The triple steak stack is back and on sale for only a buck eighty nine."

"Unbelievable. Taking me to a Taco Bell." A group of teens split like the Red Sea as I stomped down the street, mumbling to myself and waving my arms. My phone vibrated beneath my fingers.

"Hello!" I barked.

"Whoa! Hey, it's Sophie. What's wrong? Are you okay?"

"I've just had a date with a bum."

"What? This guy is a homeless person?"

"Not yet. But his ashram, life-coaching, Taco Bell-eating, weed-smoking ass soon will be, I have no doubt."

"Taco Bell? Weed? What?"

My feet swept me down the street, my arms flapping as I described the crazy date. "You know, for a few minutes I was thinking, 'This guy's really got it going on. He got the Zen thing. He's harnessed the answer to life.' I actually wanted to be more like him, until I realized he'd just smoked a joint and his blathering was a drug-induced trip. Really! How did the guy go from successful marketer to pot-smoking loser in a few short weeks? Hmm? How? Is this what they teach at ashrams?"

"I … don't … know," Sophie choked out.

"And how on Earth do I keep getting hooked up with these losers? Answer me that. Do you know anyone who's had such zany computer dates? I swear I'm attracting the lunatics. These guys look good on paper, but when we get together, it's like the crazy train comes into town."

"Um …"

"Go ahead. Laugh. I know you want to."

"I wouldn't … d-d-d"—she inhaled deeply—"dare."

I beeped my car open and angled into the driver's seat. "Humph." I took deep breaths, expelling through my nostrils. "Okay, I admit. This was a funny one."

She couldn't hold it in any longer. Laughter filled the phone lines. "Oh, Poppy." She wheezed. "I'm sorry, but you are hilarious. I can envision the entire incident."

"I suppose it was kind of funny, but, my God, how do I keep ending up with the wack-a-loons?"

"I don't know, sweetie. But you can't give up yet. If anything, it's entertaining as hell."

I sighed and rubbed a hand down my face. "You know, it's a good thing I have a sense of humor, otherwise I'd be completely demoralized."

"Oh, girlfriend. I don't know what to tell you."

I sighed. "There's nothing to say. This was my plan to find Mr. Right. But honestly, I think I've reached the end of my rope. This is the last computer date. Hell, my skydiving blind date was better than the two computer losers. I'm taking my name off the site before I leave for Denver."

"I don't blame you. We'll move on to the party idea. Wait, what Denver trip?"

Oops. I hadn't told Sophie about meeting up with my Hawaii hottie in Denver. "Uh, remember the dermatologist I told you about from Hawaii. Adam?"

"Sure, I've seen the pictures. He's a cutie. You're meeting up with him in Denver?"

"He has a medical conference and asked if I could meet him there."

"Get out. I didn't know you were still in touch."

"Yes," I cleared my throat, "actually we email and text fairly regularly."

"How come you never said anything?"

I don't know why I kept my relationship with Adam secret from Sophie. It's like I felt the need to protect it. "Dunno."

"Hmm. This is an interesting turn of events. Where did you say he lived?"

"Soph, I can tell by your voice you're reading too much into this. We're just friends. Well … maybe friends with benefits. And he lives in Ohio, which is precisely why it won't be anything more than that."

"Riiight. So, you'll be gettin' sumpin' sumpin' in Denver, eh?"

"Yeah." My stomach rumbled. "Crap. I *am* hungry. I need to get something to eat." I glanced around, but didn't see any eateries in a thirty-foot radius. "You know what? I could go for a gordita."

"No! Don't tell me you're going to go back to the Taco Bell! You just left."

"Heck, yeah. It's one thing to buy my own. It's completely different to have some guy take me there on a first date," I sniffed. "Besides, I'll go through the drive-thru. Catch you later."

I drove into the Taco Bell parking lot and kept my eyes peeled for Mr. Pothead. He didn't disappoint. As I slid by the front window, I saw John standing atop a table, arms waving like seaweed in water, with a burrito in one hand. His glasses were back on, and it looked like he was singing.

When I pulled up to the window, the kid held out his hand. "That's six twenty-nine."

"What's with the nut on the table?" I passed him a ten.

"Dunno." He shrugged. "Drunk or high. Who knows? We think he's trying to sing Tom Jones. If he doesn't knock it off, my manager's going to call the cops. Here's your change."

"Thanks." I sped out of the parking lot, laughing in relief to have escaped.

• • •

To: Adam from Hawaii
From: Poppy Reagan
Subject: Don't do drugs, kids.
Here to bring you today's entertainment. So, my latest computer date was supposed to be a successful marketer. At least that's what his profile indicated. He instead decided to visit an ashram last week, and while there, apparently found the meaning of life through yoga and wacky tobacky. He's quit his job, and while craving the munchies, decided to take me to a well-known eatery called ... El Taco Bell. Yes, that's right; he offered to take me to the Bell, the place with the Chihuahua ads.
Adam, you know me. Do I look like the type of woman you should take, on a date, to Taco Bell? I didn't think so. Here's the embarrassing part: I was actually buying his guru-intellectual-life-affirming crapola until I realized his serenity came from too many tokes from the bong. That's it. I'm off computer dating and plan to start having my friends set me up with normal people.
To top off this fun-loving week, my mom announced she's coming in for a visit after my trip to Denver. I've told you a little about her. I'm worried this is the beginning of her next divorce and all the accompanying drama that goes along with it. Ugh!
Looking forward Denver and connecting with a normal human being. I'm packing my Chanel No. 5, red panties, and nothing else. ;-)
Poppy

Adam roared with laughter. God, he loved her sense of humor. In a way he felt sorry for Poppy's bad luck. On the other hand, these crazy dates were only making him look better.

To: Poppy Reagan

From: Adam from Hawaii

Subject: You're killing me.

Where are you finding these losers? Are you sure your name is registered under a legitimate dating site? Or is it just the nutty Californians?

Don't sweat your mom's visit. Did you ever think that she might just want to see her only child now that she lives on a whole other continent? Give her a break. For me?

Adam

P.S. Looking forward to seeing the red panties.

Chapter Nine

After shoving my Rollaboard suitcase into the overhead compartment, I slid into the first class seat with a relieved sigh and nodded vaguely at the sixtyish businessman sitting next to the window. Adam was due a special treat for upgrading me.

I sent one last text to Adam before shutting off the phone:

On my way!

I rubbed my tired eyes and lay back against the headrest, wrinkling my nose against the mixed scents of burnt coffee and jet fuel. The door closed with a thunk, and a flight attendant stood in front of us demonstrating the seat belt buckle and providing emergency procedures as the plane rolled back from the gate.

It always seemed so ludicrous to me that a little margarine cup attached to an IV baggie was going to save my life in the case of drop in cabin pressure.

You know why a drop in cabin pressure would happen? Because there's a hole in the blasted plane! my mind silently screamed at the flight attendant. I closed my eyes and ignored the rest of the safety lecture.

The workweek had kept me so busy, I'd barely had time to squeeze in a visit to the salon for waxing and a mani-pedi. Worse, I'd stayed at a client's engagement bash well past midnight, the time I'd originally planned to leave, and didn't get home until after two. Subsequently, I was late getting up, but my actions the rest of the morning could only be described as shameful, and I prayed no one I knew had seen me.

Desperate to make the ten o'clock flight, I'd driven like a bat out of hell, weaving in and out of lanes, running two red lights, and, worst of all, pulling into a right turn lane to pass a slowpoke in a silver Prius. All while barking orders over the phone at poor Cody.

Once I arrived at the airport, I decided to pay for the convenience of valet parking and had to cut over three lanes to make the proper turnoff. Upon picking up the valet, I slammed my foot on the accelerator before his door was completely closed, cut off two more cars on the way to curbside drop off, and squealed to a stop in front of the United Airlines door. Because the poor kid was having a minor heart attack, I didn't wait for him to help me with my bags. I threw a tip in his general direction, hustled past a pair of septuagenarians, and practically mowed down a family with two young children to beat them to the boarding pass kiosk.

My actions didn't stop there. It was either a blessing from God, or I'm going to hell for taking advantage of another person's calamity. At the security checkpoint, TSA guards led a very loud and rather dirty, foreign-speaking couple off in handcuffs. While folks in line were distracted, I slipped under the ropes and butted in front of dozens of other passengers, saving myself at least ten to fifteen minutes.

The engines powered up, shaking the cabin as the plane roared down the runway. I reclined the seat, stretched my sore muscles, and yawned. If I could get the next two and a half hours of flight time to catch some extra shuteye, I'd be okay for whatever Adam had planned.

"Ma'am? Ma'am?" A gentle finger tapped my shoulder.

I woke to a pair of blue eyes level with mine.

"You need to put your seat up. We're about to land," the flight attendant said.

I nodded, pressed the button, and mumbled incoherently. Goodness, I'd never gotten such good sleep on a plane before—maybe I should upgrade to first class more often. Fifteen minutes later, the sleepy haze cleared as we rolled to a gentle stop at the gate.

The fasten seat belt sign dinged off, and the frenzy of unclicking belts echoed through the plane as passengers jumped up to get a place in the narrow aisle.

My fist clenched, and butterflies fluttered in my stomach. I was a short walk and taxi ride away from seeing Adam. It'd been five months since we'd seen each other in Hawaii, and I hoped I looked as good to him as I did then. It's not liked I'd gained weight or anything. I'd inherited Mom's metabolism, so I had nothing to worry about there. But, in Hawaii, Adam had seen me prancing around in bikinis and sundresses, a far cry from the heavy coat and boots I'd be wearing in frigid Denver, Colorado. After a period of time, we forget or exaggerate a person's looks and personality in our minds. I knew this was a weekend fling for the both of us, but for some reason my expectations seemed have zoomed up to Empire State Building heights. Maybe because of my dismal computer dates, I desperately hoped Adam would renew my faith that there were actually normal men in the single consortium. Would the weekend measure up to my burgeoning anticipation?

The red luggage rolled behind me as I joined the deplaning passengers. Once past security, I detached myself from the herd heading toward luggage retrieval and glanced around for signs to the taxi stand.

A sharp whistle rang out, and my head swiveled to the left. He stood with two other chauffeurs, holding a printed, yellow, sticky note that read REAGAN. Dark glasses covered up his beautiful, hazel eyes, and the orange and blue Denver Broncos baseball cap he wore stood out in the small group. He looked divine in a gray business suit with the top button of his shirt open, exposing that sexy little dip at his throat.

My heart rate picked up. I hadn't expected him to be at the airport. I came to an awkward halt in the middle of the hallway. I'd run scenarios of our meeting through my head, and now the moment was here—earlier than I'd anticipated. Subconsciously, I fluffed my hair and prayed my eye makeup hadn't smudged while I slept.

• • •

There she stood, looking as beautiful as he'd remembered. She had those long legs that he dreamed about having wrapped around him, and she emanated a sense of calm confidence that reminded him of Grace Kelly in *To Catch A Thief*. It was probably the reason she was able to handle her job so well.

"Adam?"

He grinned and removed his shades, and when she flung herself into his arms, he didn't even stumble. He wrapped himself around her and buried his nose into her hair, inhaling her signature scent, Chanel No. 5. Boy, it felt good to have her in his embrace.

"You smell divine."

"So do you," she mumbled into his neck.

"Did you bring the red panties?" he whispered.

She glanced up beneath her lashes and gave a sexy, sly smile. "I'm wearing them." Her hips wiggled against him.

Her body stirred the embers of his sexual awareness, and his lips descended upon hers. No feather-light nips. The kiss was hard and raw. He felt like a starving man. His tongue beckoned at the gates, and she opened, allowing his to dance with hers. Poppy wrapped her arms around his neck, and her slender fingers played with the hair peeking below the baseball cap, sending tingles of pleasure down his spine. He pulled her close, and she rose up on tiptoe as their bodies melded together. Finally, his lips gently retreated, and they parted.

Her lashes fluttered open, and he stared down into her jade eyes with undisguised lust. A wolf whistle echoed in the massive corridor, and her cheeks pinked. Reluctantly, he allowed her to peel herself off his chest, but Adam wasn't ready to completely let go. He shifted her into the circle of his left arm and grabbed the suitcase with his right hand.

"Is this all the luggage you brought?"

She gave a limp nod.

"Good," he growled and guided her to the exit.

The doors swished open, and a frigid breeze made her snuggle closer to his warmth.

"Since when did you become a Broncos fan?" She tapped the brim of his hat. "I thought you were a Browns fan. Isn't that sacrilegious or something?"

He grimaced. "I'd forgotten I was wearing it. I lost a bet to a buddy of mine and had to wear it while I gave a lecture this morning at breakfast."

"What was the bet?"

His eyes shifted to her and away. He cleared his throat. "I bet him he couldn't get the cocktail waitress's phone number."

"Ha!"

"Hey, I figured she spent her life fending off unwanted advances from hotel guests. How was I to know Greg's charm would work on her?"

"Are you sure she gave him a real number? Not the number to the local exterminator?"

He shook his head. "He met her for lunch today."

"Wow, he must be one smooth operator. Do I get to meet him?"

"Absolutely not. Greg can't have all the beautiful girls," he groused.

They stopped in front of a black Ford Escape. He fished the keys out of his pocket and popped the lift gate, and she pulled her peacock blue coat closer as he stepped away to load the baggage.

"Where's your coat? It's freezing out here," she scolded.

"It's not so bad." He tossed the Broncos hat on top of the luggage. "I left it in the car."

"Well, for heaven's sake, put it on. It must be fifteen degrees out. You're a doctor; you should know better. Hypothermia and all that."

"It's almost forty. That's my California girl talking. You miss your sun." He tweaked her nose.

She wrinkled it up. "Are you making fun of me?"

"Never." He swooped in and planted a fast kiss on her lips. "C'mon. Hop in before you become an icicle." The trunk slammed shut. "Normally, I'd get your door for you, but these parking spaces make for tight quarters."

They both inched their doors open and slipped in, taking care not to nick the cars on either side. Once situated, Adam cranked the engine, turned the heat up to high and flicked off the radio. Her fingers sent zips of electricity through him as she gripped the hand resting on the gearshift.

"All right, mountain man, your hands are freezing. At least put some gloves on."

"You know what they say … cold hands, warm heart. Why don't you slip on over here and warm me up?" He patted his lap and wiggled his eyebrows.

She leaned over and whispered in his ear, "Why don't you just admit it's colder than a frosted frog and put your coat on?"

She drew the lobe into her mouth.

Adam sucked wind. "Oh baby, I think you're warming me up just fine." He turned and his lips found hers again. Lust hardened his shaft. He was about to drag her onto his lap, but she pulled away before he could make good on his intentions.

"I'm not twenty anymore. I can't contort myself to do the hanky-panky behind the steering wheel. Besides, isn't there a big, fluffy bed back at the hotel?" She pulled his navy parka through the gap between the front seats. "In the meantime, try this for now."

"I suppose. But there's a good-size backseat right here."

She raised a skeptical eyebrow.

He laughed and admitted defeat. "Fine, have it your way."

He pulled on the coat while she drew on a pair of gloves, and once they were buckled in, Adam reversed out of the tight parking spot and followed the exit signs. "Unfortunately, I'll have to leave you to get settled on your own once we get to the hotel. I'm on a panel session at two thirty, but it should only take an hour."

The digital clock on the dashboard read one fifty-six. Her shoulders seemed to droop a bit. "How long does it take to get back to the hotel?"

"'Bout half an hour."

"Cutting it a little close, aren't we?"

"Your plane arrived late. I should be okay, as long as there isn't an accident on the highway." He knew it was close, but there had been a driving need in his gut to see her, so he'd risked being late for the session. Her scent filled the car, enveloping him. She rested her gloved hand on his thigh, and he felt the warmth spread up and down his leg. He released the steering wheel with his right hand to cover it.

"Thanks for picking me up. I wasn't expecting you to be at the airport. I planned to take a cab." she said softly.

"I couldn't wait. I wanted to see you."

Out of the corner of his eye he saw a feline smile spread across her face. "Tell me about the conference. You got here … Monday? How's it been going?"

"Tuesday night. Wednesday was the official kickoff of the conference. Like I said, I gave a lecture this morning. Once this panel session is over, my responsibilities are pretty much done, and I'm all yours."

"I look forward to it," she said in a husky voice.

They sat in companionable silence as the car sped down the highway; the imposing snow-topped Rocky Mountains loomed to the west, and the city of Denver lay ahead in their sights. The sun reflected off bright-snowy rooftops and trees, and she reached into her handbag to retrieve a pair of sunglasses.

"So, any more computer dates since the Taco Bell incident?" he asked with a straight face, although restrained laughter might have crept through his delivery.

She wrinkled her pert little nose and frowned. "No and no. I'm quitting the computer dating. And I don't want to talk or even think about those disasters this weekend."

His mouth twitched. *That was good news.* "Fine by me."

"Which reminds me, you never told me what happened between you and the schoolteacher."

He shifted. "It just didn't work out."

"Is that code for she dumped you?"

"It's not code for anything. We simply decided we wanted different things."

"Ah." She nodded. "Was she picturing two kids, a dog, and a white picket fence, and you weren't ready?"

"Um …" He released her hand to exit the highway and shifted uncomfortably.

"Well? Was that it?"

"Sure."

"What do you mean, sure?"

"Look, I don't want to talk about it. Okay?" he said more sharply than he'd intended.

She removed her hand from his thigh and shifted closer to the door. "Okay. Sorry, I didn't realize it was a hot-button issue."

His jaw flexed, and she looked away to stare out the front windshield. The car remained silent.

He sighed. This was not the way he wanted this weekend to start. But it was evidently important to Poppy that they clear the air about his past relationship before she could move on. "I broke up with her because I couldn't love her. Not the way she wanted or deserved."

"I see. Sorry it didn't work out."

"Seriously? Are you really sorry?"

"Well, uh …"

The light turned red, and as they drew to a halt, he tilted his head to gaze at her over his sunglasses. Her cheeks turned pink, and he caught his breath.

"Maybe I'm not." She raised an eyebrow. "Does that make me a bad person?"

"No." He retrieved her hand and placed it back on his thigh. The light changed and his muscle flexed. "It doesn't make either one of us a bad person. Sometimes things don't work out. I'd rather be here with you."

"Me too." She grinned.

At two twenty-five, he drew the car to a halt in front of the hotel. The bellhop opened her door, and a valet jogged around to Adam's side.

Adam gave the keys to the man and walked to the trunk where the bellhop retrieved Poppy's bag.

"Checking in?" he asked.

"She's with me in room twelve-twenty-two." Adam handed him a ten. "Can you please see Ms. Reagan to the room?"

"Yes, sir." The bellhop's round face beamed.

Adam escorted her into a modern, gleaming lobby. "Here's a room key." He slipped a purple keycard with a Nexium logo into her hands and pulled her in for one more, toe-curling kiss. *Damn, she tasted good.* He really wished he didn't have this session. He was ready to throw her down on the big, king-size bed in the suite he'd wrangled from Smitty.

"I'm sorry; I've got to run."

"Go, go." She grinned, shooing him away. "Don't be late on my account."

Reluctantly, he released her, slipped off his coat, handed it to the bellhop, and hurried off to his panel session.

• • •

I watched his backside stride away, admiring the strong shoulders and tight butt, bummed he couldn't come back to the room and finish what we'd started in the car.

"If you'll follow me, ma'am." The bellhop, whose nametag read Ernesto, jogged me out of contemplating Adam's fine ass, and I trailed him to the bank of elevators and into an empty car. He slipped a card into a slot on the button panel and pushed the twelfth floor.

"You're on the concierge level, so you'll need to use your keycard to get onto the floor."

I nodded.

"Is this your first visit to Denver?"

I gave a bland smile. "No, I've been to Colorado a few times. It's a beautiful state, but quite a bit colder than California."

"Yes, ma'am."

The elevator came to a stop, and once again, Ernesto led the way.

"Here is the Regency Club lounge. Coffee, tea, and pop available all day long. In the mornings there is a continental breakfast, cookies and brownies throughout the rest of the day, and hors d'oeuvres in the evenings."

He stopped in front of room twelve twenty-two, swiped the keycard, and handed it back to me. I walked into an earth tone-decorated, one-bedroom suite. Tossing my coat and handbag on a chair, I wandered over to the glass picture windows, which revealed a stunning vista of the soaring mountain range. I pushed the curtains farther apart to enjoy the view as Ernesto unloaded my luggage and rambled on about the hotel's other amenities.

"Will that be all, ma'am?"

I turned. "Yes, thank you."

"My pleasure." He gave a brief nod and left, closing the door with a soft click.

The bathroom revealed a large soaking tub and walk-in shower. Two fluffy white robes hung on hooks. I turned the tub's taps to hot, squirted some of the complimentary lavender body wash under the spray, and wandered back into the bedroom. Ernesto had left my suitcase on the bed. I put my sweaters and jeans away in a drawer and hung two dresses and slacks next to Adam's suits in the closet.

Ten minutes later, I lay dozing in the warm bath, enveloped by tiny, popping bubbles. My toes floated to the surface, and shell pink polish peeped at me.

Ah, I could get used to this type of treatment. First class ticket and a hotel suite.

I'd never considered becoming a kept woman, but with amenities like this, I understood why some girls fell into the lifestyle.

My mind wandered back to the discussion in the car about Adam's breakup with his girlfriend. It surprised me Adam had been so cagey.

We are both free agents, so why wouldn't he tell me what the breakup was about? Normally, he was a straight shooter. He never seemed to hold back in our emails and sporadic phone calls. I'd told him about Richard … well, not everything, but the overall picture. Come to think of it, when I was actually dating Richard, Adam seemed to shy away from talking about it. *Perhaps Adam isn't a relationship type of guy. Well that's fine with me. He makes the perfect go-to guy for a fling or weekend booty call. Maybe the breakup itself didn't go well and he feels bad about crushing her heart. Maybe I needed to relax and stop psychoanalyzing everything.*

I sighed and slid further down into the water.

Chapter Ten

It was four thirty, and Adam still hadn't gotten out of the seminar room when Poppy texted a selfie to him. Her hair was swept up with loose tendrils curling against her soft neck; she wore a sexy, black cocktail dress and tall boots that only served to elongate her fabulous legs. She looked stunning, and he was grinding his teeth to escape. The moderator had allowed the questions to continue beyond the scheduled time, and afterward, at least a dozen attendees had mobbed the table to ask "just one more question."

When he finally got back to the room at ten past five, he found it empty with a note from Poppy that said he could find her at the top-floor bar. He needed to change before dinner, so he stripped and turned on the shower. The bathroom smelled flowery, and bubbly remnants from Poppy's bath remained. Adam went hard thinking about her naked, floating in the tub. He turned the spray to cold and stepped in. As he showered, he wracked his brain, trying to determine the best tactic to take with her. The good news: she'd given up on the computer dates. The bad news: she planned to move on to other means. How could he put himself in the rotation? He scrubbed with the shampoo, frustrated by the limited time they had together.

Twenty minutes later, he stepped off the elevator, his hair damp and his suit exchanged for a pair of black slacks, a blue button-down and a sport coat to find two middle-aged men fawning over Poppy. One man was standing next to her doing the obvious "gut suck" while the other guy leaned in a little too close as he spoke. A spark of possessiveness flashed through him.

"Right. Right. So, Ravi asks to see the x-rays, because he's already thinking about doing the surgery himself."

"Put it in context, man. I used to work in an ER before moving into dermatology."

She jumped as he slid a hand across her shoulder and his two lips descended upon the back of her neck. The sitting guy stopped talking, and the gut sucker deflated a bit.

"You look stunning," he whispered her ear.

Goosebumps rose on the back of her neck, and she twisted in her seat to run a finger across his lapel.

"Making friends?" He grinned and draped her coat that he'd brought from the room over the back of the barstool.

"Right." She cleared her throat and dragged her eyes back to the other gentlemen. "Ravi, Ted, this is Adam Patterson, from Ohio."

He shook hands with Ravi and Ted.

"I attended your lecture on treatments for psoriasis this morning," Ravi said. "Do you really think the new drug therapy is better for acute plaque psoriasis than topical creams? There seem to be so many more side effects."

"Well, it depends on the patient, you know. You need to weigh the two carefully, and if you're getting good results with the topical, then there's no reason to change."

Ted and Ravi nodded.

Adam had no interest in talking shop with these strangers; it felt as though the weekend with Poppy was already slipping away. "I'm sorry to break up this little party, but I owe the lady dinner."

"So soon? Why don't you stay for a drink?" Ted begged.

"That's right. It's still early." Ravi checked his watch.

"Stay. Have a Coors, the silver bullet. Brewed right here in Colorado." Ted raised his glass, and a bit sloshed onto his hand.

"Sorry, guys, we've got reservations. Don't want to be late." He tossed down a twenty to cover Poppy's drink and helped her off the stool.

"Gentlemen, it was lovely meeting you. Perhaps we'll meet again and you can finish telling me the story about Peaches," she said.

Adam escorted her out of the bar to the elevators. "I think you acquired a little fan club back there."

"They were both married. Harmless. They're in the 'look-don't-touch mode.'" The elevator opened to reveal an empty car, and she preceded Adam in.

"I'm in a look *and* touch mode." His eyes raked her from the tip of her pointy boots up to the top of her ginger head. *God, she looked gorgeous. I have an urge to taste her.* He pressed the lobby button and the doors closed.

He grabbed both of her hands, plastering her between him and the mirrored wall of the elevator. Her purse and coat fell to the floor unheeded. He stretched her hands above her head and allowed his lips to nip along her perfumed skin across the jawline and down her neck. The scent of his sandalwood cologne mixed with her musky jasmine fragrance, and fire exploded in his gut as he felt her nipples harden against his chest.

"I thought I could get a preview of the red bra and panties." He breathed into her cleavage.

"Sorry to disappoint," she panted, "I changed into a black"—here she sucked in a breath as his fingers dipped into the cusp of the bra line—"pair."

"Mmm … sexy." He pulled the bra and dress down, exposing the erect nipple and sucked it into his mouth.

Her eyes closed and she mewled.

"Have you ever had sex in an elevator?" Adam's breath whispered across the rosy flesh.

She rolled her head back and forth against the hard glass.

"Maybe we should try it." His tongue flicked back and forth, teasing the sensitive bud.

"Umph," was all she seemed able to answer.

A faint ding sounded and he felt the elevator slow. "Shit." He released her hands and flipped her dress back into place. In a fluid movement he scooped up the purse and coat and pulled her against him as the elevator doors slid open. His body reeled with unquenched needs; clearly the cold shower did nothing to tamp down his desire. Poppy, flushed and still breathing heavily, leaned against him for support, and his rock hard erection pressed against her thigh.

A fiftyish couple he recognized boarded the elevator.

"Hello, Adam. It's nice to see you again," the petite, gray-haired lady greeted.

"Hi, Margo. I didn't realize you and Al were still in town." Adam shifted to try to hide his raging erection.

"We leave tomorrow. Who's your friend?" Keen blue eyes surveyed Poppy.

"Poppy Reagan, meet Margo and Al Greene. Al is on the legislative and regulatory affairs committee with me."

"Hello," she said a bit breathlessly and stepped directly in front of Adam to shake hands with each of them. "Good to meet you."

"Poppy is a friend of mine who was able to fly in from California for the weekend." He gripped her waist.

"How nice for you." Margo smiled, shifting her gaze back and forth between them.

"Where are you going for dinner?" Al seemed oblivious to the sexual tension running rampant between them.

"We're going to Elway's at the Ritz," Adam replied, greatly regretting his compulsion to take Poppy out this evening. He should have ordered room service.

Al nodded, "Yup. Took Margo there on Tuesday. Got the prime rib. Outstanding."

Margo nodded along with her husband. "We're going to get a drink in the lobby bar. Would you like to join us before dinner?"

To his relief, the elevator stopped, and the doors opened at the lobby level.

"Another time," he responded. "We have reservations."

"Sure, sure." Al nodded.

"Have a safe flight home," Poppy said as they exited.

"You have a nice weekend, too." Margo winked at them and followed her husband to the bar.

Poppy looked over her shoulder. "Do you think she knew?"

"Probably."

A giggle burbled out. "You're a naughty boy. We almost got caught."

"I know." He flashed a grin.

Her breath hitched, and something flickered in her eyes, but she looked away quickly, shuttering whatever thoughts lurked beneath.

Adam handed a ticket to the valet then turned to help her into her coat. "Better bundle up, California girl. It's cold out."

"Are we really going to Elway's?"

"Yes. Why?"

"Didn't know if you were simply putting people off."

"Nope. I've been hearing about the steaks all week long and made reservations for the two of us tonight. Although—"

"*Adam!* Where you headed, man?" A pale Brad Pitt imitation strutted across the lobby toward them.

Damn it. I do not need Greg working his chick magnet magic on Poppy right now. Adam tensed and turned in a manner that blocked her view of the approaching man. "Greg."

"Hey, a group of us are going to the Eli-Lilly shindig on the eighteenth floor. Shrimp cocktail time. I heard Joe got hold of some twenty-year-old Scotch. You should bring your date." He leaned around to give Poppy his charming smile. "Hi, I'm Greg Bowman. You must be the elusive Poppy. You're right, buddy, she's gorgeous." He slapped Adam's bicep. "He's been talking about you all week. We were starting to wonder if you really existed."

"That would be me, in the flesh."

"We can't go. I've got reservations at Elway's tonight," Adam said.

"Outstanding. Got room for another?"

He gnashed his teeth. "The reservations are for two."

"C'mon, I'm sure they could accommodate one more," Greg cajoled and then winked at Poppy. "Right, gorgeous?"

Greg was toying with him, and to his pleasure, Poppy seemed to understand. She plastered her delectable self against him. "Greg, honey, have you ever heard the saying, 'three's a crowd'?" she cooed and ran a finger along the outer edge of Adam's ear.

Adam's arm possessively encircled her waist, and he slid his hand down to squeeze her hip.

Greg chuckled. "Just messing with you, man. If I had a date as pretty as yours, I'd hightail it outta here, too."

Adam relaxed.

"Good to meet you, Poppy. You two going to the Glaxo dinner tomorrow night?" Greg asked.

"Yes. We're planning to be there."

"Great. Me, too. Trying to talk Kailey, the waitress, into coming." He winked again at Poppy. "I'll see you tomorrow then."

"I look forward to it," she replied dryly.

"Sir, your car is ready," the valet interrupted.

"Don't let me keep you." Greg loped off.

Adam glanced at Poppy; her eyebrows rose as she watched Greg depart. "Is that the Greg who made you wear the Broncos hat?"

"The very one."

"I can see why the waitress gave him her number."

He stiffened and frowned.

"But I find him … a bit too much." She kissed the ear she'd been playing with. "Shall we?"

His shoulders relaxed. "After you."

Chapter Eleven

"I thought we'd never get out of there." Adam braked as red taillights lit up the car's interior. The Ritz was only a few blocks from our hotel, but with rush hour traffic, we were forced to stop at every light.

"You're a popular guy. I can't believe that older couple almost caught us doing the dirty mambo."

He gave a wolfish grin. "I've never done anything like that in my life. You bring out the animal in me."

"I'll keep that in mind." I reached across the console and ran a hand up his thigh.

He growled, "We should have taken a cab."

"I'm surprised we didn't."

"I wasn't thinking straight."

"What about now?"

Adam slammed on the brakes and caught my hand, halting it before it could reach his happy-fun area. "We're going to have an accident if you don't watch out."

"Pooh." I moved away and slid back in my own seat.

"Why don't you tell me about your afternoon?"

"Not too much to tell. I unpacked a few things and then took a long, hot soak in the tub. I used some of the lavender body wash."

"Wish I'd been there."

My lip lifted. "Me, too."

Adam's exhale filled the car's silence. "We need to talk about something else."

"What would you like?" I took pity on him and pulled the phone out of my handbag. "Shall I read our horoscopes? What's your sign? Or I can list the headlines. Here's something mundane—the weather. Tomorrow will hang around the forties, and it looks like a warm up to fifty-nine is expected by Wednesday.

"Tell me when your mom's arriving."

"She's coming in on Wednesday."

"Do you have any plans?"

"Not officially. We'll probably have dinner and maybe do some shopping together. There are always things Mom can't get in Africa, so she tends to stock up when she comes to the States. Last time she bought a case of soup mix and a case of Dunkin' Donuts cinnamon coffee." I stared out the window. "Funny, what a person misses when away from home."

"Have you been to visit her in Africa?"

"No. I've never been invited."

"I'm sure you don't need to be invited to visit your own mother," Adam said dryly.

"Maybe not." I shrugged. "Mom and I have … an odd relationship. She dragged me from one marriage to another. When I graduated high school, I bolted. Getting as far away as possible, going it on my own, away from her marriage roller coaster. She was living in San Francisco at the time with husband number three. I went to University of Connecticut on scholarship."

"You lived on the East Coast?"

"Yeah, I guess we never talked about it, did we?"

He gave a slight headshake.

"It didn't take. You're right; I'm a California girl. I ended up back on the West Coast a year after graduation. Couldn't get past the cold winters." I shivered. "I moved to the LA area. Gave me a couple hours buffer between Mom and me. We saw quite a bit of each other that first year," I mused, remembering the time she came to help me move some secondhand furniture and paid for a couple of buckets of paint so we could get rid of the dingy yellow in that first apartment.

"Then a few months later, she divorced and took a job in Georgia. I think she finally decided the West Coast men weren't going to work out. Or she just needed to get away. Dunno. I visited her once in Georgia. She met Hamisi on a trip she took to India. I guess it was love at first sight, because they married three months later at the county courthouse. I didn't even know she was getting married until she called from the restaurant where they had a celebratory lunch. Then she moved to Kenya. I guess that's as far away as she could get from California."

"You know she didn't move all the way to Kenya to get away from you, Poppy. She went there to live with the man she loved."

"She'd move wherever the 'man she loved' lived. Up and down the California coast, Oregon, Kenya. That's why I've decided I'll *never* pick up my life and move to a different state in the name of looove." I rolled my eyes.

The car went silent and Adam's arms tensed. "Never's a long time," he finally voiced.

I shrugged. "I don't know what my mother was searching for. I hope she found it with Hamisi, but who knows. I'm telling you, this trip is fishy. Something's up."

The SUV rolled in front of the Ritz-Carlton, and the valet, with the precision of a queen's guard, opened my door the moment the vehicle came to a stop.

"Checking in, ma'am?"

"No, we're dining at Elway's tonight."

"Very well."

A snappy, uniform-clad doorman held the door, and Adam escorted me through the hotel to the restaurant. We were seated in hefty wood and leather chairs at a cozy table for two.

We both buried our heads behind the enormous menus. I pretended to read, but really my mind churned over all the emotional baggage I'd dropped on Adam.

I can't believe I told him all that. This is supposed to be a romantic weekend, and I just blathered on and on about my mom's crazy relationships. Ugh.

"What are you thinking of having?"

"What? Oh. Um," My eyes focused on the menu, and I picked out the first thing I saw. "I think I'll get the filet. After all, we're in beef country. When in Rome, you know."

"Eight or twelve ounce?"

"Eight. What about you?" I lowered my menu.

"New York strip. What about to drink? Should we order a bottle?" He perused the wine list.

"Maybe just a glass. If I drink an entire bottle with you, I may fall asleep."

"We can't have that. A glass then. How about an appetizer? Shrimp cocktail? Oysters?" He lowered his menu and winked.

My lip curled; I knew what he was getting at. "Just a house salad. I'm pretty sure we won't need oysters tonight." *Yuck.* I couldn't stand the slippery little buggers. Even watching someone eat them gave me the willies.

"So, in the car we were talking about your mom," Adam said after the waiter took our orders.

I fiddled with my napkin, re-laying it across my lap. "Boring. Why don't we talk about you? Tell me about your parents and your brother. You were supposed to go on a ski trip with them last month. How did that go?"

"It was fine." Adam wasn't to be deterred. "Back to your mom's upcoming visit."

"Look." I stared at my entwined fingers. "I know what you're getting at, and you're right. I need to cut her some slack. I'm planning to be more open-minded. Okay?"

His mouth dropped. "Okay. But, I was actually going to say that if things got too bad, you're welcome to escape by visiting me in Ohio."

My lashes swept up, and I relaxed. "Thanks. That's sweet of you."

The waiter arrived with our wine, and I turned the conversation back to Adam's oh-so-normal family. He had a younger brother who was an architect living in Chicago along with his new wife, who worked for a dental office. His parents lived about an hour outside of Chicago where his father was about five years from retirement at an engineering firm. His mother, an associate professor at the local community college, taught business writing. The family took an annual ski trip to Vermont. Still, the meal turned into a hotbed of sexual energy, with long pauses in conversation during which we sent each other scorching glances. I leaned forward, allowing glimpses down my cleavage, and sent sly winks his way. We carried on a conversation normally, but by the end of the meal, desire and tension surrounded us like an invisible cloak. I kept my legs tightly crossed to keep from leaping across the table. It was the ultimate in foreplay. We didn't shovel our food in, but neither did we linger.

As soon as the last morsel went down, Adam asked, "Are you finished?"

"Not yet. But I think I'll have dessert back at the hotel." I licked my lips.

His pupils dilated, and he signaled for the check.

"I need to go to the ladies room. Be back in a mo. Don't go anywhere." I waggled a finger at him.

"I'll be right here. Waiting."

I shoved the heavy chair back and slid out from behind the table. I got no more than a step away when my boot heel caught on something, throwing me off balance. Down I went, landing on my left knee and wrist. There was a pop, and pain exploded, shooting up to my elbow. Tears sprung to my eyes.

"Son of a mother duck." I hissed.

"Oh my God, are you okay?" Adam was beside me in a flash.

I groaned. Whatever had caught on my boot heel released when I went down, and I rolled to an ignoble sitting position on the floor, gingerly cupping my left hand.

"No." I sniffed.

"Is it your ankle? Knee?"

"Wrist."

With a doctor's gentle touch, he persuaded me to let him see the injured hand. The swelling had already begun, and with such fair skin, I could tell the bruises would arrive within the next twenty-four hours. He gently flipped my hand to see the palm side, making sure to support its movement.

"What seems to be the problem? Maybe I can help. I'm a doctor." A square, bespectacled face came even with ours as he crouched down to our level. Behind the Good Samaritan, our waiter hovered, and other diners turned our way with looks of interest and sympathy.

"I think she's injured her wrist. Can you stand?"

I nodded, and the two gentlemen helped me back in to my seat.

"Are you here for the dermatology conference?" Adam asked.

"Sure am," he drawled. "Don Beyers, from Georgia. You, too?" He was gray at the temples, and his crow's feet deepened when he smiled.

"Adam Patterson." The two exchanged greetings while inspecting the injury.

Adam looked over his shoulder at the waiter standing by. "Can we get some ice? Sweetie," Adam's concerned gaze returned to my watery one, "I think we need to go to the ER to get it x-rayed. You may have broken a bone or torn some ligaments."

"I'm sure it'll be fine if we ice it, and I've got ibuprofen back at the hotel." I shook my head and dashed away the tears with my uninjured hand.

ERs took hours and hours, and if the wrist were broken, I'd be stuck in a stupid cast for weeks. Who had time for that? It would ruin the entire weekend. Visions of habañero-hot sex at the hotel crumbled around me.

"I heard a pop. Did you hear it?"

I didn't move my head. I just stared with pleading eyes, sending telepathic messages. *Don't take me to the hospital. Don't take me to the hospital.*

Adam's brows scrunched together. "You know I have to take you in."

"A buddy of mine runs an urgent care clinic downtown. You could give that a try," Don offered.

I looked upon him as a savior. A clinic? Much better than a smelly hospital on a Friday night. "That's a better idea." My head bounced up and down.

Don dug into his back pocket and pulled out his wallet. "It's fairly new, they've got cutting-edge imaging software, and he'll be able to see if she broke anything, even cast it for her ... if she doesn't need surgery."

"Surgery?" I squeaked. "It's just a wrist sprain."

The men exchanged a look.

"Oh, God, no. Please no surgery." I cupped the painful wrist to my chest. "No surgery. I won't have it."

"Calm down, sweetie. We don't know anything yet." Adam's warm hand gripped my thigh. "That's why we need to get it x-rayed."

The maître d' arrived with a bag of ice wrapped in a clean napkin. "Thanks." Adam took the bundle and held out his hand. I laid my arm out for him, and he gently placed the napkin on the back of my wrist. The cold hadn't soaked through yet.

"May I ask how this happened?" No doubt the maître d' needed to fill out some kind of report.

"My boot heel caught on something."

The men looked around the floor and found a napkin stuck under the foot of my chair. It must have fallen when I stood up and caught under the chair leg when I pushed it back. I felt like such a clumsy fool.

"Here's a card for the urgent care clinic." Don handed the little white cardboard to Adam.

"I'm going to call ahead so they'll be ready for you. You have GPS, so you can find it?" He slipped a phone out of an inside pocket in his jacket.

"Yes. Thank you." Adam reached into his own coat pocket and pulled out a small numbered ticket for the maître d'. "Can you get our check and have the valet bring round the car?"

"Right away, sir."

"Her knee's bleeding." Don pointed.

Sure enough, my black pantyhose were ripped at the knee, and the scrape was oozing. My knee was painful, too, but nothing compared to the wrist. "It's fine. Nothing some Band-Aids can't fix. If someone can just help me to the bathroom, I'll go and wash up while we wait for the check and car."

"My wife, Betty, can help you." Don signaled a curly-haired, strawberry blonde a few tables away who'd been watching the proceedings with avid interest. She rose to join us.

"I'll have some first aid things brought to the ladies room for you." The maître d' hurried off.

"Betty, Poppy needs some help cleaning up her knee. Then they're going to go to Macon's clinic to get her wrist checked. Can you go to the ladies room to help her out?"

"Well bless your heart, you poor thing. Of course, I can help." Her brows wrinkled with concern.

I put my good hand on the table to rise but didn't get the chance. Adam scooped me up, and my face burned.

"Adam, it's all right. I can walk," I whispered frantically.

He didn't break stride.

"Don't worry, dear. I've got your purse." Betty waved it in the air and followed in our wake.

When we arrived at the bathroom door, Adam allowed my feet to glide gently to the floor. "Can you stand?"

I took a tentative step. Nothing buckled, but I felt an ache in the bleeding knee. "I'm fine. Thanks."

Betty held the door open, and we entered an opulent bathroom with marbled floors, padded stools, grandiose mirrors, and waterfall-style faucets.

"I need to go to the bathroom and remove these tights. I'll be out in a minute." I left the ice pack on one of the granite counters.

"Take your time. I'll be right here. Call if you need help."

Betty parked herself on one of the benches. I hobbled into a stall. Pulling down a pair of nylons one-handed was more difficult than I expected. I shimmied and wiggled like an off-kilter washing machine. Finally, getting them down to my lower thighs, I sat in relief. The outer door opened and closed, and I heard Betty talking in low tones with another female voice. Someone washed her hands, then the door opened and closed again.

The boots were a bit easier to remove, and the hose slid easily down the rest of the way. I kicked the torn and bloody nylons off and worked my feet back into the boots, zipping the soft leather over my naked skin. The knee had purpled with bruising, which would darken before the night ended. The bleeding had pretty much stopped, but it needed cleaning and a bandage. I took care of business, flushed the toilet, and exited the stall.

"They brought us some Band-Aids and antiseptic to clean that knee." Betty made a sympathetic noise. "Oh my, that must hurt."

I tossed the hose in the trash and washed my hands as best I could before joining her on one of the cushy benches. The bench and I wheezed sad sighs.

"Here, you put this back on your wrist, and I'll take care of your knee." She handed me the ice pack.

"Don't worry. I can take care of it. I just need a moment." The ice finally cooled through the napkin and felt good on my swollen wrist.

"It's no problem. This sure isn't the first scraped up knee I've contended with. I raised four kids." She knelt in front of me, dabbing the wound with a damp, white towel. Freckles spread across her cheeks, and her curly hair bounced as she worked. "Why, I bet my oldest daughter, Coralee, is about your age. I remember when Coralee fell out of the neighbor's tree when she was eight. 'Bout gave me a heart attack. The neighbor boy came runnin' up to the screen door sobbin', 'Coralee is dead. Coralee is dead.' She only had a broken arm, but boy was she bleedin' from scrapes and bruises all up and down her body. Tsk, tsk." Betty wrapped a big Band-Aid across my knee. "There you go, all fixed up." Blue eyes winked at me.

"Thank you." I felt the tears rising again.

"Oh, no need to cry, dear. It's gonna be okay." She sat next to me and rubbed my back. "Your boyfriend will take you to Macon's clinic, and you'll get fixed right up."

"It's just that we were supposed to have this romantic weekend, and now I've gone and ruined it," I blubbered. Betty handed me a tissue, and I blew my nose.

"Now, now. I'm sure you can still have your romantic weekend. Don't you worry. That boy loves you. He'll take good care of you. Maybe you'll just have a different kind of romantic weekend."

"You think he loves me?" I frowned, surprised by her assessment of our relationship.

She handed me another tissue. "Sure, I do. It's in his eyes when he looks at you. My son-in-law has the same look when he sees my Coralee. And he carried you to this bathroom like you were rare, blown glass. All the ladies swooned in their seats when he picked you up. Just like a hero in a fairy tale. It was very romantic."

"It was?"

"You bet it was. You're probably one of those real smart, independent ladies. Aren't you?"

"Well, I do own my own business."

"And it's real hard for you to rely on someone else?"

I gulped and nodded. How did this pixie grandmother have me pegged in a matter of minutes?

"Well, now you're just going to have to let him be a man and take care of you. Let go of some of that independent spirit—not all of it, mind, just some—and you'll find deeper depths of love that you hadn't realized could exist. Now here, let's get this mascara taken care of." She dabbed at my eyes with a fresh tissue.

I didn't want to crush Betty's vision of a deep love affair by explaining our friends-with-benefits relationship, so I let her clean me up in silence. But her observations bounced around in my mind. When we left the bathroom, we found Adam and Don waiting in the hallway.

"Everything okay?" Adam came to my side.

I nodded.

"It's fine. Just a scraped knee. Nothing to get worked up over. Though she should put some ice on it tonight. Might be stiff in the mornin'. Now you take your lady love to Macon's place and tell him Betty says he better take good care of her, or he'll answer to me." She shook her finger as she spoke.

"Wouldn't want that now, would we, dear?" Don wrapped an arm around Betty's shoulders.

"Will do. Thanks for all your help."

"Thanks, you two." I worked up a grin.

"You remember what I told you." Betty winked as she and Don turned back to the restaurant.

"What did she tell you?" Adam's eyebrows rose quizzically.

"Just some wise, girl talk."

"Do you want me to carry you?" He rubbed my back.

"No, but I could use a shoulder to lean on."

"Here, let's get you wrapped up."

I slid my good arm into the coat. Adam pulled it closed over my bent elbow and buttoned two of the lower buttons.

"Keep that ice on there. It's important now to help with the swelling. We'll get you some for your knee at the clinic."

"You know where we're going?" A cold breeze nipped at my stocking-free legs.

The valet opened the door, and Adam helped me into the car, making sure I didn't bang my head as I awkwardly sat. "I've got it in my phone's GPS." He lifted my legs into place, and the door thumped closed. The car had been running for a bit, and I thanked the saints for the warm air blowing out of the vents.

Adam angled into the driver's seat and turned to find me wrestling with the seat buckle. "Here, let me." It clicked into place. He put the car in gear and maneuvered away from the hotel's portico. GPS guided us to an urban neighborhood about fifteen minutes away.

"Are we sure this place will be open? It's almost nine."

"They usually close at nine, but Don said they're expecting us."

We pulled into a small parking lot in front of a squat, brick building with a white neon sign that read On-the-Spot Urgent Care.

As Adam helped me out of the car, the front door opened.

"You friends of Don Beyer?" a tall, lab-coated, African-American man asked.

"Yes. Are you Macon?"

"That's me. C'mon in."

Please let this be quick and painless and no broken bones. I couldn't stand it if it ruined any more of our time together.

Chapter Twelve

Thirty minutes later, the fastest I've ever been in and out of any sort of medical facility and a hell of a lot faster than any ER, we were climbing back into Adam's SUV.

The x-rays revealed no breaks, thank the Lord. It turned out my wrist had sustained a "moderate" sprain. I now wore an ugly, stiff, black brace full of Velcro closures, which would complement my wardrobe for the next two weeks. The doctor recommended continuing the ice and keeping it elevated, and gave me a handful of anti-inflammatory pain medication samples he had on hand. If the wrist got worse, he warned me to go to the hospital immediately, because it could indicate damage that would need surgery.

Adam agreed with the prognosis and promised to take care of me. For a few moments, they'd discussed casting me, which I'd vehemently opposed. I'm not sure if Macon was trying to rile me, but he concluded that the adjustable soft brace would be better with the amount of swelling.

Macon and Adam got on like two peas in a pod. Even though Adam was a dermatologist, he'd done his time in the ER during med school and got a kick out of Macon's new imaging software. Both doctors gathered around the computer, talking in terms I didn't understand, pointing out this ligament and that scaphoid bone. It was fun to see Adam in his element, with a doctor hat on, but it also made me feel a bit like a bug in a petri dish. However, Macon had worked overtime and I'd received the clinic's red carpet treatment, so I'd kept my mouth shut and allowed the mad scientists their fun.

The car cranked over, and cold air blew at us. I shivered and pulled my coat tighter.

"That Macon's got a nice little set up. Better than an ER any day." Adam backed out of the parking space.

The dismal thoughts I'd bottled up since my talk in the bathroom with Betty tumbled out.

"Oh, Adam, I *am* sorry about the mess I've caused. I've ruined our weekend, all because I'm a klutz and didn't put my stupid napkin on the stupid table." The tears I'd held in check while my wrist was twisted and turned during the exam threatened to tumble out. It was unusual for me to be klutzy. All those ballet lessons I took growing up provided me a lithesome grace.

The car stopped, and he stared at my profile. "Sweetie, it was an accident."

"I know. But I feel like such a fool."

He gripped my chin between his thumb and forefinger and forced me to face him. The car was dimly lit by the exterior lights, so I could only see half of his face through my watery view. "It's okay, you know. Not everything is going to be perfect, and as for ruining our weekend, there's no such thing."

I sniffed. "But, I wanted it to be perfect."

"Now we have the perfect excuse to order room service and lie around in bed all day. I'll feed you grapes." He kissed my quivering lips.

I melted under his touch. "Oh, Adam. You're such a good sport."

"Good sport, nothing. I should be thanking you for taking one for the team." He tucked a hair behind my ear then returned his attention back to the street.

"What?"

"Yeah, not only is the Ritz going to pay your medical bills, the restaurant comped our dinner. I suppose they thought you might have grounds for a suit or something. Thanks, beautiful, you saved me a couple hundred."

I giggled. "Really?"

"Really. I'll have to remember that ploy. Forget dropping a cockroach in the salad. Take a dive on the way to the bathroom."

"Ugh. Don't remind me."

"It was a little funny. There you were, shimmying your breasts in my face …"

I gasped. "I did no such thing."

"Who do you think you're kidding? You were taunting me the entire meal. You're lucky I didn't reach across the table and ravish you right there in the restaurant."

"Okay, well, maybe I did a little."

"As I was saying, you shook your tuchas at me then, wham! You were down."

I mashed my lips. "It wasn't funny. It was humiliating."

"Okay, it wasn't funny. But, you were very ladylike when you fell."

"Ha!"

"I heard that pop and knew it was bad. Actually, I thought it was your knee and we'd be taking you out on a stretcher. You're lucky it was only the wrist and your left hand instead of your dominant right hand."

"I just hope it's better by Saturday. I have a luncheon on Thursday that I can have Sierra take care of, but Saturday I've got a wedding. I need to be on the ball."

He shook his head as he pulled to a stop at the light. "Hire some assistants. You don't want to overdo it. Your wrist needs time to heal."

"Sure, sure, doc." I dismissed his concerns with a wave of my good hand.

"I'm not kidding, Poppy." He placed a firm hand on my shoulder. "If you reinjure it, you may end up with that surgery you didn't want. Then you'll be down for six weeks or more."

"Mmm hmm."

"Poppy." His voice held a warning note, and he glared at me.

I sucked in a breath. *So serious.*

"I promise. I'll be careful. Scout's honor."

The light changed, and he returned his attention to the traffic. "I have a hard time picturing you as a Girl Scout."

I couldn't stop my bark of hilarity, and I peered at his profile. "I never was. How did you know?"

A headshake. "I just do. Your childhood didn't seem to support that type of activity. I know you better than you think."

God, he's adorable. I can't wait to get back to the hotel and get him naked.

"Oh, yeah? What am I thinking now?"

He glanced at me then back to the road. "Something X-rated if I had to guess."

"Maaybee." I licked my lips.

"*Poppy.* Don't mess with me while I'm driving. I'd like to get back to the hotel in one piece so we can do some of those dirty things clogging up your brain."

I gave a resigned sighed. "Okay. I'll be good."

• • •

Instead of the manic, clothes-slinging frenzy Adam had envisioned, he treated her like breakable crystal. With her injury, everything needed to be slow. The doctor in him knew he should probably put her to bed and leave her be, but the two of them had been smoldering like a powder keg since he picked her up at the airport, and his base nature knew he wouldn't be able to leave her alone.

Once they crossed the room's threshold, he helped her shrug out of the coat then, scooping her up, gently deposited her on the bed. One at a time he unzipped those sexy boots, gliding his fingertips down her calf. The boots dropped to the ground, and he kissed the tops of her pink toes.

She giggled and wiggled them at him.

He leaned in to kiss each one separately before moving on. His hands kneaded her foot and worked their way up her strong calf muscles. He could feel her body relaxing beneath his touch, and she sighed at the gentle massage. His gaze caught on the bruised and battered knee, and he paused his fingers.

"Poor baby. Does it hurt?"

"No." He knew she was lying.

He kissed around the boo-boo and continued north, sliding the dress up her thighs, kissing and kneading the supple skin. She moaned, and desire made him harden. The dress slid over her head, and, gently, he encouraged her to lie back against the fluffy comforter, the soft crush of material whispering beneath their bodies. His hands reached the panty line and dipped under the delicate lace, pulling it aside. He played his fingers along the outer edges of her womanhood.

"You need to tell me if I hurt you. We need to be careful … very careful of your wrist." His breath drifted along the shell of her ear before nibbling a path down to the hollow of her throat. Her eyes closed as his fingers delved into the moist valley, his thumb rubbing along her engorged clitoris. Her hips lifted off the bed to meet the pressure.

"Mmm hmm," she whimpered.

Adam continued his assault, slipping the straps of her bra from her shoulders; his greedy mouth followed the descending elastic's path, tugging aside the thin lace covering her breast. Out popped an orb, and her breath hissed as he sucked on the distended nipple while his fingers continued their onslaught below.

"God, you're so wet," his voice whispered across the hardened peak.

She moaned, rocking harder into his busy digits. He moved to suckle the other breast, tugging the pink bud into his mouth. He lavished his attention on them like a butterfly sucking nectar, moving from one to the other while continuing to stroke her. Her head thrashed from side to side and her fists clenched the bedding.

"Adam, stop … I can't." She panted.

"Yes, baby, you can." His wily fingers picked up the pace.

"No. Not without you."

"Sh …" His breath blew across her hardened peak; he sucked it in once more, and she yelled his name and shuddered in ecstasy.

As she lay on the bed with her eyes closed, half naked, he took a moment to let her catch her breath before he gently slid off the rest of her lingerie. Once the ethereal beauty of her body lay before him, he couldn't hold back any longer. He quickly stripped off his own clothing and slid into her still-quivering, wet tunnel.

Her eyes flew open, and she wrapped her legs around him, pulling his hard shaft deeper.

"Oh, yes, Adam," she rasped.

Slowly, he stroked in and out. It took every last bit of effort to restrain himself from pounding her like a rutting teenager. She felt so hot and tight around him, it was difficult to remember he had to be gentle. She was injured, but oh, Lord, she felt good. Just like in Hawaii and his dreams … only better.

She ran her good hand up his back, kneading and massaging as she went. Her hips moved in rhythm with his.

"More, Adam. Faster."

"I don't want to hurt you, sweetheart. We need to be careful." He grit out through his teeth.

She bowed up from the bed while digging her heels into his thighs, pushing him in deep and hard. "I can handle it."

Thrusting into her, he picked up the pace. His muscles quivered with strain as he desperately tried to hold on when she called his name, shattering apart in his arms, her passageway clenching around him like a tender fist. He let go and dropped over the precipice with her.

After her trembling subsided, Adam rolled to her uninjured side; she rolled along with him. Her half-lidded, jade eyes gazed at him, and she licked her kiss-swollen lips before murmuring in a husky voice, "Again?"

• • •

My eyes shot open to pain throbbing up and down my left arm. The bulky brace felt like a boa constrictor squeezing its next meal. Adam's chest rose and fell beneath my head, and the aching wrist lay splayed to my side. The room was dark, and I rolled my head to find the clock. It read 5:04.

His slow, sensuous lovemaking had tugged at my heartstrings. He spent half the night distracting me from the injury, and he'd done such a thorough job, I'd completely forgotten to take some of the pain meds before falling into a pleasurably sated slumber.

Now it was time to pay the piper. I rolled off Adam and whimpered. My injured knee was stiff and sore, too. Hobbling into the cold-tiled bathroom, I blinded myself when I flipped on the light. Through squinted eyes, I made my way to the robes and wrapped myself up to ward off the chill. After a few minutes, my eyes adjusted, and I found my hand swollen almost twice its normal size.

Oh, snap!

I stripped off the Velcro straps and removed the brace. Once the brace was off and the pressure released, the hand felt imminently better, but the wrist still throbbed. My heart started to race; the circus-clown hand was kind of freaking me out.

"Sweetheart? What's wrong?"

"Um…" Fear made my voice shake. "Noth-thing. Do you know wh-where the pain pills are?"

Adam pattered naked into the bathroom. Unfortunately, I was in too much pain and busy trying to hide the swollen appendage to enjoy his manly attributes.

"C'mon. Let me see."

I turned and allowed him see the puffy mess.

"Christ, Poppy." His mouth turned grim and a V formed between his brows. "This is my fault. I should have had you elevate it before going to sleep. Damn it, I forgot to give you the pills, too."

"No, no. It's my fault. It wasn't hurting when I fell asleep," *Nothing was hurting when I fell asleep.*

"I know better. The pills are in my coat pocket. I'll be right back."

My legs felt kind of shaky, so I plopped down on the side of the tub to wait. He returned, wearing a pair of boxers, with a handful of pills and bottled water. He handed me the water, and after wrestling one out of its Fort Knox-style, plastic-and-tinfoil wrapping, passed along a little oblong pill.

After I swallowed the tablet, Adam held his hand out to me. "C'mon."

"Where are we going?" I said in a panicked voice as I rose.

"Back to bed. I'll get you set up."

"Is this normal?" My voice shook.

"It can happen. Swelling can be pretty bad in the first twenty-four hours. I should have had you loosen the brace before bed, too." His eyes were tight, and he frowned as he flipped on the lamp by the bedside and helped me climb in. "Here, lay back and I'm going to elevate your wrist with pillows."

He built up a pillow stack and tenderly laid my wrist on top. He eyed the injury for a moment, and then he pulled on the slacks he'd worn earlier and my gut clenched.

Had he changed his mind? Was he going to make me go to the hospital?

"I'll be right back. I'm going to get you some ice."

Whew.

A few minutes later, he returned with an ice pack wrapped in a towel from the bathroom. He laid the pack on the wrist, and I flinched.

"Damn. I'm so sorry, sweetie."

I stared at him with wide, frightened eyes.

"I told myself to leave you alone." He ran an agitated hand through his hair, making it stand on end. "But then I laid you on the bed, and I couldn't seem to help myself. I'm such an asshole." He looked miserable.

"Um, Adam."

"Yes?"

"Is my wrist going to be okay?"

He sighed. "Yes. The swelling should come down. But I'll need to keep an eye on it. You can take another pill in six hours."

Thank heavens. Relief flooded my system. "Okay. You shouldn't really worry about the acrobatics earlier tonight. They were …" *Mind-blowingly fantastic?* "Really great," I whispered.

He sat down next to me, taking care not to jostle the injury.

With my good hand, I ran a fingertip along his forearm. *Mmm, his toned swimmer's chest really was a lovely sight. Even at 5:00 a.m.*

He seized my hand and kissed the palm. "You're too good. Most women would tell me I was a selfish jerk, and they'd be right." He looked so cute with his hair a mess and concern for me in his eyes.

"I'm a big girl, Adam." I laid my palm against his scruffy cheek. "And you're a wonderful lover. I don't regret it a bit. We fit together like a Chinese puzzle box. Just like in Hawaii."

He kissed my forehead. "We'll talk in the morning. Try and get some more rest. Hopefully, when you wake the swelling will have gone down."

I nodded and patted the other side of the bed. "Join me."

• • •

He turned off the bedside lamp but left the bathroom light on. It emitted a soft glow into the room. Adam slid into bed next to Poppy. Her uninjured hand sought his, clasped it. He gave her a reassuring squeeze as he lay, wide-awake, waiting for the pain meds to kick in and for Poppy to fall asleep.

Damn. He really screwed up this time. His mind would never be able erase that expression of fear he'd seen in the bathroom as she observed the swelling. He knew he should have left her alone when they came back to the room, but he'd thought with his dick, and look what had happened. Now she was in a mountain of pain, and it was all his fault.

How could I forget to give her the pain meds? If she didn't improve by morning, he'd have to take her into the hospital, and he knew she'd hate that. If it happened, Adam had no idea if he would be able to salvage the rest of this weekend, much less entice her to come out to visit Ohio.

She shifted and whispered, "Adam?"

"What?" His head popped up. "Do you need something?"

"Nothing. Just … I can't fall asleep. Tell me a funny story about you and your brother growing up."

"Hmm." His reeling brain shifted focus, and he dredged the back of his memory to find something funny that would take her mind off the pain. "I know. There was the time we stayed at a resort in Jamaica. I was ten, my brother seven. They had these peacocks wandering the property. Beautiful but noisy. Have you ever heard a peacock screech? Ulk. At the crack of dawn, too. Worse than a rooster. Anyway, my brother was fascinated by this one peahen. I don't know why. He named her Matilda and would literally follow her around.

"There were signs all around the resort saying 'Don't Feed the Birds.' One morning, my nodcock of a brother snuck some toast out of the restaurant and decided he was going to feed it to Matilda. I told him it was a bad idea. That's me, always following the rules. So he held out his offering and softly called to Matilda. Sure enough, the bird approached. Peacocks don't gently take something from your hand. They zoom in like a homing bee and peck at their food. Well my brother screamed and dropped the toast, upsetting Matilda. She expanded her tail feathers and started screeching at my brother. The next thing I know, instead of my brother chasing Matilda, Matilda's chasing him all around the park area, both of them screeching their heads off. My mom ..."

Her breathing turned heavy and even.

"Poppy?" he whispered.

There was no response. He brushed a lock of hair off her alabaster cheek. "God, you're amazing."

Chapter Thirteen

When I woke again, around ten in the morning, to my great relief, the wrist had reduced in size and pain level. I'd found Adam in the main room fully dressed, working at his computer, drinking a cup of coffee, and nibbling from a tray of pastries and fruit he'd ordered from room service.

"How are you feeling?" His eyes smiled at my mussed hair.

"Better." I yawned and held out my arm. "Look, no more clown hand."

He nodded. "I know. I checked on it this morning while you slept. I think you're in the clear, but I want you to continue taking the pain meds every six to eight hours. I don't want the swelling to increase like that again," He poured me a cup, and I snuggled up on the couch next to him while he finished working.

"What do you have to do today at the conference?"

"Nothing. Once I finish these emails, I'm all yours."

I gave a ghost of a smile. "Yay. Since my wrist is better, I could get dressed, and we could go out and do something fun. I read an article about a Native American art museum in the paper yesterday."

"No."

My brows rose at the succinct answer. "You don't like art?"

He sat back from the computer and pulled me close. "I like art just fine. Tell me, when was the last time you had an injury like this?"

"Um …" I cast my mind back then snapped my fingers. "Oh, I sprained my ankle in dance class when I was in seventh grade. I had to use crutches for a week. It was awful."

"That's what I thought." His jaw flexed. "One of your strengths, Poppy, is your energy and ability to get things done. You're a go-getter. That's why your business is so successful. But you don't know when to slow down and relax."

"What do you mean? It's past ten, and I just got up. I'm a lazy sloth." I leaned against his chest and looked at him from beneath my lashes.

He grinned and tweaked my nose. "You're recovering from a busy night and a painful injury. You need to rest."

"So, what do you want to do?"

"Stay in. Order room service. Watch bad movies. Let me take care of you."

"I'm sure we could find something more interesting to do."

I climbed into his lap, but he wrapped his hands around my waist and wouldn't allow me to burrow up against him.

"As much as I would love to feast upon your delectable body again, you need rest."

I stuck out a pouty lip and ran my good hand up his chest.

"Poppy." His voice held a warning. "I felt like an utter jackass when you woke up with your wrist swollen twice its normal size. I never should have allowed it to happen. Today my job isn't to seek sexual gratification, yours or mine; it's to take care of you."

My mouth pinched together. *It wasn't his fault my wrist swelled up. It was mine. My responsibility.* Why would Adam take it on? It's not as though we had any sort of commitment to each other. It was probably his medical training.

"Your health is my responsibility, Poppy, and not just because I'm a doctor. You're my guest for the weekend, and that makes me accountable for your well-being."

Was he reading my mind?

"Okay, if you're sure. Don't you think you'll get bored?"

He laughed. "Sweetie, you're anything but boring. It doesn't matter to me how we spend our time, as long as it's together." He brushed a hair behind my ear, and my breath caught at the tenderness in his eyes.

I nodded, mute.

We ordered room service and watched HBO movies. He gave me a foot rub, which left me moaning in pleasure. I taught him naughty ways to fold napkins, which left him doubled over in laughter. I thought there might be some more canoodling, like the night before. However, except for a lot of snuggling and a smokin' hot make-out session that left me gasping during the climax of *Lethal Weapon 2*, Adam kept us in the realm of PG ratings.

Most of all, he took care of me. It was a completely novel concept to me. After my shower, he helped me into a pair of jeans and a sweater. He watched the clock and made sure I had something to eat and drink when it was time to take my meds. He checked the brace and swelling every few hours. He asked my movie preferences and made sure I kept the injury elevated.

Not since I was a kid had someone else taken care of me. For the most part, I was a healthy person, but when I did get sick, I powered through with over-the-counter drugs. Or, if it was really bad, like when I had the flu in January, I barricaded myself at home. Sophie had brought soup, medicine, and drinks, but otherwise, I'd been on my own. Even Richard had feared getting sick and had stayed away.

However, by late afternoon, cabin fever set in, and I decided to work my wiles on Adam. If he wouldn't allow sex, I'd talk him into the next best thing.

"Shopping? You want to go shopping?"

"I need to get up and move. As fun as this little movie marathon has been, my butt fell asleep during the last twenty minutes of *Captain America*. Unless you want to do something more fun … in the bedroom." I gave him my best lascivious look.

He ignored it, tugging at his bottom lip. "Okay, I guess we could go out. Originally, I'd planned to take you shopping for something special today anyway. I guess there's no reason we can't still do it."

"I'm game. Go where?"

"You'll have to wait and see."

Twenty minutes later, we pulled up to a large, beige building with a sign that read "Sheplers, Western Stores Since 1899." I made an effort to keep the horror from showing on my face.

"What are we doing here, Adam? Because, let me be clear, plaid shirts do not fit into my wardrobe."

"Originally, I had reservations for us to go horseback riding today. We were supposed to have a picnic on the trail."

"Aw, you did? How sweet. I haven't been riding since I was a little girl. Maybe we could go tomorrow."

"Doubtful." He shook his head. "Anyway, I didn't figure your repertoire of shoes housed a pair of real cowboy boots."

"You would be correct."

"Even though the horseback riding is out, we can still get you a pair of genuine leather cowboy boots. What do you think?"

This wasn't exactly the type of shopping I'd expected. However, Adam's original plan sounded really sweet, and I felt bad for ruining it, so the least I could do was give it a try. "Sure, what the hell?"

Sheplers turned out to be an enormous warehouse filled with all things western, including shirts, boots, cowboy hats, and jeans. A myriad colors, sizes, and textures of boots lined the walls. We probably would have gaped at the selection the rest of the afternoon if a staff member hadn't come up to offer help.

She got me sorted out with a half dozen pairs to start.

"You should go pick some to try on, too," I told Adam.

"I will. But first, you'll need some help getting those on." He sat next to me on the bench.

"Nonsense. I can do it." I toed off my flats and with my good hand reached for a pair of black and red boots. After a few minutes of struggling to get the boot on properly without using my left hand, I gave up.

"Damn it," I mumbled and gave a frustrated huff. I glanced at Adam, who patiently waited, eyebrows raised and a tiny uplift playing around his lips. "Fine. I need help,"

Without a word, Adam got down on his knees to help me take the boots on and off. Considering the last time he'd been in this position it had led to some mind-boggling sex, a little fire lit in my belly. I had to shake off the dirty thoughts to focus on the task at hand.

I must have tried on more than a dozen pairs before he shoved a brown and turquoise boot onto my heel. "What do you think about these?"

The leather scrollwork was exquisite. I twisted my ankle to admire the tooling up the side. "They're gorgeous. I'd no idea cowboy boots could be so beautifully crafted."

"They look good on you. Walk around like the saleslady suggested. Make sure they don't pinch or rub." His warm hand pulled me to my feet, and I paced the store, stopping to admire the cowboy hats. *I wonder how Adam would look in one.*

"Well, what do you think?" He came up from behind, placing a hand at my waist.

His touch sent a warm tingle through me. "I think you should try on a hat."

"Focus, Poppy. What about the boots?"

"Boots are perfect. I think we have a winner. But I want you to try on a hat." I snatched a black one off the rack and plopped it on his head.

"Hey there, little lady," he adjusted it backward and said in his best John Wayne drawl.

"No, black's not right. Here, try this tan one." I plunked it on, and it fell down past his ears. "Too big, but I think we're on to something. Try a smaller size." I browsed the selection.

"How's this one?"

Whoa! The stone-colored Stetson suited him, and, quite frankly, made him look sexy as hell with his dark sweater and jeans. I never thought I could be turned on by the western look, but Adam pulled it off. "I think I'd like to see you wearing that hat and nothing else, cowboy."

He laughed, placing the hat back on the rack. "I'll splurge for boots, but not a $150 hat that'll never see the light of day. Come on. If those boots are a go, it's time for me to look for a pair."

I pouted, following him back to the bench. The helpful sales associate appeared as I slid back into my own shoes. She suggested we start browsing the men's boots while she put my mine up at the checkout counter.

In typical male fashion, Adam found his after trying on only three pairs. He chose a black cherry-colored pair of lizard skin and leather boots. No surprise, the boots also made him look sexy. *Man, with the hat and the boots ...*

"What are you grinning at?" Adam poked my ribcage and pulled me out of the horseback-riding fantasy spinning through my head.

I blinked. "Nothing."

"Were you thinking dirty thoughts about me and a pair of boots?" His breath whispered along the sensitive part of my ear and I shivered.

"Yup."

As he kissed my neck, his phone beeped, killing our little interlude. "Let's see if we can find you a bottle of water—that's your pill reminder."

I could tell it also reminded Adam about my injury and his promise to leave me alone. *Crap.*

"If you don't mind, I wanted to look over the fancy leather handbags before we leave."

"I'll go up to the checkout and see if there's a Coke machine or something around here. Why don't you shop purses and join me when you're done?"

"Fine. I'll be up to pay in a few minutes."

"My treat." He walked away.

"Hold up there, Tex." I grasped his elbow to halt his retreat. "Those are $280 boots. I can't let you pay for those. I'll buy them."

"Forget it. You took one for the team last night. Remember, free dinner?"

"Dinner's very different from buying me a pair of boots."

"Why?" He frowned.

"It just is."

"I planned to spend more on the horseback-riding trip. What's different about a pair of boots instead?"

"I don't know." I flapped my good hand at him. "It's just … well they're … you know … for my feet."

He continued to frown and stare at me.

"All right. I have no idea why not. It just seems weird for you to buy my boots."

"If I bought you a piece of jewelry, would you mind then?"

"Maybe, maybe not. Boots, shoes, pants, dresses, it seems a bit strange for you to buy for me. It's more like …

"Something a husband might do?"

"I guess."

"You haven't had many men buy you things, have you?" He caressed my cheek.

Men had bought me dinners, paid for tickets, maybe sent flowers, but I wracked my brain to think of a physical item that a man had purchased for me. Jewelry? Clothes? At Christmas Rich had bought us tickets to *The Nutcracker*. The last man who bought me something physical was Matty Callahan in freshman year in college. He gave me a gold necklace with a tiny heart for Valentine's Day. I still had it in my jewelry box.

"I guess not."

"I want to do this."

"I don't know …"

"Sweetheart, let me do this."

An idea popped into my head that made his insistence on purchasing the boots more palatable. "Okay, if you insist. I'll check out the handbags and be with you in a minute."

He kissed my nose and headed off to the front of the store. Once he was out of sight, I dashed back to the cowboy hats. The stone Stetson was on the same rack, and I pulled it off.

"Can I help you with something?" I turned to find a salesman, wearing the requisite western gear and hat, standing at my elbow.

"As a matter of fact, you can." A few minutes later, I met up with Adam just as he finished signing the credit card receipt.

"Jim here says there's a Coke machine in the back near the restrooms." He hooked a thumb over his shoulder.

"Great. Do you think you could get me a bottled water or diet soda? Someone's getting a bag from the stockroom for me. You can go ahead and leave the boots here while I take care of the bag."

Amenable, Adam loped off to the bowels of the building while I executed my plan in his absence. Everything was sacked up and ready to go when he returned.

"So do I get to see the purse you bought?" Adam asked as he held the car door open for me.

"Sure." I whipped out the Stetson and plopped it on his head.

"This doesn't look like a purse." His brows creased.

"I lied," I said in singsong, sending him one of my sunniest smiles. "If you can buy me boots, I can buy you a hat."

"Why the hat?"

"Well, I think two hours spent in the country store turned me into a convert. You looked hot in it, and now that I see you wearing it, I understand that song 'Save a Horse, Ride a Cowboy.'"

His hazel eyes turned a stormy green, and the brim came toward me. I tilted so it wouldn't hit my forehead as his lips descended upon mine. *Wow! Who knew it was so sexy to kiss under a hat?* Heat bloomed in my belly, and soon all thoughts flew out of my brain as he sucked on my tongue.

We were both panting when he finally retreated.

"Maybe you're on to something with this hat. I thank-ee, ma'am." He drawled and doffed the Stetson.

Whooee. No kidding.

Chapter Fourteen

The stockings' pink packaging stared back at me from the bed. *How on earth am I going to get them on?* They'd been the devil to take off one-handed yesterday. There was no way I could pull them on single-handedly without ripping a hole. And, of course, they were the last pair I'd brought with me. Too bad I forgot to pack some thigh-highs. I might've been able to handle those on my own.

The shower turned off. I gave up and sat down on the bed in my matching green-and-cream, lace underwear to wait for Adam to help me get dressed.

He came out wearing a towel around his waist, and I lost my train of thought. Water dripped off his hair, down his collarbone, into the fuzzy, sandy blond hairs on his well-defined chest.

His eyes darkened, and he whistled. "That's a sexy little getup."

I sighed. "In keeping with today's theme," I held up the pink package, "I think I'm going to need help with these."

He flashed a playful grin. "Are you sure you need to wear hose tonight? You have beautiful legs. Or you could wear your fancy, new boots."

"First off, though I love them, the boots don't go with the outfit. Second, seeing as I'm a pasty-white redhead, yes. Yes, I do. Also, it's cold. I'm going to need their warmth."

"Very well. If you insist." He pulled on a pair of black boxer briefs then knelt at my feet.

Seeing him at my feet sent my mind to the gutter … again. It didn't help that he slid the hose up my legs in slow, sensual increments. My body squirmed by the time he reached my upper thighs.

"Adam," I ground out.

The stinker knew exactly what he was doing. He kissed both my thighs, planted a hot kiss between them, pulled me to my feet and then in one fell swoop, tugged the nylons all the way up to my waist.

"There. All done. That wasn't so bad, was it?"

I grit my teeth. "Just dandy. Thanks." Two could play this game. I brushed my good hand against his boxers and felt him twitch at my touch.

Adam sucked wind, grabbed my hand and pulled it up, planting a soft kiss on the inside of my wrist. "Don't play with me." His warm breath blew across the sensitive skin sending goose bumps up my arm.

"Me? You started it. And who says I'm playing?" I gave him a sultry stare.

His head moved slowly from side to side. "Maybe tomorrow. I told you, I don't want mess around and risk your injury today."

"I don't care about my injury." I swayed closer, but Adam stopped me with a stern hand on my shoulder.

His eyes hardened. "I care."

I let out a huff. "You're no fun."

"You're cute when you pout." He smacked my bottom. "Now be a good girl and get dressed. You're going to make us late."

"Yipe!" I rubbed my ass. *Well, that's one way to dispel the sexual tension.*

I was able to get into my emerald-silk sheath dress and a pair of silver and black stilettos without Adam's help. Luckily, the dress fell below the knee and covered most of the bruising.

Fifteen minutes later, we gathered in the lobby with more than a dozen other doctors and their spouses/girlfriends/dates. Adam's buddy, Greg, introduced me to Kailey, an attractive brunette with big doe-eyes. I could see why the guys went for her; she wore a tight, cleavage- revealing blouse and short, yellow skirt that she constantly tugged at. However, she stood out among the rest of us dressed in appropriate cocktail attire, and I pitied her immature clothing choice.

The ugly, black brace contrasted with my alabaster skin, and Kailey's first question was about it. For about thirty seconds, I debated telling everyone a different story: Got into a bar fight. Slipped on some ice and am suing the hotel. Adam dropped me while dancing. Wretched car accident on I-70. Since it looked like we'd be with these people for most of the night and I wasn't sure Adam would back up my BS, I decided to come clean with the truth.

"Tripped and fell down last night."

Kailey's brown eyes got even wider. "Really? Where?"

"Elway's."

Her eyes got wide and then she giggled. "Ouch, that must have hurt. Did you break it?"

"Nope. Just a sprain."

"I can't believe you fell at Elway's. Weren't you embarrassed?"

"Mortified," I said through my teeth.

"Where were you sitting? Like right in the middle of the restaurant or closer to the door? Did everyone see you? How exactly did it happen? Did anyone laugh?" She leaned in, salivating to hear about my ignoble fall.

It was then I decided I didn't like this twenty-something Bambi, with her butt-hugging micro mini and shampoo-commercial hair. Before I could say something cutting, Adam swooped in.

"Poppy, I want you to meet Brian MacDonald, our host for this evening."

I turned to find a man of average height, with a full head of salt-and-pepper hair and a weatherworn face.

"Hello." We shook hands. Adam explained Brian was a drug rep at GlaxoSmithKline, the company who had sponsored his lectures.

"Lovely to meet you. Adam was just telling me about your little adventure. How are you feeling?" he asked with sympathetic eyes.

"Much better, thanks to his expert medical care."

"You let me know if there's anything I can do for you while you're in town."

"That's sweet of you."

"Any time," Brian said.

A tall, lanky man with messy brown hair joined our trio. "Walt! Glad you could join us." Brian greeted the newcomer.

"Look what the cat dragged in," Adam said.

"Wouldn't miss it." Walt eyed me.

"Poppy, have you met Walter Smith?"

"No, I haven't. Poppy Reagan." I held out my hand.

"You must be Adam's California girl. Right? Adam told me all about you." Walter's grip was firm.

I looked at Adam and grinned. "He did? Good or bad?"

Adam stared hard at Walter and ever so slightly shook his head.

"Good. All good. Though we thought he was exaggerating a little. But I can see he's not." He continued to hold my hand, covering it with his left. His six-foot-five frame bent closer. "Explain to me how this schlub hooked such a beauty?"

I grinned. Walt's flattery was fun, and it didn't give me the slimy feeling that Greg's had.

"Luck and good, clean livin', buddy." Adam's teeth flashed.

Another person in the party hailed Brian, and he excused himself.

"Well, if you're ever ready to move into the big leagues, you give me a call, little lady." He released me.

"Forget it, Smitty." Adam slid a proprietary hand around my waist. "I'm not letting her out of my sight with you around."

"You might not have a chance. What with Poppy living in my neck of the woods." He winked.

"You live in California?" I perked up.

"Yes, ma'am. As a matter of fact, you're my new best friend."
Walter smiled. "Convince your boyfriend to move out to the
sunny City of Angels. I've been trying to talk him into leaving
dreary Ohio for five years. Now it looks as though I have a chance
to get him to at least come west for a visit."

My eyes bounced back and forth between Walter and Adam,
whose mouth had turned into a hard line. Something seemed off,
but I couldn't put my finger on it. "Interesting. Where do you
work, Walter?"

"Call me Walt; everyone does, except for this guy." He gave
Adam a shot to the shoulder. "He's the only one allowed to call
me Smitty."

"Hey, you were the one who suggested it for your jersey."
Adam's mouth softened.

"Yeah, I just didn't expect it to stick around for so long. Anyway,
to answer your question, I've got a practice in West Hollywood.
I'm always looking for good doctors to join us, but so far, I haven't
been able to convince Adam here to move away from America's
Heartland." He grinned at me as though he knew a secret I didn't.
"Until now."

Adam remained mute, shaking his head.

"Really? Tell me, Walt, how did you two meet?"

"I'll tell you where we met." Adam spoke up, cutting off
whatever Walt was about to say. "I pulled his fat out of the fryer
when we were interns. I believe it was a matter of a pretty blonde
resident, an angry head nurse, and a chimpanzee."

Walt threw back his head in laughter. "Ah, the research lab
monkey. What was his name?"

"Cha Chi." Adam deadpanned.

"He was a fast little bugger, wasn't he?"

One of Adam's brows rose. "You're lucky we didn't get thrown
out on our asses."

"Pshaw. You never would have gotten thrown out. You were the top of the class. I was lucky my father ponied up a load of cash to fund a new MRI machine, or I would have gotten thrown out."

"The joys of family money."

I watched as the two friends bantered. "Are you married, Walt?"

He shook his head. "Divorced. Came to the conference stag this year."

Oops. "Oh, sorry."

"Tell me, how do you like your hotel suite?" he asked.

Adam stiffened, and I felt his fingers dig into my waist. His eyes narrowed, but I didn't have a chance to answer, because Brian's voice rose above the din.

"Okay, folks, I think everyone is here, so we'd best get going. Our chariot awaits."

Brian had arranged for the hotel's shuttle van to take us to a swanky Italian restaurant in the heart of Denver. As I climbed aboard, Adam whispered something urgently to Walt, which was met by a good-humored guffaw and, "Okay, buddy. I'll stop."

When we arrived, a waiter led our group to a back room with a large table that could accommodate all of us. Brian began splitting up couples, in order to "mingle," but Adam resisted his request.

"I'd prefer to sit next to Poppy in case she needs help. She's not very good at asking for it." He wrapped a protective arm around my shoulder.

The table fell into varied conversations. Adam, Brian, and I talked about our favorite Colorado ski slopes. Brian favored the black diamonds at Copper Mountain, whereas Adam was a fan of Steamboat Springs. I'd only skied at Breckenridge, which both the boys pooh-poohed as too "touristy." But they couldn't sway my vote. I adored the little town with its boutique shops and great nightclubs.

A chiming glass interrupted the debate, and our heads swiveled as one to Kailey.

"I know what we can do to get to know each other better. Let's go around the table and play truth or dare."

People shifted in their seats, and nobody seconded the motion. Truth or dare seemed a bit parochial for this crowd. I surmised Kailey liked being the center of attention and Greg was spending too much time on his other seatmate.

Brian cleared his throat. "Um."

"Why don't we share our first job instead?" I suggested.

Kailey shot me a dirty look.

Brian latched onto the idea like a vise. "Excellent notion. Katherine, why don't you start? Introduce yourself and then tell us about your first job." He pointed to the woman next to Greg, and we went around the table sharing our first job experiences, which brought much laughter to the table.

By the time our first course arrived, we'd gone back to small-group conversations, and I noticed Kailey now dominated Greg's attention. Her talons had a firm hold of his forearm, and she leaned at such an angle that I'm sure he had a bird's eye view of a handful of cleavage. Her high-pitched giggle constantly rose above the din of conversation. At one point, Walt and Adam exchanged a look that I interpreted to mean Greg had been an idiot for bringing her.

Halfway through the evening, my wrist started to swell; after the main course had been cleared I excused myself to visit the ladies room to check on it. I loosened the Velcro brace when Kailey walked in. She checked under the stalls then sauntered over to the sinks and washed her hands.

"Jeez, what a crowd of duds, eh? I didn't know doctors could be so boring. Except for our two dates, everyone else seems to be a loo-ser." She made an L on her forehead with her thumb and pointer finger.

Some women liked to bond with other women through gossip and snarky comments. I was not one of them.

"Oh, I don't know. The folks at my end of the table seem to be pretty interesting." I turned and left the bathroom.

I returned to the table and whispered to Adam that my wrist had become painful and asked him if we could skip dessert and go back to the hotel. The darling man didn't hesitate. He rose immediately. We thanked Brian for the meal and said our goodbyes. Walt walked us to the entrance of the restaurant.

"Don't forget, Adam, if you come west, you could keep a closer eye on this filly."

"I'll think about it." They shook hands.

Walt turned to me. "Here's my card. Maybe we can have drinks some time."

"Not on your life," Adam piped in.

I grinned and shook Walt's hand. "Maybe."

Chapter Fifteen

"Let me see it," Adam said once they were situated in the back of a cab.

She held out Walt's card.

"No, silly. Your wrist."

"Oh, it's not that bad." She waved him off. "I just couldn't stand being around that catty little monster for a second longer."

He threw back his head and let out a bellow of laughter. "Meow. I assume you mean Kailey."

"Look, I work in a world of women like her. I deal with them all the time. I simply don't want to do it while on vacation." She searched his face. "You don't mind leaving early, do you?"

He pulled her head against his shoulder and kissed the top of it. "Not at all. I understand. She's a bit much to take."

An eyebrow rose. "A bit."

"Honestly, I think Greg regretted bringing her. Especially once he found out Katherine is getting divorced." Glad she'd left her hair down, he buried his fingers in it.

"The attractive lady at the end of the table?"

"Yep. They've played a flirtatious cat-and-mouse game for years at these conferences. This is the first year they've both been available. I have a feeling Kailey's going home as soon as Greg can swing it."

"Well, maybe Greg isn't so stupid after all." She sat up. "Tell me about Walt's practice."

He rubbed his chin and debated telling Poppy about the deal he'd made with Walt for the hotel suite—the deal that included a promise to come out to California and listen to Smitty's pitch. A deal that was becoming more and more attractive the longer he spent with Poppy. Thanks to her telling comment in the car yesterday about "never moving for a man," if he wanted to be in her life, he might have to make the sacrifice and move. It would be a life-changing decision. One he didn't take lightly.

"I'm not going to lie; it's very lucrative. Besides dermatology, he provides facial reconstruction and plastic surgery, wrinkle injections, cancer care, the works."

"He's in the right place for all the plastic works," she mused. "Not your thing? Is that why you didn't take him up on his offer? I have trouble envisioning you among the wealthy, yummy mummies begging for Botox injections to compete with their husbands' younger secretaries."

He let a ghost of smile cross his face as he studied Poppy in the darkened cab. "My family's in the Midwest, which was the main reason I settled where I did. There's been no reason for me to move to California."

"And, now?" Her voice was barely a whisper.

Adam battled with the answer that sat on the tip of his tongue. "I'm giving it some serious thought." He said it softly, but loud enough for her to hear. Loud enough to know she heard. Unfortunately, her eyes were shadowed, and the car was too dark to read her face.

• • •

Heat prickled around my neck, and the cab felt overly warm. I sucked in a breath. Suddenly, we were talking about more than a playful weekend. We were talking about feelings that had been coming at me in waves ever since the airport. Feelings that rose to the surface, even now. We continued to stare at each other, unsure what to say.

"What about you? Would you move to Ohio?" he asked.

I released the breath I'd been holding and glanced down at my hands. "I don't have a job offer in Ohio, and I've got a successful company where I live." I picked at a piece of invisible lint on my coat.

"If you did?"

Would I? I swore I'd never move for a man.

The question hung between us as the cab pulled to a halt in front of the hotel. My passenger door popped open, and the doorman held it, waiting for me to exit.

Adam grabbed my good hand, halting me. I met his questioning gaze with my own troubled one.

The cabby turned his head. "That'll be ten fifty."

Releasing me, Adam dug out his wallet, and I took advantage of his distraction to stumble out of the taxi. The cold winter air filled my lungs, leaving puffs of smoke as I exhaled. The frigid temperature only served to cool my overheated body, not clear the thoughts tumbling around my head. I stuffed shaking hands into my pockets as I waited for him to join me.

A silent, frowning Adam escorted me to the elevators.

One opened, and I stepped in, but he didn't follow.

"You go on up. I'm going to get a drink at the bar." His eyes had turned flat and indecipherable.

My heart dropped, and I barely had enough time to plant my good hand on the closing doors. "Please come up. We need to talk."

I hadn't wanted or expected the weekend to turn serious, but my question in the cab had changed the atmosphere. Or maybe it hadn't. Maybe I'd been denying what had been happening right in front of my face. We needed to figure out what was going on with our relationship. Now. If I left his question unanswered, the weekend would probably continue just fine. He'd come back to the room in an hour or so, and we'd pretend nothing happened. But, when we parted on Monday, our friendship would surely flounder and die if we didn't figure this out.

He crossed his arms and looked like he would refuse.

I played my ace in the hole. "Please. I need help." I held up the brace.

His eyes softened, and he gave a sharp nod.

The ride up remained silent. When we entered the room, I dropped my handbag on an end table, but left my coat on and went directly to the couch where I plopped down.

Adam, also still wearing his black overcoat, entered the living area and stood stiffly behind a burgundy chair directly across from the couch.

"I don't know," I answered.

He remained motionless, his green eyes unreadable.

"When I agreed to this trip, I thought it would be like Hawaii. A weekend fling. Friends with benefits. But, it's not ... is it? It's different. It's more."

"Astute of you." His mouth barely moved.

I ran a hand down my face. "I don't know what you want from me, Adam."

He came around and sat in the chair. "Yes. It's more," he ground out. "I think about you constantly. I adore having you near me and taking care you. I want you ... and I'm not just talking about sex. I want more than friendship from you. I want you in my life."

My heart stuttered to a halt. I opened my mouth, but nothing came out.

He grimaced. "I guess that wasn't very well done of me. Was it? Not exactly how I'd planned it."

"Hawaii?"

He shook his head. "Afterward. Over email."

"But ... but what about your ex-girlfriend?"

"A diversion. When you started dating Richard and things seemed to get serious, I decided I needed to move on. But in my mind she couldn't compare to you."

I sat back, replaying the conversation in the car after he picked me up from the airport. "I broke up with her because I couldn't love her. Not the way she wanted," he'd said. *He couldn't love her because of me.*

"Well, it's out there now. What do you have to say about it?" he challenged.

I shook my head. "I don't know. It's all … it's just that … I'm overwhelmed."

He threw his head back against the chair and stared up at the ceiling. "I'm sorry. It's a lot to take in. But, I think you've answered the question that's been on my mind since I picked you up at the airport."

"What's that?"

"You don't feel the same way."

"I didn't say that."

His head rolled forward, and his expression changed to hopeful. "How do you feel? Willing to take the next step? Willing to become serious about us? What do *you* want, Poppy?"

I rubbed my eyes as he pounded me with questions. *Jesus, how am I supposed to know? I wanted a fling.* Or at least I thought I wanted a fling. Now I didn't know. Was I willing to sacrifice the friendship to explore our feelings further? What about the long distance? That stood in front of me like a brick wall. The thought of moving made me sick to my stomach. "I don't know. I care about you, and I know I feel something for you. Something deeper than I'd expected."

"You're scared."

"I beg your pardon."

"You're afraid to commit to something beyond a weekend fling. For years you watched your mother bounce from one man to another, up and down the coast."

"How do you know?"

"You told me."

I knew I'd regret that conversation; I just didn't realize it would be so soon.

"She moved all over the place from one husband to the next. So, you've decided to stick your pole in the sand and stay right where you are. You spent your childhood bouncing around with your mom, so as soon as you were able, you created a lifestyle of inflexible control. I can understand wanting to plant roots." He ran his hand through his hair. "But you don't realize you're doing the same thing in California, bouncing from one bad relationship to another. Searching for the right guy, in the right place. Do you know how infuriating it is to know I'm not part of that plan because I'm not in the right place, therefore I'm out of the running? "

His statements slammed into me like an NFL linebacker. My mind couldn't keep up with the information overload.

"Do you know how much it pained me when you said you were going to get serious about finding a relationship through computer dating? You can't believe my relief when each one failed."

"Gee, thanks." I said dryly.

"But you know what really kills me? You can't even fathom the thought of coming out to Ohio to see me, see where I live, and maybe see where this … us … might lead. Maybe find another place to plant roots."

"What the hell are you talking about? You've never invited me to Ohio."

"Of course I have! Dozens of times in email, text, and most recently, last night at dinner."

"I … I …" My mouth bobbed. He had invited me. But I'd brushed his invitations off as simple kindness or a joke. I lived in an area where people always said, "We should meet for lunch," you agreed, and then it never happened. I never suspected he really meant it … did I?

"You're afraid to take a chance, because you know it might mean uprooting your perfectly planned life. But you know what I think? I think maybe you care more than you're willing to admit and are tempted to explore this, just a little." He pinched his thumb and forefinger together. "And you know what, Ms. Planner? Life doesn't always go according to plan."

The resentment in his voice bit at me. "I think I've realized that. Thank you very much," I spat, holding up my injured wrist and rising to my feet. My stomach fluttered in a panic, and I felt like a cornered rabbit. Then my confusion turned to anger. "Who do you think you are? Talking about me and my mom? *You* don't know her. *You* don't know how *I* feel. Hell! You don't know what you're talking about. How *dare* you!"

By now I was pacing the floor in front of the couch.

He clenched his jaw and crossed his arms. "I know that you don't choose relationships that will last for the long term. You're constantly dating the wrong type. Like that biker guy in Hawaii."

Umph. He made a direct hit with that painful truth, and I lashed back at him. "You think you know me. You don't know shit! You don't know *a damned thing* about me, Adam Patterson."

He flinched.

That was a low blow. I knew the moment it slipped out of my mouth. Besides Sophie, Adam probably knew me better than anyone. Our weekend, our friendship, seemed to be crumbling around me with every word that came out of my mouth. *What the hell am I doing? A wonderful man is asking me for a chance, and I'm panicking like he told me I'm dying of a ghastly disease.* I flopped back down on the couch.

"I'm sorry." My head ached, and I rubbed my temples. "That's untrue. You do know me. Maybe better than I know myself. What are we doing, Adam?"

"Apparently, I'm making an ass of myself." He sighed.

"No. You're not. If I'm honest, I've been wondering about your feelings toward me."

"Now you know," he murmured.

"Now I know. What I don't know is where do we go from here? I can't say the words you want to hear, because I don't know my own mind. I need time to process all"—I made a circle in the air—"of this. Only … I don't want to lose you while I try and figure it out."

A wry smile crossed his face. "Don't worry. I'll always be here for you."

I closed my eyes, pressing against them with my fingers. "I'm tired, and my arm aches." It was a cop-out, but I knew he would fall for it. I looked at him. "I think I need to lie down."

Concern swept over his features. He checked his watch. "It's past time for your pain meds. Let's get you a pill, and I'll help you get changed."

Fifteen minutes later, I snuggled beneath the comforter. My silk nightie slithered across the cotton sheets.

"Get some rest. We'll talk in the morning." Adam kissed my forehead.

I pulled him down to meet my lips. The soft kiss turned into an emotional roller coaster and left us both panting. My hand caressed his cheek, but he removed it and turned away.

Sometime later, I woke to darkness as Adam climbed into bed, and the sound of the heat vents hummed through the room.

"What time is it?" I whispered.

"Just past midnight." He had the scent of whiskey on his breath.

I rolled over and curled my leg across his thigh. The hairs on his chest tickled my palm, and I kissed his shoulder. His stomach muscles shuddered beneath my touch as my fingers headed south, encountering the waistband of his boxers. I slipped beneath the elastic and wrapped my hand around the growing erection.

"Make love to me."

I didn't have to ask twice. His hand cupped my cheek as his lips sought mine in the darkness.

The lovemaking was soft and tender. I wept silently after it was over and Adam had drifted off to sleep.

Chapter Sixteen

"What's going on?" He had a panicky feeling in his gut as he stood, shirtless in a pair of jeans, staring at Poppy.

Her hand smoothed away a wrinkle on her slacks as she seemed to contemplate her next words. Luggage, packed and ready to go, sat next to the couch. She must have gotten up early to shower and pack. He cursed the Johnnie Walker he'd indulged in before coming to bed. It must have been the reason she'd been able to do all of this without waking him.

"Adam, I've been up half the night thinking about us, and I need time. Alone. I don't think it's fair to you, if I stay."

No, no, no. This can't be happening. I'm losing her. He skirted around the luggage and sat next to her on the couch. His fingers fiddled with her pink-polished nails. "What if I said I didn't want you to go?"

"I would say that you could probably talk me into staying. But it would be a mistake. Your presence overwhelms me, and I can't think straight."

"Then stop thinking and just feel." She chewed her lower lip and stared down at their entwined fingers.

"Running?" he asked.

"No," her eyes swept up.

She'd done a good job with cosmetics, but up close he could see they were swollen from crying, and sleepless circles rimmed the bottoms.

"I don't know," she whispered. Her tortured gaze locked on his. "Maybe."

"Don't go." He tucked a soft red curl behind her ear. "Stay."

Tears welled up, turning her eyes to a soft, grass green, and she mashed her lips together.

He couldn't stand to see her so conflicted. Maybe she did need time alone to come to the right answer. There was an old saying that if you loved something, set it free. He sighed, and his shoulders slumped in defeat. "Give me ten minutes. I'll drive you to the airport."

"I'll take a cab," she choked out.

He knit his brows, absorbing this punch to the solar plexus. "Your wrist …"

"I'll get help."

"When can I expect to hear from you?"

"By Friday. I don't want to leave this blowing in the wind longer than that,"

"Promise?"

He caressed her jawline with his thumb, and she looked to waver for a moment. But then she sucked in a deep breath. "I promise. By Friday I'll have my head straight."

"I'll wait."

The leaden pain in his gut was indescribable. As he splayed across the empty bed, he struggled to figure out how she'd slipped through his fingers. He mentally flogged himself regarding the scene in the cab and the subsequent discussion in the room. *Damn!* He knew she wasn't on the same page. He'd do anything to take back his words. To wait and tell her when he came out to visit Smitty. But no, he'd jumped the gun, and she'd skittered off like a scared deer. Now all he could do was wait and hope for the best. Friday seemed like a million years away.

• • •

All the way to the airport, through the interminable lines, and during the entire flight, I questioned my decision to leave Adam. My thoughts went in circles like a merry-go-round, and my stomach roiled with uncertainty. I still questioned my choice as the

Lexus rolled to a stop in front of Sophie's gated drive. As I pressed the call button, I prayed she would be home

"State your business." Ian's tinny voice came through the metal box.

"Ian, is Sophie home?"

"Poppy, are you okay?"

"No." I sniffed.

"Come on up."

The gate rolled open, and I motored up to the house.

Sophie, clad in jeans and a white, Juicy sweatshirt, stood in the open doorway. Her eyes searched my sleep-deprived features, and she pulled me in for a hug. The familiar scent of strawberry shampoo calmed my nerves.

"Come in. It looks like you need some wine."

I followed her flip-flopping wake into the kitchen.

"Sit." She pointed to one of the counter stools. Ian was nowhere to be seen. "Red or white?"

"You got anything stronger?"

Her eyes widened, but she didn't say a word; she just laid out two crystal tumblers in front of me and pulled a bottle of Ketel One out of the freezer. Her eyebrows rose in a silent question.

I nodded.

The colorless liquor splashed into the glasses, and she left the bottle on the counter.

I threw back a gulp and grimaced. Cold fire burned down my throat, landing in my churned up belly.

"Talk."

"Adam wants a serious relationship with me,"

Her nostrils flared. "And."

"And nothing. I panicked and fled the scene."

A low whistle of air blew out between her teeth.

"I'm a fool."

"Do you want to?"

I stared at the clear liquid left in the glass; the light shifted through the cut crystal. "I don't know. I don't know." My anguished voice cracked. "Maybe. Yes. Oh God, I don't know. You're right. He's right. I don't know how to be in love. And the fact that he lives in Ohio scares the shit out of me."

She nodded sympathetically. "Long-distance relationships are hard. You both have lucrative businesses and careers where you live. If this is going to go anywhere, one of you would have to make a sacrifice."

"Exactly!" What a relief to have Sophie verbalize my fears. "It's coming at me so fast. I went into this weekend thinking it would be a fun-filled sex-a-palooza. It's a mess; it turned into something more. Now we may be talking 'rest of our lives' shit. I am so desperate *not* to make the same mistakes my mom did that I'm afraid I'll miss out on my chance at love. My heart is begging to take the gamble, but my head gets in the way." I plunked both hands on the offending noggin, gripping it tightly.

"What happened to your wrist?" Sophie indicated with her glass before taking a sip. Her nose scrunched as she swallowed.

"Oh, this? I slipped and fell. It's a moderate sprain."

"Is it going to be okay?"

"Yes, yes." I waved her question away.

Her eyes narrowed. "Adam didn't have anything to do with it, did he?"

"Heavens no!" I assured her. "It was my own clumsiness. As a matter of fact, he did a wonderful job taking care of me. Better than I could have asked for."

"Good. Because if he had done that to you, I would have sent Ian to kick his ass," Sophie threw back the last of the vodka. After rescuing her sister from an abusive relationship last year, I should have realized she would look at any sort of injury with a suspicious eye.

"Thanks, doll, but you don't need to worry. Adam is not abusive. But you're a good friend for asking." My lips curved in a half-smile.

"So how did you leave it? Since you're home a day early, I imagine not well."

"You're right. He's not happy with me for fleeing, but I promised to get in touch with him by Friday. I figured I'd have my head on straight by then. Maybe come up with a plan."

Sophie's laughter trilled through the air. "Oh, Poppy. You know I love you dearly, but if there's something I've learned, it's that love *cannot* be planned. I understand you're a woman who spends her life organizing everything. Maybe when it comes to Adam you need to let go of the reins."

I bit the inside of my lip. "I'm not much of a fly-by-the-seat-of-my-pants gal."

"Maybe it's time you give it a try."

"Well. But … but I mean …"

"But, but, but …" She gave me a goofy, wide-eyed, pinched-mouth look.

"Stop it." I swatted at her.

"You've been planning to meet Mr. Right through computer dating, and how's that been working out for you?"

I grimaced and rolled my eyes.

"Precisely. You didn't plan Adam, and he may turn out to be the love of your life. Are you going to let that pass by because it wasn't planned? Or because you're chickenshit?"

I sucked in a deep breath through my nostrils. "I'm not chickenshit."

"Okay then." She nodded with emphasis.

"I have to figure out some of the logistics. My mom's coming in on Wednesday, and I have a wedding this weekend. I can't just take off to godforsaken Ohio."

"Book a Sunday flight and go."

"Go? I don't even know if I should go. Like I said, I don't know how I feel. What if we do this and screw up a perfectly good friendship?"

"That's crap. I've never seen you get so knotted up over a guy. All your other relationships were passing time. This guy's in your head." She tapped my forehead. "Look at you. You're a wreck. I bet you were up half the night stewing and chewing on it."

I spun the tumbler, but I didn't deny her accusations.

"When was the last time you lost sleep like this over a guy? Ever? You didn't give Richard this much thought."

She had me there. Even the physical distance I'd put between us didn't lessen these achy feelings swirling inside me.

Ian padded into the kitchen, wearing shorts and a sweaty T-shirt. "Sorry. Ignore me. Just popped in to nab a juice." He ducked his head into the fridge.

"Ian?"

"Red?"

"Your mom moved to New York to marry your father."

His Adam's apple bobbed as he took a gulp.

"Was she angry that she'd made the move after the divorce? I mean she moved back to Ireland, right?"

"Well, my mum had a job in New York when she met my father. So, technically she didn't move to New York to be with him. She quit her job when I came round and moved back to Ireland when I was still in nappies."

"Oh. Never mind then."

"Why?"

"Poppy's in love with her dentist in Ohio," Sophie interjected.

"Dermatologist," I corrected.

Her eyes twinkled.

Ian tilted his head. "Hmm. I can't see you in Ohio."

"Ian!" Sophie winged the vodka's silver bottle cap at him.

"What? Look at her. She's a city girl ... New York, Chicago. That's where clients are going to be for your party business, right?"

"Not helping," Sophie said through gritted teeth.

I laughed. "He's got a point. I have a hard time visualizing myself in Ohio. Like I told Adam, I love my sun."

"See?" Ian said defensively.

Sophie made a tsking noise. "You're no help. Go finish your workout." She flapped a hand at him.

Ian shrugged and headed upstairs to his exercise room.

"Ignore him."

"No, he's right."

"No, he's not. *You* need to go out there, and *Adam* needs to come here." She jabbed her finger on the counter for emphasis. "You've always met on neutral ground. You won't know anything for sure until both of you visit each other's turf." She poured another finger of vodka in our glasses.

I swallowed the shot in one gulp and shuddered; I was really more of a tequila girl. "You're right. I'm going to call him later this week and make plans. We'll visit each other's territories."

"You're going to leave him twisting in the wind? Why later in the week?"

"I need to talk to my mom."

Comprehension dawned in her eyes.

"There are a few questions I need answered."

Chapter Seventeen

A knock pulled me away from the invoice I was reviewing.

"Boss, there's someone here to see you." Sierra stood in the open doorway.

I scrunched my eyebrows; I didn't remember having a meeting. I even looked to the open calendar on my computer. No meetings scheduled.

"What's it regarding?"

Sierra shrugged. "Don't know. He said it was personal, and he's a cutie." She whispered the last part.

"Show him in." Hastily, I pulled the pencil out of the haphazard bun at the back of my head, shaking the hair loose. I swiped at the cracker crumbs littering my blouse, a remnant from a quick snack a few hours ago, when a six-foot man with silvery blue eyes stepped across the threshold. The Armani silk suit he wore fit him better than a James Bond tuxedo, and I realized he looked very much like the online photos.

His presence in my office surprised me; what with the weekend in Colorado, my mom's impending arrival tomorrow, and the upcoming wedding, I'd completely forgotten we'd rescheduled our Match.com date for tonight. However, if I recalled, we'd agreed to meet at seven. It was only ten past five now. Whatever the case, my tumultuous relationship with Adam had changed the game. I should have contacted Paul Chapman and canceled. Rising, I straightened my skirt and came around the desk. "Paul, right? I'm sorry, I thought we weren't supposed to meet until seven," I stalled. Strong, chilly fingers encircled mine.

"Poppy, it's nice to finally meet you. Let me begin by apologizing in person for missing our last date. It was inexcusable, and I'm a desperately lucky fellow that a beautiful woman like you is good-natured enough to give me a second chance." His smile softened the rugged planes of his face.

"It's quite all right. I think it was your taste in wine that decided it for me."

"I'm glad you enjoyed it. I apologize for dropping in on you like this. But I was hoping to talk you into leaving a tad early for our date."

My stomach rumbled. The paltry crackers had been my lunch, eaten hours ago. "How early?"

He flicked his wrist and glanced down at a slim silver watch. "Fifteen minutes?"

I chewed my lip. *It's just dinner, what can it hurt?* "May I ask why?"

"I'm not doing this very well." He cleared his throat. "I've come into some tickets to the opera, and would like to have time for dinner first."

Opera? My eyebrows rose. "Which opera?"

"Mozart's *The Magic Flute.* Do you enjoy opera?"

"Yes, I do, as a matter of fact." I loved musicals, operas, plays … you name it. Yet very rarely did I get a chance to attend the theater.

He cleared his throat again. "Would you be available to join me tonight?"

"This is a bit last minute, Paul. I don't know."

"Absolutely. Forgive my presumption. I should have called in advance to run this by you. It's just that the tickets came across at the last minute …" He trailed off, and his ears pinked.

I decided to give him a break; he probably had that CEO mentality—snap their fingers and everything fell into place. Dinner and the opera wouldn't be so bad. Would it? Adam would never find out. I needed to eat. What possible harm could come from a night at the theater?

"Paul, it just so happens that I have fifteen minutes of work left to complete, and then I believe it would be possible to join you for the opera tonight." I gave him a half-smile.

"Fantastic." His shoulders relaxed.

"Would you like to have a seat while I finish?"

He shook his head. "No, I have a car outside to take us. I'll wait there. Would that be acceptable?"

"Normally, I would prefer to meet you."

"Yes, I understand your need for independence and safety. I can place the car at your disposal should you wish to leave at any time." His eyebrows scrunched together as he gave me a serious stare.

"Hmm." I tapped my chin. "I think you've got a high enough profile that I don't need to worry. I'll join you in fifteen."

As soon as he was out of sight, I closed my door and zipped around to the computer to start the shutdown process, while at the same time unbutton my wrinkled cotton blouse.

A short rap at the door made me pause. Cody slipped in, closing the door behind her.

"What's with the sexy guy Sierra sent back here? New client?"

"My date for tonight. We're going to the opera. What should I wear?" A small cupboard in the corner of my office housed fresh blouses, jewelry, makeup, and a full-length mirror. I whipped off my wrinkled shirt, tossed it into the dry cleaning bag, and lubed up with deodorant.

Cody scooted over to peruse the closet's offerings. "Is he one of your Internet dates?"

She held up a cream-colored button-down, but I shook my head, pointing to the purple bra I wore. The next choice, a coppery, silk blouse with a waterfall neckline, would cover the bra and worked with my black pencil skirt and tall boots. I slid it over my head and tucked it in.

"He's the one who stood me up at Osteria Mozza." Lipstick, dangly earrings, a mist of Channel No. 5, and a couple of swipes with the hairbrush completed the ensemble.

"The one who bought you that outrageously priced bottle of wine."

"The very one." I stood back to assess.

"Nice. I'll keep my fingers crossed for you that he doesn't end up being as disastrous as your other computer dates. By the way, you haven't given me a debrief on your weekend expedition. And what's the story on your wrist?"

I'm a horrible person. Adam would be hurt if he found out about this. I stuck my tongue out at myself. "It's a long story."

"Tell me the bare minimum. Did you have smokin' hot sex?"

Guilt ate at me, and the Jiminy Cricket on my shoulder whispered in my ear. I sighed. "I fell on my ass and sprained my wrist. And, yes, the weekend included mind-blowing sex."

Cody rubbed her hands together. "Details, details. Did you leave the room at all? Is he as good in bed as you remembered? Do you think you'll plan another weekend hookup?"

I closed my eyes against her barrage of questions and pinched the bridge of my nose. "It's complicated. We had good sex, but … it may be more than a weekend sexcursion."

"Oooh, really? You and the doctor? Sooo … what about this guy? Is he just a free meal, or are you leaving your options open?"

"Um … let's say free meal … and networking connection and … possible future business opportunities." *Yes, that's the ticket. This is business; it's not personal.* After all, Paul Chapman was a millionaire. Surely he held private and corporate events and parties throughout the year. *Whew. Guilt trip averted.*

At least that's what I told myself.

"Gotcha." Cody clicked her tongue and winked at me.

My fifteen minutes were up. "Do me a favor; call me in about half an hour. If I don't pick up, everything's fine. If I do, you'll be my emergency exit strategy."

Cody gave the thumbs up as I tucked the phone into my purse and hustled down the hall to reception.

"Sierra, I'm leaving early. Please send all my calls to voicemail, and if it's slow, feel free to leave early yourself."

"Sure, boss. You going out with that silver fox?" She wiggled her eyebrows.

"We're going to the opera."

"Don't do anything I wouldn't do. Which pretty much leaves you wide open."

Sierra's snorting mirth followed me out the door. A Mercedes-Benz limousine idled across four parking spaces. A stocky driver, who looked like he'd taken a left hook to his nose, stood by the back door and opened it as I approached the vehicle. His jacket shifted, and I caught a flash of a holstered gun as I slid onto the leather seat next to Paul.

"You look stunning."

"Thank you. Are we in danger?"

Paul's brow furrowed, and his lips turned down. "Not that I know of."

"Then, what's with Odd Job and the gun?"

His expression cleared. "Joe is my driver and bodyguard."

"I figured that. Are you a target for someone in particular, or just in general? You're not going to use me as a human shield or anything if the bullets start flying?"

A smile lit his features. "Nothing in particular tonight; it's just general security. And no, I won't be using you as a human shield."

"Well, that's a relief."

"I can't speak for Joe, however."

"Good to know."

Chapter Eighteen

"I'm sorry sir, but the part has to be flown in from Michigan and won't be here until tomorrow. You'll need to make alternative plans if you have to return to LA tonight." Edgar, our skinny, middle-aged pilot explained.

Paul grimaced, and my shoulders drooped.

Our evening began with a ride up to San Francisco on Paul's private jet. I took it in stride, as though these kinds of things happened to me every day, but I'll admit I was impressed with the fancy cream-colored jet. For dinner, the flight attendant served a delicious filet mignon with baby greens. The meal was plated as beautifully as any five star restaurant, and the place settings included crystal wine glasses. Following the flight, another limousine picked us up and drove to the Opera House, where Paul had obtained orchestra seats, dead center, a dozen rows from the stage.

As nice as the evening had been, it was now close to midnight, the tiny airport was practically deserted, and my wrist ached from the long day. Paul was a nice man, and the evening had gone better than I'd come to expect from my computer dates, but he was no Adam. I'd spent the evening comparing the two and felt like a fool for agreeing to go on this date. The pilot's bad news made me want to cry. I was desperate to get home to bed, and I didn't relish the idea of a six-hour car ride back to LA.

Paul and the pilot were discussing the possibility of a helicopter, when the door to the tarmac swooshed open.

A bowed head wearing an LA Lakers ball cap and beat-up bomber jacket entered. "Yeah, yeah, I can do that. Have Joan call me Friday to confirm," his gruff voice rumbled into the phone.

Paul and the pilot stepped out of the way, but I recognized that gravelly voice and remained in the newcomer's path.

"Chuck?"

The head popped up, and a familiar grizzled mien met mine. "I need to go. I'll call you back." A wrinkled finger pointed at me. "Campbell's redhead, right?"

I smiled, pleased he'd remembered.

"How are you?" he asked.

"I'm good. How about yourself?"

His callused hand gripped mine. "Well, I'm not dead yet."

"And that's a good thing, right?" I laughed.

"It is today. You look mighty snazzy. What are you doing here?"

"I'm here with my friend Paul. We just saw *The Magic Flute*, at the Opera House." My head swiveled, "Paul Chapman, meet Chuck. Chuck likes to throw people out of his plane."

Chuck shook a finger at me. "Only when they're wearing parachutes and if I don't like them, young lady. The rest of the fools get out all on their own."

"That's an interesting hobby." Paul's voice rumbled over our laughter, and the two shook hands.

"Is that your Gulfstream out there?" Chuck asked.

Paul cleared his throat. "That would be mine."

Chuck whistled through his teeth. "She sure is a pretty one."

"Unfortunately, it seems there's a bit of a mechanical issue, and it doesn't look like we'll be able to take off," I explained. "What are you doing here?"

"Just flew a couple of the stunt guys up here for a shoot in the morning."

"You wouldn't happen to be flying back tonight?" I asked with slim hope.

"It would just so happen that I am flying back tonight." Chuck grinned. "You need a lift, little lady?"

I returned Chuck's grin. "I would love one."

"You have space for two?" Paul asked hopefully.

"Nope."

I had to bite my lips to keep from laughing at Paul's disappointed expression.

"Of course, I could pay you. Name your price," he said.

"A million dollars," Chuck deadpanned.

Paul's pilot, who had been watching the exchange, gasped.

"Do you take credit cards?" Paul pulled a wallet out of his coat pocket.

"High roller you got here, Red." Chuck let out a wheezing laugh and slapped Paul on the shoulder. "Tell you what, you chip in for the fuel and we'll call it even."

"How about I cover all the fuel?"

"You're on. I've got to hit the head," Chuck hooked a thumb over his shoulder, "and run through the flight checklist before we take off. Why don't you two wait here?"

"Will do," I said.

Paul and I looked at each other.

"You're quite a resourceful woman to have on hand."

My brows rose. "I try."

"So, skydiving? Is that how you hurt your wrist?"

Bless Paul for being such a gentleman. His eyes had drifted over to the brace on numerous occasions, but he'd never brought it up, and I hadn't explained. I snorted. "Not on your life. I met Chuck on a blind date setup. After embarrassing myself and hyperventilating, Chuck took pity on me, and instead we went for a leisure flight along the coast. This," I held up the brace, "I acquired tripping over my own two feet."

He nodded.

"By the way, we should probably arrange for some transportation. Chuck flies into a little airport in Malibu. You still have Odd Job and the limo on the clock, or should we call for a cab?"

"No problem. I'll take care of it." Paul pulled a phone out of his pocket and turned away to make his call.

A few hours later, the limo rolled up to my townhouse.

"Sorry, this night didn't go as smoothly as I'd hoped."

"Forget it. I'm a party planner, I know all about unexpected twists to original plans." I opened my door.

"Can I see you again?"

The question of the night. I'd had a perfectly fine time with Paul, and if he'd shown up for our original date, I might not have accepted Adam's weekend invitation. Things might have gone very differently. But Paul hadn't shown up, and I did meet with Adam. And like lenses shifting into focus, the epiphany came to me. I was falling for Adam. I'd thought about him all night because I wanted to be with him. Going on a nice date made me realize the truth. I was sitting in a big limousine with the wrong guy.

I shifted to face Mr. Not-so-right. "Paul, I had a nice time tonight."

"I feel a 'but' coming."

"When we made this date, there wasn't someone in my life."

"And now there is?"

I sighed. "Yes, I'm afraid so."

"I kind of thought you were keeping me at a distance. When? Sounds recent."

"A man I've known for a while, but this weekend I realized that it's turned into something more."

"Is it serious?"

"Perhaps. But I need to pursue it, or I'll regret it."

Paul let out a breath. "I really blew my chance, missing our first date."

"No ... well, maybe." I turned down my lips sympathetically.

"That'll teach me."

"Sorry. Keep me in mind for your next corporate event." I exited and closed the door.

"Poppy."

I leaned down to peer through the lowering window.

"If things don't work out, give me a call." He handed me his business card with his private cell number scribbled on the front.

"You're at the top of the list, Paul."

A niggling of doubt itched my brain as I keyed into the house. *Should I tell Adam about my date with Paul? Was I willing to risk his wrath, or worse, hurting him?* It would be ridiculously late to call him now, and I didn't want to write it in an email. Moreover, I still felt the need to talk with my mom. Even being all grown up, some childhood hurts ran deep, and I needed to move past them before moving forward with Adam. I flopped down on the couch, threw an arm across my eyes and groaned. Relationships were much harder than jumping out of an airplane.

Chapter Nineteen

All settled at the hotel. I'm in room 264.

The luncheon was in full swing when Mom's text arrived. I'd wanted to pick her up at the airport, but her flight arrived at eleven, and there simply wasn't enough time to fetch her and get to the venue on time for prep. Mom waved away my concerns and insisted a taxi would be fine.

Good. Dinner at 7? I'll come to your room.
Fine. Going to take a nap. See you later.

"Excuse me, can you tell me where the ladies room is?" One of the white-haired attendees drew my attention, and I slipped the phone back into my pocket.

"Yes. Go down this hall and turn right. It's the second door on your left." I turned my attention back to the DAR party at hand.

A few hours later, my knuckles rapped against the plywood underneath the numbers 264. The door swung open, and the soft scent of orange blossom and jasmine wafted out. Tatiana, Mom's signature scent, hadn't changed; the smell evoked visions of childhood when I'd watch her dress up for an evening out. Spraying the perfume was always her final touch. She looked dressed to the nines, as usual, in a blue-silk wrap dress that drew out the blue in her eyes. Her hair was shorter than last time, trimmed into an attractive chin-length bob. Even approaching sixty, her features and form held an elegant beauty, and it was easy to see how she'd induced so many men to walk her down the aisle.

"Darling! You look beautiful!" my mother exclaimed and held her arms open.

Even in my flats, I towered a good six inches above her as I leaned down to be enfolded into a surprisingly strong hug. "Hi, Mom. You look great, too."

She stepped back. "Oh, it's so good to see you. I've missed you.
"Yes, me, too."

"What happened to your hand?" She held up the arm with the brace.

I'd been answering this question for days now. "I tripped and fell. It's nothing. Just a sprain. It hardly hurts at all, but the doctor says I need to wear the brace to keep it stabilized."

Mom tsked. "That's so unlike you."

"Tell me about it." I sighed.

"You used to be so graceful, fluttering across the stage in your ballet tutus. Remember when you wanted to be a dancer? I always wondered why you didn't pursue that dream."

"We kept moving around. It was tough to establish myself at a ballet school and get solid training," I stated flatly.

A stricken look crossed her features, and I immediately regretted my choice of words. I didn't want this to be an awkward trip; after all, I promised Adam I'd behave and give her a break. "Besides, I grew too tall. I'd have looked like a giraffe among all those petite, little dancers." I said with breezy nonchalance.

"What am I doing keeping you in the hall? Come in."

I followed her into a nice but generic hotel room with a rumpled, king-size bed in the center. "So, where shall we eat? Any place you've got a hankering for?"

"Why don't we eat here in the hotel? They've got Italian or Thai. Do you fancy one over the other?"

"How about Thai?"

"Wonderful. Let me put on some lipstick and get my purse. Have a seat."

I plopped down on one of the easy chairs as Mom headed to the bathroom. Jeans and a T-shirt lay wadded up at the end of the bed, and bottles of lotions and cosmetics stood in a soldiers' row on top of the dresser in front of the large, flat screen TV. At least a dozen shoes piled up underneath the desk.

"Geez, Mom. How long are you planning to stay?"

"A little while. Why?" Her voice echoed out of the bathroom.

"You've got enough shoes for a month."

"I know. I got carried away. I had to pay extra for the bags because they were overweight. Don't tell Hamisi."

"My lips are sealed."

She came out with eyeliner and fresh lipstick and perused the pile of shoes, settling on a black and white spectator. "Shall we go?"

Down the hall and in the elevator Mom chattered on about her flight. The young seatmate next to her apparently had visions of grandeur with big plans to come to LA and make it in the music scene, a demo tape in one hand and a beat-up guitar in the other. Sure, I wished her luck, but realistically breaking into the music business was almost as difficult as opening a can of Spam without a key. We made small talk until we were seated and the waiter had taken our orders and returned with drinks.

"Mom, I need to ask you something, but I don't want you to get defensive."

"Okay, shoot."

I blew out a breath and wiped my sweating hands on the cloth napkin in my lap. "Why did you keep marrying all those men?"

Her lips pursed, and her eyes closed for a moment before snapping open to zoom in on me. "I know you think your old mom's a fickle flake, bopping from one husband to the next."

I didn't contradict her assessment, simply remained mute, with a neutral face.

"Initially, I wanted to find you a good daddy who could love you like you deserved and help me raise you. So I'd be the woman I thought they wanted. They'd fawn over me, and I tricked myself into believing it was love. But I wasn't being true to myself. I realized I wasn't in love and they deserved better. Then the relationship would start to break down, or I'd get bored and … well, you know." Her gaze wandered over my shoulder. "Later … I don't know … I guess I was searching for happiness from them. You see, sweetie, what I didn't realize until years later is you can't go looking for happiness from a man. You have to find it in yourself; a man can only add to your happiness. The wrong man can certainly make you unhappy; that's for sure. But if you're not happy with being yourself … it'll never work."

"Did you regret having me?" I clenched my jaw, my gut roiling.

Her flashing eyes came back to mine. "Oh, baby, *no!* Absolutely not. Is that what you think?"

My eyes blinked furiously as the tears rose to the surface; I looked down and surreptitiously swiped at them and cleared my throat. I don't know what I thought. Or that it mattered, or that I'd allowed it to matter.

"You're the very best thing I've ever done," she fervently whispered. "You were my rock though all my foolish turmoil. I always knew I'd never be lonely, because I had you and the two of us could take over the world together. Look at you. You're beautiful, strong, smart, independent. Lord, I remember you were always such an independent little thing. You started making dinner before the age of ten, and you were always so good about getting your homework assignments done without help. And look at you now, a successful businesswoman. I hope I had something to do with it."

I didn't mention that she never seemed to show interest in my schoolwork, much less any of her husbands. During high school, I realized that if I didn't want to be like my mother, I'd have to study hard to get a college degree and make it in the business world on my own. I didn't get straight As to make my mother proud. I got them to insure my own future success. Sad to say, most of the decisions I'd made in my life were made in a conscious effort *not* to become like her, which created different issues.

It's not like I didn't love her. I did, just as any daughter loves her mother. But I'd grown to do it with quiet exasperation and tolerance.

Our Korean waiter arrived with our Thai meals, effectively ending the discussion.

After a few bites, and without much forethought, I dropped another bomb on her. "Mom, are you here to start divorce proceedings with Hamisi?"

Her fork clanked against the plate, and she sat back in her chair like I'd slapped her. "Is that what you think? I came here to see a lawyer?"

"Honestly, I don't know what to think." I pegged her with a solemn look.

She licked her lips, then mashed them together, then licked them again. "You may not believe this, considering my history, but Hamisi is my one and only. My swan. My soulmate for life." She leaned forward, and her words held a ferocity I'd never seen from her. "As much as it pains me to live so far away from you, I'm afraid it's got to be this way. Hamisi understands me like no other man ever has. And I understand him. He's the love of my life, until death do us part."

"No more divorces?" I was pretty sure I'd heard similar sworn tributes of love about her past relationships.

She shook her head. "No more divorces. This may sound morbid, but years from now, I hope I'm the first to go. Because I don't think I could live without him."

Wow! This was a new side to my mother. One I'd never seen, or one that I'd never bothered to notice?

"So why are you here? It's not just to see me."

"Well, I am!"

"And … what else?"

She chewed her lip.

I knew it.

Her shaking hand reached for the wine glass. "I planned to tell you after dinner, but it seems it can no longer wait."

At last, we get to it.

"I have an appointment at a clinic tomorrow with a specialist." Her features had paled. A spark of fear shot down my spine, and the dreaded word *cancer* sprang to mind.

"What for? What's wrong?"

"It's nothing really. I just need to have some things removed from my face."

"What things?" I squinted at her perfect complexion, and for the first time, realized she wore heavy foundation. Something she hadn't done since I was very young.

"I have a squamous cell carcinoma right here on the edge of my nose, and up above my eyebrow."

That seemed simple enough—scary, but not like being told you have brain cancer. "Why didn't you have it done in Kenya? Don't they have doctors?"

"Not like the plastic surgeons here in LA. You know, sweetie, they're some of the best in the world, and since they're on my face …" She shrugged.

I guess I could understand her need to have a good surgeon working on her beautiful face.

"I'm having this special surgery called Mohs, which should keep the scarring down to a minimum. And they might have to do some skin grafts."

"Holy crap, Mom. Why didn't you tell me before?" Being of pale complexion, I knew the dangers of the sun and religiously slathered on sunscreen every morning. Something I'm sure my mom's generation didn't do when they were younger.

"I didn't want to worry you. Really, it's no big deal. I'm also going to see if they can do a little tuck underneath my eyes. I figure if I have to have work done on my face, I ought to get something good out of it."

"When do you see the doctor?"

"I'm having the procedure done tomorrow."

My mouth dropped. "So soon?"

"Well, there's also a little melanoma on the back of my arm that they want to get at immediately."

I felt as though I'd been punched in the gut. All the air went out of me. "Melanoma?" I squeaked. I knew that word. Melanoma was the bad skin cancer. The kind that could eventually kill you. My voice came back full force. "Where? How big? Why did you wait so long to get it removed? Show me."

"Sh. Calm down, relax."

"Relax," I hissed. "How do you expect me to relax after you drop the cancer bomb on me?"

"It's not that bad. It's smaller than a dime, on the back of my arm. The doctors are pretty certain it hasn't spread and they can remove it all. But they're going to have to carve out a fairly large chunk."

"What time?"

"I need to be there at eight."

I mentally ran through tomorrow's calendar. There were a million little details to see to before the weekend's wedding extravaganza. Sierra was going to earn her salary this week, because she was about to get a bunch of those details dropped onto her lap. I trusted her implicitly; it just killed me that I wouldn't be overseeing every bit and bite before the big day. Control freak, I know.

"I'll pick you up at seven thirty."

"It's not necessary." Her hand waved through the air.

"You're having surgery tomorrow. It's necessary." I frowned. "Why didn't Hamisi come with you to have this done?"

She pursed her lips, and her eyes darted around, finally landing on her plate. Her fork scooped up a broccoli tree, and she shoved it into her mouth. I waited patiently, watching her chew at turtle pace. Her gaze remained glued to the spicy Thai beef broccoli in front of her.

I placed my palms down on either side of my plate and cleared my throat.

"I didn't want to bother him. He has so much going on at the moment. I don't want to burden him further with a trip to the States. Besides, I told you, it's no big deal."

Alarms whistled in my head, and my eyes turned to slits. "You didn't tell him, did you?"

"No."

"What was all that crap about Hamisi being your main duck?" I leaned forward, my hand fisted, pressing into the tablecloth so hard I could feel the material's fiber gritting against my skin.

"Swan, dear, they mate for life."

"Whatever. Why didn't you tell your life mate that you've got cancer?"

She wiped her mouth with the snowy white napkin and deliberately smoothed it on her lap before looking me in the eye. "Like I said, he's very busy right now. The business is going through some changes, and I don't want him to see me until after it heals."

"Vanity? This is all about your vanity? If Hamisi loves you like you say he does, then it won't matter to him what you look like."

"But I'll remember. If he sees me with the stitches and bruises and … and swelling, he'll never forget it, and he'll always worry about more cancer. I don't wish to put pity or worry in his eyes. I don't want to bring any sort of stress or pain on him." She looked away and murmured, "He has enough to worry about."

"Mom! I don't understand you."

She opened her mouth, but I cut her off.

"No, really, you just fed me all that crap about being happy with yourself and Hamisi being the one 'until death do you part.' What happens if you die on the operating table tomorrow? Did you think of that? There's always the possibility you won't make it out of the anesthesia. How's Hamisi going to feel if he finds out his wife came here to have cancer removed, and she died without telling him?"

The tirade silenced her, and I could tell I'd brought up some issues she hadn't thought of.

Her mouth bobbed a few more times before responding. "To begin with, I'm not going under general anesthesia. It's all done with local. So there's one of your arguments shot down. Second, I'm sure this isn't life threatening. If it had been, I can assure you, I would have told Hamisi. The doctors all assured me the procedure has minimal risks."

I threw up my hands and rolled my eyes. "Fine. I can see you know exactly what you're doing." Sarcasm dripped like honey.

"Come on, dear. Don't be that way."

"What way?"

"So, fatalistic. When did you become such a drama queen?"

My eyes flared. *Me? A drama queen? Hello, kettle.*

"Everything's going to be just fine," she continued. "You'll see. And when I go home, Hamisi won't know any different."

"What if there is scarring?"

"Well, then, I guess I'll tell him when I get home, after it's had time to heal. But I'm sure it'll be fine. The doctor sent me before and after pictures, and it's amazing the tiny white lines it leaves behind. There was one woman I couldn't even tell where they had cut."

"Mmm hmm."

"Now, let's discuss something else. How's your love life? Anyone special these days, or are you still playing the field?"

She'd switched topics so quickly her question threw me off.

"Yes. No."

"Which is it? Yes or no?"

"It's yes."

"Intriguing. Tell me more." She leaned in, eyes wide, ready for the scoop.

"Fine." I huffed. "Yes, there is someone. His name is Adam, but he lives in Ohio."

"Do you have a picture of this gentleman?"

I found one that we'd had our waiter take at Elway's before my fall and slid the phone across the table at her. "Here."

"Very nice. What a wonderful smile." She tapped to the next photo, also taken by the waiter, but while I still smiled at the camera, Adam had shifted his eyes to me, and his look could only be described as ... hungry.

"Oh my."

I held my hand out, and she passed back the phone.

"What's the problem?" Mom asked.

"Didn't you hear me? O-hi-o."

"So?"

"I'm not like you, Mom. You move at the drop of a hat." I snapped my fingers. "You seemed to like it. I grew to hate it; and the thought of picking up my life again ..."

She made a moue with her mouth. "Don't allow my mistakes to affect your choices. I know you like having your roots here in California. But don't close the door on a future that could be fabulous. Remember what I said about finding your own happiness?"

I nodded.

"You've already found happiness. You're happy with your life, running your business, right?"

When I looked at it that way, I was perfectly happy. I didn't need a man to make that happen.

"The right man can only enhance that happiness. Tell me, how does he make you feel when you're with him?"

"Beautiful, happy, like floating on clouds." The words popped out of my mouth without thought.

"How are you when you're with him?"

"What do you mean?"

"Do you feel like your best self when you're with him?"

"I'm not sure … maybe. We haven't spent enough time together."

"You need to figure out if he's worth the time to find out. Find out if being with him makes you a better person."

As much as it pained me to admit, my flaky mother was right. The woman who flitted from one marriage to another in my formative years seemed to have finally figured it out.

I left my mom at the elevators around eight thirty and drove directly home. After searching on the Internet for an hour, I managed to turn myself into a shaking, tearful wreck. I'd heard all my mom's protestations about the simplicity of the surgery, but the doom and gloom I'd found on the web about melanomas and even squamous cell carcinomas had me freaked out all over again. Mom might not die on the operating table tomorrow, but the melanoma could metastasize and kill her next year.

Chapter Twenty

It was after midnight when the ringing phone woke Adam from another fitful night's sleep.

"Hello?" he rasped, sitting up to turn on the bedside light. Sobbing on the other end had him pulling the phone from his ear to check the caller ID. *Christ!* His gut clenched when he recognized the number. "Poppy? What's the matter? Is it your wrist? What's wrong, sweetheart?"

"It's m-my M-mom." She sniffed.

"Is she okay?" The tension eased off slightly when he realized Poppy wasn't hurt.

"C-c-cancer."

"I'm so sorry. What kind?"

"Hold a sec." It sounded like she put the phone down, and he could hear her blowing her nose in the background. "M-m-melanoma." A sigh whispered across the lines.

"How far advanced?"

"She said it's smaller than a dime, on her arm. What's the prognosis?"

Not good. He debated his response, but the doctor in him couldn't sugarcoat the news, even for Poppy. "I'm not going to lie to you, it would be better if it were smaller, but I've removed bigger."

"She said she's having Mohs surgery. She also has some squamous cancer on her face."

"Who's doing the surgery?"

"Dunno, but she's going in to have it removed tomorrow." She provided the name of the clinic.

"That's an excellent facility. I'll call Smitty, find out who's in charge of the Mohs surgery unit. It's a specialty, so there's bound to be only one or two guys running it."

"What is this Mohs all about?"

"It's a way of removing the least amount of skin. The cancer is mapped and removed microscopically, a layer at a time. Then the surgeon will evaluate the skin removed and determine if more will need to be done. They might carve four or five times to make sure to get all of it. With basal cell carcinoma, there's a ninety-nine percent likelihood that they'll get it all." He made an effort to sound reassuring as he explained the surgery.

"What about the others?"

"Squamous has a high cure rate as well. Melanomas are … trickier," he hedged.

"Trickier how?"

He sighed. "Some doctors disagree on the Mohs's effectiveness. The cure rate can be lower."

"How much lower?" she pressed.

Adam ran a hand through his hair. He should have known she'd want to get all the details. Poppy was too smart to take the surface-layer explanation. She'd probably been researching everything online already. "Depends on the surgeon."

A sob caught in her throat.

"Aw, sweetie, I wish I could be there for you."

"Me too," she whispered.

Her answer was music to his ears. "Listen, I want you to stop worrying. Your mom's in good health. The clinic's got excellent doctors. I'm going to call Walt and get more information about the surgical staff. I want you to get some rest. Doctor's orders. Your mom's going to need you to be there for her tomorrow. Okay?"

"You're right." She sucked in a big breath. "I need to be strong. It's going to be fine. She'll be fine." Poppy's voice cracked.

It was just like when she held it together at Elway's after that fall. Indeed, she was one of the strongest people he knew. "How's your wrist doing?" he asked in an effort to divert her.

She blew her nose again. "It's fine. Sore by the end of the day but nothing I can't handle."

"Just be careful not to overdo it, sweetheart."

"I won't. Poor Sierra's doing most of the heavy lifting. I've hired one of our part-timers to work full time the rest of the month."

That was a relief. "Good. I'll call you tomorrow and tell you what Walt has to say."

"'K." She sniffed.

"Promise me you'll get some rest."

"Promise. Sorry for waking you."

He closed his eyes and whispered, "Don't be. I'm here for you. Remember that."

Silence.

"Seriously, I'm here for you."

"I know. Adam … when my mom's drama is over, I want to talk. I've come to realize some things in the past seventy-two hours."

His heart stuttered, and the tension in his gut coiled into a tight knot. "I'm awake. Want to talk about it now?"

"No. After Mom's surgery tomorrow. I need this to pass so I can focus on us and give it the attention we deserve."

Adam had no way to interpret that declaration, whether for good or bad. Their issues would have to wait, even though it was ripping him apart.

"I understand. Focus on your mom. It's most important right now. I'll touch base tomorrow."

After she hung up, Adam stared at the phone, debating his options for about thirty seconds before dialing.

"Smitty, it's Adam. Yeah, I know it's late. Listen, buddy, I'm paying up one favor and calling in another."

...

I felt imminently better having heard Adam's calming voice at the other end. After a few minutes, my breathing steadied, the tears dried up, and my stomach slowed its quivering. I shuffled to the kitchen to pour myself a glass of wine; on the way, I spied the map of the world I kept in the hallway. I got my wine and backtracked to the map. Pushpins dotted the atlas, designating all the places I'd traveled to in red—international places like Ireland, Mexico, and Russia—as well as all the places in the States that Mom and I had lived.

The places I wanted to visit had little yellow pushpins, like Paris, Amsterdam, and Kenya. I moved the one from Paris to Ohio, then stared at that little yellow pushpin stuck in the dot for Nairobi and waged a mental debate. Kenya was eleven hours ahead of California. It would be late morning there. Mom would be furious with me. I didn't know if it was the smart thing to do, but it felt like the right thing to do.

"*Jambo*." A deep voice rumbled across the phone lines.

"Hamisi? It's Poppy, Amalina's daughter."

"Yes, of course. How are you? Enjoying your visit with your mother? Lina insisted she couldn't wait another day to come see you." His accent held a distinct English cadence from spending a dozen years studying in England, and I heard the affection when he spoke the nickname he used for Mom.

"It's great to see her. That's why I'm calling. Um, I'm afraid I may be overstepping bounds here, but I felt you should know."

"Know what?"

"Mom's not here only to see me. She's here to have some skin cancer removed, on her arm and face."

My declaration met silence.

"What kind of cancer?"

"One of them is a melanoma."

"Why wouldn't she tell me?" His voice held hurt and confusion.

"I think because they're going to be cutting her face; she's worried about how she'll look afterward."

He made a noise at the back of his throat. "Lina and her vanity. Did she think I wouldn't notice when she returned home?"

"I don't think she plans to return until she heals."

"I see." There was a pause. "When is the surgery?"

"Tomorrow. But, listen, please don't call her tonight." I rushed on, "I don't want her to get upset before the procedure. She's probably asleep by now, and I'm picking her up very early in the morning to take her to the clinic."

The line remained silent with disapproval.

"Hamisi, please?"

"I will do as you ask, only because I don't want to upset her at a time like this. It is good she'll have you with her."

"Yeah." I sighed with relief. "She says I'm her rock. I'd better go; it's getting late, and I need to get some rest myself. I just thought you should know. I'll call you tomorrow after it's all over."

"Yes, thank you for phoning. *Kwaheri.*"

"Goodbye, Hamisi." I disconnected and flopped back onto the bed, covering my eyes with my hands. *What did I just do? Mom's going to be furious with me when she finds out. Well she's just going to have to suck it up. Her swan mate should know she's got cancer, for crying out loud.*

I sat up, scooped the wineglass off the bedside table, and chugged the remains in a single gulp. My iPod's headphone wires dangled from the stem of the glass in a jumbled muddle. I pulled the mess off and untangled it. Jamming the buds in my ears, I scrolled through the menu searching for something soothing, finally selecting a Vivaldi piece. Halfway through the soft violin strains of the concerto I drifted off into an uneasy sleep.

•••

The reflection of the mirror caught the light from my phone, and I glanced down to find it vibrating along the countertop. I silenced the hairdryer, and the iPhone's tinkling notes echoed in the bathroom.

"Hello."

"Poppy," a voice boomed. "It's Walt Smith. We met in Denver."

"Yes, of course. Adam said he was going to contact you about my mother. I hope he didn't wake you."

"Not at all. Do you know who's doing the procedure?"

"No, my mom wasn't very forthcoming about details. I'll find out this morning. "

"Well, I wouldn't worry, all the docs there are top notch. When you find out, give me a call at this number. It's my cell."

"Will do ... and thanks, Walter."

"Sure thing, and call me Walt." He hung up.

I finished drying my hair and got dressed in a pair of comfortable slacks and a stretchy, green T-shirt. My stomach felt like a dirty lump of coal lay in it, and fear shuddered down my backbone. Not knowing how long I'd be in the waiting room, I forced down a cup of yogurt and stuffed an apple in my handbag before heading off to pick up Mom.

An hour later, we sat side by side in the busy waiting room, sipping Starbucks coffee. The uncomfortable, plastic molded chair had me shifting positions in an effort to keep my butt from falling asleep. On the way over, I'd wormed the doctor's name out of my mother and promptly texted it to Walt at the next red light. As I dropped Mom off at the front door, he called back.

"No worries, my dear. Your mother's in good hands. Dr. Rowan is one of the best in the nation. We've met a few times, and I attended his lecture at a recent symposium. He uses cutting-edge technology and has a high cure rate."

I sighed with relief as the Lexus slid into an open slot. At least she hadn't picked some field hack.

"That's good news, Walt. I really appreciate you taking the time to call me."

"No problem. I'll stop by around lunchtime to check on you two."

"Thank you, but it's not necessary. I'm sure you have better things to do with your time."

"Nope. Besides, I told Adam I would. Catch you later."

He hung up before I could protest any further.

"Amalina ... uh ... Kuh ... Kuh" A Hispanic nurse wearing pink scrubs and carrying a file folder struggled to pronounce Mom's last name.

"That's me." My mother popped up.

The nurse smiled and waved her back.

I rose and laid a hand on Mom's arm. "I'll be here if you need me. If I'm not here, have someone check the courtyard. I need to make some calls."

"I told you, honey, just go to work. One of the nurses can give you a call when it's all finished."

"I'll wait," I said with finality.

"Suit yourself. But like the doctor said, it'll be a few hours." She followed the nurse into the prep area.

Three hours later, I paced a corner of the triangular courtyard, dictating instructions to Sierra. It was the only place that received decent cell reception and didn't smell like antiseptic, so I'd spent the bulk of the morning on the hard concrete bench or standing in one of the three corners in an effort not to disturb other visitors.

"Confirm with the florist—they will have access to the church at two thirty, and the reception site should be turned over by four, so they can set up the table arrangements starting at four. Oh, and be sure to note that the bride doesn't want any carnations in the arrangements; she wants to substitute peonies."

"Got it," Sierra said.

"Don't forget to confirm the string quartet for the ceremony. They need to be there an hour in advance. Also, the harpist should be setup at the reception, ready to perform, by six thirty."

"Will do. What about the band?"

"I confirmed with their manager yesterday, but it wouldn't hurt to send an email."

"I'll take care of that."

"I think that's everything for now. Keep your phone close just in case."

"Will do. How's your mom doing?"

"Good, so far. They started with the cancer on her arm. They've cut on it three times. It looks like we'll be a while. We're working on hospital time, you know."

"What do you mean?"

"I've come to realize there's normal time and rat-race time. Our business fluctuates from rat race to normal. Hospital time is a whole different story. There's no hurry to do anything, and there's a lot of waiting around. The procedure only takes ten minutes. But it's another whole hour before we get back to business. Things apparently only happen fast around here if you're bleeding out or having a heart attack." I kicked at a loose stone. "Remember that, Sierra. If you ever really need to see a doctor at a hospital, complain of chest pains."

She snickered. "I'll keep that in mind, boss. You take care."

"Bye."

"Workin' hard or hardly working?"

I glanced up from my pacing to find Walt standing a dozen feet away wearing a serious mien. We met in the middle, and he clasped my hand in his big mitt.

"Thanks for stopping by," I said warmly. "You didn't need to, but it really means a lot to me."

"No problem. I'm trying to work my way into your good graces."

I worked up a wan smile. "Did you talk to anyone yet?"

His mouth turned down. "I heard they had to go in three times on the melanoma, and the cut was deep."

I nodded. "The doc said something about testing the lymph nodes."

"It's a precaution. I'm surprised they hadn't already done it."

"I'm not sure what kind of care she was getting in Kenya. Don't get me wrong, I'm sure they have good doctors, but my mom might not have let them do any more once she found out she needed work done on her face."

A crease formed between Walt's eyebrows. "Cancer's not something to fool around with."

My head bobbed, and a sigh escaped. "I know. What can I say? Mom has her vanities." I shrugged. "Do you have a minute? Can I buy you a cup of coffee?"

Walt checked his watch. "I've got about fifteen minutes."

Walt and I slid into a padded booth across from each other, sipping a cup of coffee that tasted more like black sludge than its namesake. I stirred in another yellow packet of sweetener, hoping to dull the bitter flavor. Walt must have grown immune to the taste of bad hospital coffee, because he drank it black and knocked it back without a ghost of a grimace.

"So, tell me about you and Adam. He said something came up and you had to leave Denver early."

The sip I just took caught in my throat, and I spluttered, choking and hacking into a napkin.

"You okay?"

I nodded and wiped at the tears forming in my eyes. "Wrong pipe." My voice croaked.

Walt watched as I got the coughing under control. "You know, I wasn't kidding about Adam joining the practice."

My brows rose.

"You think you have any influence over that?" Walt asked.

"Walt, you old dog. I might have a little. But it seems an awful lot to ask Adam to leave his own practice in Ohio."

He waved his hand. "California would be good for him. You and I know what he's missing out here. Do you think you could talk to him?"

I frowned. "I don't know. I'm not sure I'm comfortable with that right now. Adam and I have a few things to sort out."

"What's there to talk about? He's obviously smitten, and you seem perfect for each other." He leaned back and slung his arm across the seat.

I waggled a finger at him and shook my head.

"Can't blame me for trying. I've known Adam since med school, and I've been trying to get him to join the practice for years. This is the first time I've really seen him head over heels for a girl, and you're here. What better incentive than that?" His mouth opened wide, and I could see his fillings as he yawned. "By the way, I'm expecting an invite to the wedding."

"You're fishing."

He issued a snort. "Okay, Red. Whatever you say." His cell vibrated. "My time's up. I've got to run."

We both rose.

"Thanks for the coffee." He gripped my hand for a brief moment. "And say hi to Adam for me."

"I will, the next time we talk."

He gave me a funny look and opened his mouth to say something, but his cell vibrated again and he took off instead, tapping a message as his long legs strode toward the cafeteria's exit.

I cleared our coffee cups, dumped them in the trash on the way out, and headed back to the waiting area to see if there were any new developments with Mom.

Chapter Twenty-One

"Is this seat taken?"

Poppy swept a lock of hair aside, and, glancing up from the iPad, stared dumfounded as he slid into the chair. Then her eyes went blank, as though unable to comprehend his existence in the waiting room.

Concerned, he scrutinized her and closed her gaping mouth with his finger.

"Adam. Who? What? How did you get here?"

"This big thing called an airplane." He flashed a lopsided grin.

"But ... but ... what are you doing here?"

"I can leave if you prefer." He frowned and moved to rise.

"*No.*" She clutched at his hand. "I just can't believe you're here."

"You seemed in need of support. You sounded pretty torn up last night." He searched her face for something positive he could cling to.

"I do. I was. I am. I can't believe you came all the way here, especially after ..." Her mouth bobbed, apparently she wanted to avoid their uneasy parting in Denver.

"Was it wrong to come?" *Please say no, baby.*

"*No.* Not at all. It's really..." Her beautiful bottle-green eyes misted over, and she sniffed. "It's possibly one of the sweetest things anyone has ever done for me." She reached out to cup his cheek, and their lips met in an unhurried kiss.

"Thank you," she murmured, rubbing her nose against his.

Relief flooded his system as he encircled her shoulders. "You're welcome. So, tell me, how's Mama doing?"

"Good. They've taken care of the melanoma and are working on the ones on her face. They seem to think it'll be another hour or so. Then I can take her back to the hotel."

His eyes widened in surprise. "She's not staying with you?"

"No. Stubborn cow. She's insisting on staying at a hotel. Says she wants to be able to order room service whenever she wants." Poppy rolled her eyes. "Originally, she thought she could talk the doc into giving her an eyelift along with the surgery. But he put the kibosh on that, thank heavens. Really, not sure what she was thinking there."

"One-stop shopping?"

"I guess so. You missed Walt. He came by and drank a cup of sludge with me."

"Gee, I'm sorry I missed that." Her humor in the midst of all the worry tugged at him.

"You should be. I think it gave me heartburn." She put a fist below her breastbone and pushed. "Ugh."

"I'll keep that in mind."

"What about your patients? Aren't you backed up from last week?" Her brows V'd and her pink mouth turned down.

"I called in a few favors and got coverage through the weekend." He gave a nonchalant shrug, refusing to admit to her the hoops he'd had to jump through to make the morning flight. There were a number of favors out there that he now owed.

She searched his face, looking for something; he knew not what. "No man has ever done such a thing for me," she murmured, and he shifted uneasily.

"How's the wrist?"

Silently, she pulled off the brace for his inspection.

His mouth pursed as he smoothly flipped it over, inspecting the injury. "Swelling's down and the bruising looks better. How's the pain?"

"Not bad. I take the pain pills at night to help me sleep. I take ibuprofen during the day if it hurts."

He nodded and efficiently rewrapped the brace.

"Did Walt know you were coming?"

"Yes, I texted him when I got on the flight. Why?"

"Just wondering. He looked at me funny, and that explains it. Why didn't you tell me you were coming?"

"I wasn't sure if I could make it, and I didn't want to get your hopes up."

"Oh."

"I also didn't want to give you a chance to tell me no."

"I don't think I would have."

His brows rose. "No?"

"No." She shook her head and stared at him some more.

Emotions seemed to flit in and out of her eyes, but he couldn't put a finger on her thoughts, and the uncertainty kept him tense and guarded.

"Adam, I want to pursue this relationship thing with you. I think it's possible … you could be my swan." Her beautiful lips formed the words he'd been aching to hear since Denver.

He didn't understand why she was talking about waterfowl, but the relationship part sent him to the moon. Joy surged through his body as he stared at the shock on her face. It was as if she couldn't believe she'd just said that.

"Really?"

Her head bobbed.

He allowed a grin the size of the Grand Canyon to split his face. "That's the best news I've heard all week. Is it my coming today that tipped the scales?"

She shook her head. "You see, I figured it out during my date on Tuesday night."

"What date?" Grand Canyon turned south, joy deflated, and his eyebrows scrunched up.

"My last computer date. I'd forgotten about it, and when he came to pick me up, I didn't have the heart to say no."

What the hell? I swear this woman is going to kill me with her damn computer dates.

He opened his mouth, but she held up a hand, and he snapped it shut.

"Let me explain. We went on a delightful date to the opera. He was a normal human being and actually a charming gentleman. I may introduce him to Sophie's sister," she mused, tapping her chin. "But it was during the date that I determined what I really wanted."

"What do you want?" he asked through a clenched jaw.

"I want you. I want us to figure this out." She made a circling motion with her hand. "I don't know where it'll lead, and I'm not making any long-term plans. But I want us to follow it. If that means we'll be flying back and forth for now, that's what we'll do. I figure military couples are separated by oceans and war. What's a couple thousand miles and a mountain range? Oh, and we'll need to start using Skype so I can actually see you." She grinned.

The anger receded, and he pulled her into a bone-crushing embrace. Her breath expelled in a whoosh, and it was a few moments before Adam registered her finger tapping his shoulder.

"Too tight," she wheezed.

He eased the hug slightly.

"I guess letting you leave was the right thing to do," he murmured into her hair.

"Yes. I needed the space to figure out my head. You really blew me out of the water with your confession in Denver."

"I'm just glad you came to the same conclusion."

"I'm not sure there was any other conclusion to come to. You're fast making me realize that you're the best thing to enter my life. I don't know anyone else who would drop everything to fly to my rescue."

"I'm not so sure you needed rescuing. You're always so independent. It can be a little intimidating how self-sufficient you are."

"Maybe you're right. But I needed a friend, and getting a lover along with it ain't too shabby." She grinned.

A doctor in green scrubs entered the waiting area and approached.

"How is she, Doc?" Poppy asked.

"She'll be fine. We're going to keep her overnight."

"What's wrong? I thought she'd be released today."

"I want to run some more tests."

"On the melanoma?"

"Yes."

He seemed hesitant to say anything more, glancing at Adam.

"Oh. Dr. Rowan, this is Adam Patterson. Adam's my ... boyfriend, but he's also a dermatologist."

They shook hands.

"I don't believe we've met. Where's your practice?" Dr. Rowan asked.

"Ohio. I flew in to be with Poppy and her mom."

"How did the facial surgery go?" Poppy asked.

"We had to do some skin grafting, and keeping her overnight will allow me check on it first thing in the morning."

"Can we see her?" Poppy asked.

"Yes, of course. As soon as the staff gets her situated in a room, someone will be down to let you know where to go."

"Thank you, doctor."

He left, and wide, fearful eyes turned to Adam.

"Is this bad?"

"Not necessarily, sweetheart." He rubbed her back. "Sounds like it's merely a precaution. Perhaps, since she's from out of town, he wants to keep an eye on her. Some out-of-town patients fly the coop, and it can turn out badly."

"Will you come up with me?"

"If you want and you don't think she'll mind."

"No. I think she'll be interested in meeting you."

...

I walked into the nicest hospital room I'd ever seen: the walls were painted a soft, baby blue, there was a comfy easy chair next to the bed, and three other padded guest chairs. The requisite television hung, dark, in the left corner.

Mom lay in the bed, covered up to her chin, with her eyes closed. Bandages decorated her pale face, and her red hair splayed across the pillow.

Adam remained just inside the doorway as I approached on cat feet.

"Mom?"

Her eyes opened. "Hi, hon. They're keeping me overnight."

"The doctor told me."

"You should go on home. I'll be fine. I'm kind of tired from the medication." She started to yawn, then winced when her mouth opened too wide.

"Mom, I wanted to introduce you to a friend of mine."

Her head started to shake, but I forestalled any refusal by waving Adam forward. "Adam Patterson, this is my mother, Amalina Kwambai."

"Hello, Mrs. Kwambai, it's nice to meet you."

"Adam? Adam? Where have I heard that name?"

"He's the dermatologist friend I told you about, Mom."

Her eyes sparked, and a minute smile played at her lips. "Adam, from Ohio?"

"Yes, ma'am," he said.

"When did you arrive?" Mom asked.

"Not long ago."

"It's so good of you to come."

"I thought I might be able to help," he said with a grin.

"Thank you, but it's getting late and I need to rest. Why don't you two go get something to eat?" And with that, her eyes fluttered shut.

I leaned down and kissed the unbandaged portion of her forehead. "Get some rest, Mom. I'll be back tomorrow morning."

"See you tomorrow, Mrs. Kwambai." Adam gave Mom's hand a gentle squeeze.

"Call me Amalina," she murmured in a faded voice.

"Bye, Mom."

"Bye, dear."

I hooked my arm through Adam's and we left the room. As soon as we'd exited, I heard her voice calling me back.

"Just a sec, she needs something. Why don't you wait for me downstairs?" I turned away from Adam, but he pulled me back for a quick kiss before heading toward the elevators.

The bed made a low hum as the upper half shifted into a sitting position.

"What's up? Do you need some help?"

"No, I'm good. That's the guy, isn't it?" she whispered conspiratorially, looking bright-eyed and chipper, all semblance of fatigue gone.

There was no need to beat around the bush. "Yes."

"And, I'm to assume, he flew all the way from Ohio to be here for you. Didn't he?"

"Yes."

"He's a keeper, my dear." She scrutinized my face. "You need to give him a chance. I know you have issues with the whole long-distance. But who else do you know who would rearrange his life to fly out and provide support to you when your mom's dealing with some minor cancer issues?"

I sucked in a breath. "First off, there is no such thing as a 'minor cancer' issue. Second, I am. We're moving our relationship forward."

Her face split into a grin, and she immediately winced. "Are we talking engagement? Wedding bells?"

"Mom! No! Sheesh, we're just opening ourselves up to explore our relationship further. I'm going to spend some time in Ohio. He's going to come here. We're taking it to the next level,"

"Oh, my dear. I'm so happy for you. He's taller than I expected. I hope you find what you're looking for."

"At the moment, I'm not looking or planning, or … or … anything. We're simply going to take things as they come. One day at a time."

"Very sensible. Are you sleeping with him?"

"*Mom.*"

"Well, honey, you're a grown woman. It's not like I think you're a nun or anything, and he is quite handsome, isn't he?"

"Yes, he's handsome."

"I just wanted to caution you to use protection."

Ew! I stared at the ceiling and sucked in a breath. "Thanks, Mom. But you're about fifteen years too late for the birds and the bees talk."

"Okay, okay, I get it, and I know I haven't been the best mom to you, but be careful and keep an open mind."

My shoulders relaxed and my face softened. "I'll do that. And you are a good mother. I took your advice at dinner the other night to heart. Now, is there anything I can get you?"

She adjusted her sheets then clutched my hand, giving it a squeeze. "No, I'll be fine. You go on. I can't wait for the morning to hear what happens."

Chapter Twenty-Two

The band music rose to a crescendo as happy, drunk couples danced around the floor. Hotel wait staff circled the tables, laying down servings of white wedding cake with chocolate ganache filling at each place. I reached down for my phone, but it wasn't in the pocket of my dress where it should have been. As a matter of fact, I wasn't wearing a dress. I looked down; the only clothing I wore was a pair of white granny panties and a funky bra I didn't recognize.

Where was my dress?

With a squeal, I slapped my arms across by body and crab-walked behind a group of potted Ficus trees lined along the wall. The dance music suddenly transformed into a Black Sabbath song, its head-banging bass drum shaking the walls around me.

"Where did my pants get to last night? Poppy, *wake up*. Do you know where you threw them?"

My eyes sprung open, and the shaking walls morphed into a quivering bed as Adam crawled over me and hung halfway off, scrabbling with something on the floor. A muffled version of the Black Sabbath song continued to emanate through the room.

"What's going on?" I mumbled.

"It's my phone. I can't find my pants. You tossed them away after stripping them off me last night. Do you remember where you threw them?"

"Over my shoulder."

"Ha, ha. Very helpful."

"Try over by the closet."

Adam's naked body hopped off the bed and crouched on the floor by the closet. "Got it." He held the phone up and the song quit as he rose to full height.

Yum.

"Hello … hello? Nuts, I missed him."

"Who was it?"

"Smitty. We're supposed to get together this morning. I need to call him back."

"By all means." I yawned, stretching my arms high above my head, and the sheet fell away revealing my breasts.

Adam's eyes turned dark and hungry, and Mr. Happy perked up. "Maybe later." He dropped the phone and slid himself up my body.

An hour later, the toaster popped, and I laid a raisin bagel on a plate; its clean, square lines and bright whiteness lay in stark contrast against the black quartz countertop.

"You sure you don't want some of these eggs?" Adam stirred an egg, cheese, and ham mixture around the hot pan.

"I'm sure. I'm not much for big breakfasts." The toaster popped again. I pulled out a perfectly tanned piece of wheat toast and laid it on Adam's plate sitting next to the stove.

He scraped the egg confection out of the pan, and I nabbed a small bite with my fingers. The fluffy eggs slid down my throat. "Mmm, this is pretty good. I didn't know you could cook."

"I have a few dishes I do well. Breakfast is one of them."

"Well, aren't you a useful fellow? Good thing I decided to keep you around."

He grabbed me by the waist and slid a hand underneath my silk blouse, tickling along the sensitive skin of my stomach.

I wriggled and giggled, trying to pull away from his torturous fingers.

"What did you say?"

"S-stop it. I never sh-should have told you I was ticklish."

"You didn't tell me. I discovered it. Now,"—his fingers rose higher—"what did you call me?"

"U-useful," I wheezed. "I promise never to do it again."

The fingers ceased, and his lips moved across mine. "I don't care why you decided to keep me around."

He started nibbling the edges of my mouth, then moved from corner to corner planting feathery kisses. I moaned, and once again heat shot straight to my hoo-ha.

"Adam," I whimpered.

"Hmm?"

"If we keep going at this rate, we'll never leave the house."

"That's a nice thought." He sucked on an earlobe.

I sucked wind. "Seriously, I've got a wedding tomorrow. I need to get to work today."

He released me and held me at arm's length. "Oh, all right. If you must."

"Sadly, I must," I said with a frown and leaned in to kiss his nose.

We carried our plates to the breakfast bar.

"What's your plan today?" He scooped up a big hunk of egg on his fork.

"I'm going to the hospital this morning, and after I check on Mom, I need to head to the office. What time are you meeting Walt?"

"Ten thirty. Can I catch a ride with you to the hospital? Walt said he'd swing by and pick me up there."

"That's fine. I plan to leave as soon as we finish eating." My cell phone rang. "Hello."

"Poppy, it's Hamisi."

"Hello, Hamisi. How are you?" I'd texted him last night to let him know that Mom's procedure had gone well and she was remaining at the clinic overnight.

"I'm fine, thank you. Could you please tell me the name of the hospital where Lina is staying?"

I told him the name and her room number. "But I'll be picking her up today, possibly this morning, so I don't think she'll be there much longer. If I can't convince her to come back to my home, I'll be dropping her off at the hotel. You can call her there or on her cell phone. Do you need the hotel number?"

"No. I've just left LAX. I'll go straight to the hospital."

"Wait, what? You're in California?" But as he'd already hung up, my questions met dead air.

I stared at the phone.

"What's up?" Adam's sandy eyebrows arched across his forehead.

"Hamisi's here."

"Your Mom's husband, right? That's great. She'll be glad to have him here, especially since you've got a wedding and will be working all day tomorrow."

"No, no, no, it's not great. It's awful," I wailed. "Mom's going to have a conniption fit when she finds out I told Hamisi."

"What do you mean?"

"I called Hamisi after I got off with you, on Wednesday night, and told him the truth about why she came here. She'd told him it was to visit me. She never told him about the surgery."

"So?"

"*So?* She's going to be pissed! Get your stuff. We're leaving. *Now.* I need to do damage control." I scrambled out of my chair and raced around the kitchen, gathering my daily trappings. "We have to go." The iPhone got tossed into my handbag.

Unperturbed, Adam continued to eat.

"You don't understand. I need to get to the hospital before Hamisi." I shoved the tablet into a black-and-white tote. "To explain to Mom." A notebook and file folder stuffed with wedding materials followed the tablet, and then I slung everything over my shoulder.

"Hurry up. C'mon." I spotted my blazer on the back of a kitchen chair and snatched it up. "Breakfast is *over* if you want to get a ride with me." I removed the tote, slipped one arm through the jacket, and returned the tote to my shoulder.

"My keys, my keys." I rotated 360-degrees twice, trying to remember where I'd left them. They weren't sitting on the counter in their usual place. "Where the hell did I leave my keys?"

"Whoa, whoa, slow down. You dropped them by the front door when we came in last night. I remember them hitting the tile floor."

Of course, my mind had been on other things, like Adam's tongue dancing down my throat. I bolted down the hall and spotted them in the corner. "*Adam*," I hollered.

"I'm coming. I need to get my shoes on."

"Fine. Just hurry!"

My feet paced the front foyer; each second seemed like an eternity. Finally, I heard Adam's shoed footsteps.

"Okay, let's go," he said, calm as a cucumber.

I set the alarm, and we hustled out. Once again, I'm embarrassed to admit, I squealed out of my complex and drove like a maniac. Not exactly the type of behavior I'd wanted to introduce to Adam this early in our relationship, but it couldn't be helped. A block from the hospital, I wheeled around a corner way too fast, and Adam had to grip the "oh shit" handle to keep from flying into my lap.

"Christ!" he exclaimed. "Take it easy. You're no good to anyone if you're dead."

I wheeled the Lexus to a halt at the front entrance and threw the gearshift into park. My harried eyes met Adam's gaze. He seemed to be struggling between alarm and amusement.

"I need you to park the car." Without waiting for an answer, I angled out of the driver's seat and hurried through the sliding doors.

Bypassing the receptionist, I went directly to the elevators and pressed the "up" arrow. The elevator didn't seem to be moving fast enough, so I held my finger on the little button. Subconsciously, I knew this wouldn't bring the elevator any faster, but it made me feel like I was doing something. It finally arrived, and the lone occupant, an elderly lady with white hair and a walker, shambled forward. I smiled with gritted teeth as she moved, one, slow inch at a time. The walker became stuck on the silver plates that separated the elevator from the floor.

"Let me help you." I shifted the walker over the threshold.

"Thank you, dear," she replied in a wobbly voice, shuffling forward.

Finally, she cleared the entry. I pressed the button for the fifth floor, and just as the doors were about to close, a hand gripped one of the doors and pushed them back open. A stocky nurse in purple scrubs entered.

"Two, please," she said.

I gnashed my teeth and pressed number two. The nurse exited at the second floor. The moment she stepped off, my thumb held down the close-door button. I didn't want any last-minute riders.

"C'mon, c'mon," I mumbled under my breath.

The elevator made no more stops, and once the doors spread open at the fifth floor, I speed walked down the hall to Mom's room. My feet stopped short in the entryway. The bed was empty. I reversed and strode back to the floor nurse.

"Hi," I chirruped with my friendliest smile.

The nurse looked up.

"I was wondering where my Mom went; her room is empty. Amalina Kwambai?"

The nurse turned to her computer and tapped at the keys. "They needed to run some tests. She should be back in a few minutes. You can wait in the room if you like."

"Oh. Okay." I returned to Mom's room, plopped into the easy chair, and ran my hands through my hair.

Guilt ate at me, and I gnawed my lower lip. *It can't be that bad. She's medicated. Physically, she can't get that upset. Right? It was the right thing to do. I did it for her own good. How bad could it be?*

Bad. It could be very, very bad.

"Sweetie, you're looking a little wild-eyed. Where's your mom?" Adam strolled in.

"They're running some tests. She should be back in a few." I continued to chew my lip, and my fingernails tapped a beat against the arm of the chair.

A light bulb went off in my head, and I hopped up. Instead of waiting for Mom to return, I could head off Hamisi, and let him know that I needed a few minutes with her before he arrived.

"I'm going to go down and wait for Hamisi. Text me when they bring Mom back to the room. Okay?"

Adam shrugged. "Fine. But I think you're making too much out of this. How angry could she get?"

"Trust me. You don't want to know." I didn't know how angry she'd get, but our rocky relationship seemed to be on an upswing, and I feared what this betrayal would do to it.

Twenty minutes later, I still paced the front entrance when a taxi slid to a stop. Hamisi's six-foot-two physique exited, and he turned and bent to retrieve a small suitcase before shutting the door.

"Hello, Poppy." His deep voice reminded me of a fifty-year-old bottle of Scotch, smooth and comforting. A smile brightened his golden brown eyes, in contrast to the smooth dark skin of his cheeks. "You look as beautiful as your mother."

He slung an arm up and pulled me into a shoulder hug.

"It's good to see you," I said. "I wasn't expecting you to come."

"Of course I came. Your mother is the most important person in my life. I still can't believe she came without me."

We strode through the front doors.

"About that." I halted our steps "She doesn't know you're here. I was hoping you could wait a moment before going up to see her. I'd like to ... prepare her for your arrival."

The smile returned. "In trouble, are you?"

"Maybe a bit." I pinched my thumb and forefinger together.

"I planned to go to the flower shop first."

"Perfect."

"But that is all the time I'm willing to give you."

"That's fine." I silently prayed Mom would be back in her room by now. "The gift shop is down the hall on your left. I'll head up and see you in a few minutes."

Hamisi loped down the hall, suitcase in tow, as I headed back to the elevator bank.

I texted Adam.

Is Mom back yet?

Yes.

Argh! Why didn't you text me earlier?

All I received back from Adam was a smiley face emoticon. Sure, it was funny to him. He wasn't the disgraced daughter.

The elevator was free when it arrived and made no other stops as it rose to the fifth floor. Once again, I speed walked down to Mom's room and found Adam rearranging the pillows for her.

"Morning, Mom." I walked directly to her bed and kissed her on the forehead. The low ponytail she wore enhanced the sleep circles ringed beneath her eyes. "You look tired."

"They kept coming in to take my temperature and blood pressure. Really, I'd heard jokes about nurses waking people up to give them a sleeping pill, but I didn't believe it. Midnight and four in the morning, they came in …"

Adam and I exchanged a look, and I bit my lips to keep from laughing. I knew if I allowed it, she'd continue on her hospital care rant, but time was not on my side. I pulled up a chair and cut her off. "Mom, listen. There's something I need to tell you."

"Poppy," Adam said, but I shushed him with a hand.

"Yes?" Her brows rose.

"I ... I have a surprise for you." I made an effort to produce a big smile, but I'm not sure it achieved the desired effect.

Adam grimaced.

"And what would that be?" Mom asked.

"You see, the other day ... well, I thought ... you see..." I struggled for the right words.

"Poppy," Adam said.

"No, dear boy, let her get it out," Mom chided gently. "I'm dying to hear what she has to say."

I released a big huff of breath. "I called Hamisi the other night, and he's here now." It came out in a rush.

Mom pursed her lips. "He's here? In California?"

"At the hospital as a matter of fact. Isn't that wonderful?" I smiled brightly. "He was worried and came to see you. What a wonderful husband you have. You're right—Hamisi is your swan. He dropped everything and came to you at your time of need." I laid it on thick.

"Poppy." A warning highlighted her tone. "Do you remember me telling you that I didn't want Hamisi to know? I didn't want to bother him with this." Her eyes bore into me, and the knot of panic that had formed this morning when Hamisi phoned morphed into a big, fat lump of guilt.

"Yes, but after all that bird stuff, I thought maybe you were wrong and that he should know. I only did what I thought was best for you."

"Daughter."

Uh-oh, I was in real trouble when she called me daughter.

"One of the reasons I didn't bother my husband with this minor procedure was because he is in the middle of merger negotiations with his company, and having him fly out here in the midst of them could endanger the merger."

Oh dear. I gulped. "You didn't mention that part."

"I didn't think I needed to." She frowned as much as she was able considering the bandages and stitches. "I expected my only daughter to respect my wishes."

"Now, Amalina," Adam interrupted. "Don't you think that's enough?"

"Yes, I suppose so." She sighed. "You're lucky Adam already explained everything."

"He did?" My eyes shot to him, and my lips turned down.

"Yes, and it's probably a good thing he did. Otherwise, I might have lost my temper when you told me. Really, dear, I know it's your life's work to plan everything, but you need to learn that sometimes those around you don't wish to be a part of your planning. I'm very angry with you right now, even though I'm not blowing my top."

"Yes, Mother."

"Don't you Mother me."

"Lina, leave the poor girl alone. She only did what she thought was right." Hamisi carried a vase full of red roses.

"Oh, Hami." She put her hands to her face. "I didn't want you to see me like this."

Hamisi passed the flowers to me and took Mom's hands in his own. His long fingers dwarfed her petite ones. "Lina, *upendo wangu*, you should know better. These," he lightly touched the bandages, "don't matter. You should have told me."

"What about the merger negotiations?" Her eyes clouded, and she blinked.

He placed a finger on her lips. "They have been postponed."

"Oh, *no*. Does that mean the deal's fallen through?"

I laid the vase on the table at the end of the bed.

"Not at all. The negotiators felt it's an excellent tactic, more likely to make the other company concede to some of our demands. I'm not sure they even believe the real reason I'm here. However, that is not the point. I am upset with you, Lina. You lied to me." His deep voice resonated in the room.

Adam and I'd slowly backed out of the room as they spoke. With Hamisi's last statement, we quietly closed the door and slipped down the hall.

Adam's phone buzzed. "Walt's here. Are you going to be okay? Crisis averted?"

"Yes. Thanks for breaking the news. It was a brilliant stroke."

"I thought she might take it better from a stranger. Less chance of producing fireworks." He wiggled his eyebrows, and that beautiful smile flashed at me, making my insides turn to JELL-O.

"You were right." I hooked my arm through his. "I'm beginning to believe you're always right. Aren't you?"

He gave an exaggerated sigh. "Yes, I'm afraid it's my cross to bear. I'm always right."

I gave him a shot to the arm. "You're kind of a wiseass, too, aren't you?" He grinned and kissed my head in that sweet way of his. "I'll walk out with you. I need to head to work."

"Here are your keys." Adam dug them out of his pocket. "You're parked in aisle H about halfway up."

The elevator opened, we stepped inside together, and turned as one. A sense of rightness came over me. I laid my head on his shoulder. *Not only is he adorable, he's smart, funny, and fast becoming one of the few people in the world I know I can rely upon.*

The doctor released Mom at lunchtime, and I ran her and Hamisi back to the hotel, which both of them insisted on returning to over my assurances that they could stay with me. Mom was supposed to have follow-up appointments over the next few weeks. Hamisi, it turned out, was even more efficient than I. He arranged for a car service while they remained in town, and would be moving them into a furnished rental condo close to the clinic.

The wedding rehearsal ended by six, and with it, my responsibilities for the night. The groom's family was in charge of the dinner and had chosen not to contract with me to make those arrangements. Considering all the things going on in my life this week, I was relieved not to have that duty on my plate.

During the rehearsal, Adam had texted to tell me he was at a local sports bar having a drink and asked me to pick him up when I was done for the day. The bar was across town from the church, and what should have taken ten to fifteen minutes took me thirty-five in rush hour traffic.

I found Adam and Walt bellied up at the bar, laughing raucously.

Walt slapped Adam on the back. "Good one, buddy!"

"What's so funny?" I smiled.

Adam slid his hand around my waist and pulled me to him. I leaned down and gave him a smacking kiss on the lips. As I drew away, Adam pulled me back and plundered my mouth with his tongue. He tasted of yeasty beer. The passionate kiss made my toes curl and my belly flutter.

"Get a room," Walt hooted.

Adam released me. I covered my passion-induced muddlement by grabbing his beer and taking a good, long slug.

"How was your day, dear?" He shot me a heart-dropping smile.

"Fine, dear. How about yourself?" I returned the smile.

"Excellent."

Walt snorted, then dug a wad of money out of his pocket. He threw a couple of twenties on the bar. "Well, ladies and gents, I'd better be getting along." He gave me a shoulder hug and whispered in my ear, "You're a magic maker. I owe you one." Then he kissed my cheek.

I leaned back and gave him a confused look.

"Later, Adam." Walt waved and loped away.

"See ya," Adam called, barely taking his eyes off me.

I slid into the seat Walt had vacated. "What was that all about?"

Adam shrugged. "Ol' Smitty can be an odd sock sometimes. What do you want to do for dinner?"

"I'm famished. If you don't mind, can we eat here?"

"No problem." Adam signaled the waiter.

"So, what were you two up to all day?"

The waiter arrived. I ordered a hard cider on tap and requested some menus, which he pulled from beneath the bar and handed to us.

"Checking out his practice," he said evasively.

"How did it go?"

"One of his partners is retiring at the end of the year. Guy decided he's made enough money and is moving to Hawaii to live the life of leisure." Adam perused the menu.

"Must be nice."

"Mmm. I think I'll have a steak. What about you?"

My eyes shifted to the menu and I chose the first thing they landed on. "I'll get the salmon."

"How was your day?"

"Busy. Everything's in order so far." I shrugged. "We'll see."

"I'm sure it'll go off without a hitch."

I sipped my cider. "I've been in the business for fifteen years. In all that time I've never, ever had a wedding go off without a hitch. Something always goes wrong. It just depends upon if it's a big something or little something. Or if the bride, groom, M.O.B., F.O.B., F.O.G. or M.O.G., maid of honor, or some other non-related wedding guest decides to make a big deal out of the little something. It's funny how the littlest thing can turn into a huge blown-out-of-proportion deal."

"When does that normally happen?"

"You never know." My shoulders lifted. "Sometimes the mousiest bride will turn into the biggest bitch because the flowers didn't open properly or she didn't like the way her makeup was done. And the one who you expect to turn into a screeching monkey from the *Wizard of Oz*, as she watches a windstorm turn her chuppah into a parachute that flies off to Never Never Land, turns into a Zen master and happily holds her wedding vows in the foyer of a busy hotel without the blink of an eye."

"Who's the worst to deal with?"

"M.O.B., sometimes M.O.G., and every so often the M.O.H. who really wants to push her own wedding agenda."

Adam stared at me with this silly grin on his face.

"What?"

"You're cute, F.O.B., M.O.G., M.O.H. I have no idea what you're talking about, but it's really cute."

I gave him a shove. "Get out. Mother of the bride, mother of the groom, father of the bride"—I held up a finger as I ticked each one off—"you know, all those extraneous people that insist on getting into the action."

"Right, those pesky parents."

I rolled my eyes and took another sip. "I get it. Boring. So tell me more about your day with Walt."

"I never said it was boring. Frankly, all the things you have to organize for these parties boggle my mind. I don't know how you keep it straight."

"Copious notes. And after you've done it for a few years, you get into a rhythm. My first events had some hiccups along the way, but I was cutting clients such a good deal just to get started, they didn't complain."

"Do you think you could start a new company in Ohio?"

I stared down into the amber drink, running my fingers up and down the glass. "I don't know. It would take a while to build a new clientele in a new city. If I sold my business here, I might have enough capital to buy a partnership with an established event planner."

"Doesn't sound ideal."

I made a noise at the back of my throat, neither agreeing nor disagreeing. This was the hardest thing for me to get on board with. I loved my job here in the LA area. I was good at it. I had an established clientele as a boutique-style planner in a niche market. However, it was dawning on me that more and more I wanted

Adam in my life. And it was probably leading me to give up the career I'd established here in California. I didn't want to put a damper on our evening together, so I changed the subject.

"Tell me the full story about you, Walt, and the chimpanzee, Cha Chi."

Chapter Twenty-Three

Adam: Has the bride turned into a screaming monkey yet?
Poppy: Not yet. I'll keep you posted. How are Mom and Hamisi?
Adam: Fine. All settled. We're debating what to order for dinner. Any suggestions?

I stood in the back corner of the church as tuxedoed ushers seated the guests to the soft airs of a Bach concerto. It was T minus ten minutes. The groom was safely ensconced in an anteroom with the minister and best man. Thanks to a shot of tequila snuck in by the best man, he seemed relaxed and ready to roll. The giddy bride had arrived about fifteen minutes ago, buffed, painted, and shellacked in all her white-wedding glory. She waited in a parlor suite with her parents, bridal attendants, and Sierra.

There's a great Italian place around there. Mama something. Check the Internet.

"Boss, we have a problem." Sierra's calm voice spoke in my ear bud. "Bring the sewing kit."

Gotta run. Will be home around midnight. Text u later.

"On my way."

I hustled out a side door and down the hall to the parlor. Sierra stood in the hall next to a shame-faced bridesmaid named Carmen, who held up a wad of periwinkle satin in her hand. A ripped gash showed near the hem. I pulled out the sewing kit and went to work.

An hour later, I greeted guests as they began arriving at the reception site. Sierra had remained behind with the wedding party for post-ceremony pictures, and I surveyed the waiters circling trays of hors d'oeuvres through the ever-growing throng. A quick glance at the bars assured me they were doing a swift business.

A guest wearing a bright orange dress caught my attention and asked for directions to the restrooms. Whoever said orange was the new black hadn't seen this sad sack. After setting her on the right path, I turned and walked slap into Richard.

Yes, loathsome, detestable, cheating Richard. He hadn't been on the guest list, so I assumed he came as a plus one.

We were both so shocked to see each other that neither one of us said a thing for a solid thirty seconds. Had I still been cut up by his cheating, it would have been a crushing blow to have run into him this way. However, his appearance only made me feel guilty over the last time we'd seen each other. Now that I'd clarified a number of my relationship issues in the past few weeks, maybe Rich wasn't fully to blame.

I took a deep breath and plunged in. "Rich."

His eyes were guarded, and he turned slightly like he was about to bolt, but I laid a hand on his arm to stay him.

"Can we talk in private for a moment?"

His eyes darted to the bar. "I'm supposed to be getting drinks."

"I'll hook you up. Just a moment of your time. I promise I won't bite."

"You're not hiding any syrup back there are you?"

I shook my head.

He shrugged and stuffed his hands in his pockets.

I led him out of the reception room and into a quiet alcove. "Rich, I wanted to apologize. Your actions hurt me, and I behaved badly."

His shoulders slouched forward, and he stared down at his shoes. "I shouldn't have cheated. We were great together, and I fucked it all up. I always do that."

"Can I ask why?"

"'Cause it's what I do. C'mon, I know Ian warned you about me. I'm an asshole. What can I say? I'm the emotional equivalent of a fifteen-year-old."

"Richard, look at me."

His eyes swept up.

"Seriously, why? Was I too clingy? Controlling? Didn't pay enough attention to you? Was it the sex?"

He snorted then thought for a minute. "The sex was great. But I always felt you held me at a distance. As though there were a part of yourself that you kept hidden and I could never reach. It doesn't excuse what I did. But you never let me in, and I was never sure how serious you were about our relationship. Sometimes, I felt as though you were just biding time with me."

I nodded. He was right. "I'm trying to work on that. It's hard for me to let people in. And I wasn't being fair to you. There was someone else who may have been in my heart, but my head wasn't aware of it."

"That Ohio guy?"

My brows flew up. Rich was more perceptive than I'd given him credit for.

"Maybe."

"Are you seeing him?"

"I am now."

"Well, I give you full credit for creativity. I've pissed off a lot of women, but you certainly took your revenge to creative new heights."

I mashed my lips together to hold back the grin. The syrup and feathering was pretty funny. "Listen, I won't keep you any longer. Why don't I hook you up with some drinks now?"

"Uh, Poppy?"

"Hmm?"

"You're not going to post that picture on Facebook or Twitter or anything, are you?"

"I thought about it when I was really mad." I mused, tapping a finger against my chin.

Rich's eyes got big, and he shifted his weight.

"No, I won't do that." A sad sigh escaped.

"Uh, thanks. I guess."

• • •

The click of her heels against the hardwood woke Adam as she entered the dark house. He listened to her footsteps move around; the rip of the Velcro closures from the brace sounded loud in the quiet. She must have walked into the kitchen, because he heard running water, and a few minutes later her shoeless feet padded down the hall into the bedroom, where she quietly changed into a silky nightgown before sliding beneath the sheets up against his warm body.

Adam rolled over and curled his arm across her belly. "What time is it?"

"Quarter past one."

"How'd the wedding go?"

"Fine. Only a few hiccups. How'd the move into the condo go?"

"Hamisi and your mom are all set, although I've never seen a woman travel with so many shoes."

"I know."

"She had a suitcase just for shoes. Who travels like that? When I travel, I take two pairs. Black and brown. Maybe some sneakers. That's it."

"We're women. It's different."

"If you're planning to travel with a separate suitcase for shoes, we may have to break up."

She snorted. "Don't worry. I'm a little more down to earth. I travel with just the right amount of shoes."

"Good. By the way, their condo has a nice setup. The kitchen is full of stuff; they could probably host a dinner party for a dozen. Speaking of dinner, your mom wants us to come for lunch tomorrow, but nobody knew if you had to work. She said something about a post-wedding brunch?"

"There is one, but I wasn't contracted to organize it. Thank God. So I'm free."

"That's good."

He nuzzled her hair. "Mmmm, you smell good. Like …" he sniffed, "cake."

"You caught me. I had a piece before I left."

"Yum. Did you bring me a piece?"

"No, sorry. I forgot."

"Mmm." He nibbled her chin. "Then I guess I'll have to get my own piece of cake."

She giggled. "Stop it."

"Are you sure you want me to stop?" His tongue slid down to top of her breast.

"No," she whimpered.

Chapter Twenty-Four

The drive over to Mom's new rental condo was silent. I chalked it up to the fact that we were both tired from our nocturnal activities and that we'd be saying goodbye in a few hours when Adam caught his flight home.

"Listen, I wanted to find some time to come out and visit you. Check out your digs, see what it's like to live among friendly country folk." I gave a cheeky grin. "What is your work schedule like over the next few weeks?"

"It'll be heavy next week. I have to work a couple of late evenings and a full day Saturday to see patients I had to reschedule."

"I understand. Maybe next week isn't good. Perhaps the following week? I've got weddings every weekend through March and into April, so I'll probably need to visit during the week." I pulled into a sprawling condo complex. Adam pointed to the right, and we snaked through the lot.

"Why don't we figure it out after lunch? There's no rush."

The gear shifted into park, and my gaze turned to Adam. A strange feeling of premonition came over me. "You're not backing out of this, are you?"

Adam's eyes widened in surprise. "No. Not at all. I'm just saying let's compare calendars after lunch. Okay?" He rubbed the back of my neck.

"Okay."

We got out of the car and loaded ourselves up with two bottles of wine, a flower bouquet, and the deviled eggs I'd made for lunch.

Hamisi greeted us at the door. "*Jambo!*" He took the dish of eggs out of my hand. "What have we here?"

"Mom's favorite. Deviled eggs."

"Did I hear you made deviled eggs?" Mom's voice floated through the condo.

"Yes, you did."

"You're my favorite daughter."

"I'm your only daughter."

Her laughter trilled as she flip-flopped down the hall toward us. I imagined the hall led to a bedroom. We walked into a beige living room with a high ceiling and stairs on the right that led to a loft area overlooking the seating area. To the left was an open concept kitchen with oak cabinetry and golden-flecked granite. I laid the flowers on the counter and eyed the rest of the apartment. Neutral beige tones with modern furniture decorated the home. Rather bland, but perfect for a rental property.

Mom's bandages were gone, and the swelling had reduced since the surgery. I understood why she'd flown all the way to LA. The surgeon did a bang up job. Only a slight puckering showed around her nose area. As the swelling continued to go down, the scarring would become unnoticeable, which would be a relief to Mom.

While the boys retired to the living room to talk about man things, I helped Mom get the food ready and set the table. She'd prepared a ham, biscuits, and a salad. It was almost like that last year she'd lived in California, when we worked around each other, held a conversation, and laughed like I imagined normal mothers and daughters did. When the meal was ready, we called the men in to the dining room and sat boy-girl around the square table.

Once our plates had been filled, Mom led into a discussion about an African safari she and Hamisi had taken last year. They'd seen all sorts of wild animals and slept in canvas tents with cots. Hamisi remained quiet, allowing his effervescent wife to control the conversation while he watched with a tolerant smile, only speaking when asked direct questions.

I finished the last bite of ham and slumped back in my chair with a satisfied sigh. "That was a tasty meal, Mom. Thank you."

"I second that comment. Amalina, you made a delicious meal," Adam said.

"You're both heartily welcome. Hami, would you like anything else?"

"No, thank you." My mother and Hamisi exchanged a look. She raised her eyebrow and Hamisi nodded. Adam didn't seem to notice the exchange, but perhaps because I'd grown accustomed to Mom's subtleties, my radar actively engaged.

"What's going on?" I asked.

Mom, who sat across from me, snapped her gaze away from the silent conversation she'd been having with her husband to me. She sucked in a breath, laid her napkin on the table, and pushed her plate toward the center.

"Poppy, I've had some news from the doctor."

"What kind of news?" My heart plummeted.

"Some of the tests they ran … showed the melanoma was larger than they thought."

"What does that mean? Do they need to go back and cut more skin away?"

Hamisi laid a hand on my mother's, and my eyes zoomed in on the protective gesture.

"No, they found cancer in the lymph nodes."

The filling meal that had just sated my appetite threatened to come back up and I had to fight back the nausea.

"The good news is, I'll be staying here in the States for a little longer than originally planned."

My gaze swept to Adam, whose face had turned calm and compassionate. The type of manner I suspected he put on for his patients. "What does this mean? What kind of treatment are they going to do?"

"Surgery. Medication. There's a new drug therapy specific for melanoma on the market." His hand covered my cold fingers and gave a reassuring squeeze.

"When did you find out?" I asked Mom.

"Yesterday."

"Did you know?" I directed my question back at Adam.

He nodded.

"Why didn't anyone tell me?" I snatched my hand back and stared accusingly at Adam.

"Sweetheart—" Adam tried to retrieve my hand, but I hid it in my lap.

"Poppy, dear, we're telling you now," Mom said.

The gut-wrenching fear had me lashing out. "What the hell? You *knew* yesterday. Was this a conspiracy to keep me in the dark? Am I not a part of this family?"

"*Poppy!*" Mom reprimanded.

I regarded her, my jaw set in a mutinous line.

"You were working all day for an important client. There was no reason to provide this type of distraction on top of the other stresses you were dealing with. I decided to wait until today. And before you go ripping up Adam, you should know I swore him to secrecy because it was important to me to tell you myself."

I rubbed my temples and closed my eyes. Perhaps she was right. If she'd told me yesterday, I would have spent the entire day thinking about the fact that my mother had cancer. *My mother had cancer.* The dreaded C word. The insidious, silent killer of the human world. An awful disease we couldn't cure but that would affect every person on this planet in some manner. Mom was right. Complaining about when I was told, or who told me, would do nothing to change the facts.

Adam's warm hand gripped my shoulder.

"Are you okay?"

I drew three, deep breaths, releasing them slowly, opened my eyes, and returned my attention to him. I asked him because instinctively I knew he wouldn't lie or sugarcoat the facts. "Sorry, hon. What's the prognosis?"

"Depends upon how far into the lymphatic system the melanoma has spread. The doctors are hopeful it's localized and they'll be able to remove the affected tumors. If that's the case, the prognosis is good. If she can tolerate the new medication, it gets even better."

"When do you go back to the hospital?" I asked Mom.

"Tuesday."

I turned to Hamisi. "How long are you remaining here?"

"As long as necessary." Hamisi's dark gaze remained bonded to my mother as he answered the question.

As romantic as that sounded, I was a realist and knew at some point he would need to return to Kenya to sort out his business dealings. My mind turned over plans to locate in-home nursing care for Mom's recovery while I worked.

"I can already see your brain ticking away, making plans to organize your life around this, and I'm telling you to stop that right now, Poppy Sidwell Reagan," Mom snapped.

I frowned and drew my brows together.

"Sidwell?" Adam said.

"Her great-grandmother's maiden name. What a wonderful lady. She was married at sixteen, widowed in her early thirties with three children to feed, eventually opened her own maternity shop. So ahead of her time." Mom's eyes glazed over as she reminisced. "When Poppy was an infant, she would get this determined look on her face. It reminded me of Grammy's determination. Little did I know, she was just having a bowel movement."

My face burned in mortification.

Adam grinned, unrepentant, at my discomfort.

"*Mom,*" I ground out through gritted teeth.

"Dear, it's the truth, and the Sidwell name has been fitting. Look at your success. I swear you received your business acumen from Grammy Sidwell."

"Back to the matter at hand, on Monday, I'll look into private nurses for times when Hamisi has returned home and I'll be working."

Mom opened her mouth to speak, but Hamisi cut her off. "That's kind of you, but unnecessary. I will remain, though I'm sure your mother and I will appreciate your visits. Her healthcare is not your responsibility. It is mine. I will take care of everything. As it should be." He said this in his deep rolling voice.

If Mom had made these statements, I would have argued with her. Hamisi's delivery closed the discussion with finality. I gladly relinquished the reins of Mom's medical care into the capable hands of the man who was fast becoming my favorite of her husbands. We discussed her situation for a bit longer before she declared herself "done" talking about this morbid topic and demanded I tell us tall tales about life in the event-planning world. All too soon, it was time for me to drive Adam to the airport. Mom and Hamisi said their goodbyes, and I promised to join them for dinner the following evening.

• • •

Adam pondered the turn of events as a Coldplay song blared through the speakers and Poppy threaded her way through the busy I-405 traffic. A week ago, he lay on that empty hotel room bed, crushed, with little hope that he'd see Poppy again. And here he was with her in California, considering one of the biggest changes of his life.

Poppy muted the stereo. "Adam, I know we talked about coming to visit, but I'm not sure with my mom and her issues …"

"Don't worry about it." He shook his head.

"No, I'm sure I can work something into my schedule once we figure out what's happening with Mom."

"Poppy, stop." He placed his hand on her thigh. "Seriously, don't worry about it. You have enough going on right now. I'll make arrangements to return in a few weeks."

"You can't keep coming to my rescue, Adam," she reasoned. "It's a two-way street, and I promised I'd come check out Ohio. So I'll figure out how to make it happen."

As much as he wanted her to visit, he had a fair idea of what she and her mom would be going through over the next months. He didn't wish to add to her stress. "Do you ever shift out of planning mode?"

"Only when we're in bed." Her lips turned up.

"Then perhaps that's where I should keep you."

"Mmm, sounds good to me." She shifted lanes and slowed to exit. "But, as I was saying, I'll email some dates to you in a week or two."

He sighed and skimmed a hand through his hair. "I wasn't going to say anything until things were … more finalized, but I'm planning to talk with my partners when I return to Ohio."

"About what?" She glanced at him then back to the road. "What are you talking about?"

"I'm talking about Smitty's deal. He wants me to replace the partner who will be retiring at the end of the year."

She shifted lanes, slowed, pulled off onto the shoulder, and then turned to face him. "And you're thinking about doing it?"

"Yes."

Her nose wrinkled, and their eyes met. While her clear gaze searched his, a buzz of fear and excitement skittered up his spine. As usual she had forced his hand.

"Why didn't you say anything?"

"Like I said, I needed to finalize some things."

"Things?"

"In my mind."

"This is a big step, Adam." Her rings nervously tapped the steering wheel. "Why are you doing this?"

"You're here."

"Oh, no." She waggled a finger under his nose. "Don't make this decision solely because I'm here. That's a lot of pressure to put on a fledgling relationship."

"I'm not." He grabbed the finger and kissed it. "I thought it would sound romantic,"

"It did. You get points for romance, but I need to know more. Sounds to me like Smitty's been on you for years to make this move. Why are you considering this now?"

He shrugged. "Smitty can be very persuasive, and I'm growing to like the California sunshine. The thought of not having to shovel snow every winter appeals to me."

She snorted. "Don't kid yourself. Earthquakes and wildfires bring their own adventure."

"I think I can handle it."

"And?"

"And," He pressed his head back against the seat and closed his eyes. "It's a fantastic opportunity, the practice is state of the art with an excellent reputation, and the money is unbelievable. My jaw unhinged when Smitty threw out the numbers."

"So, it's about the money?"

"You make me sound so mercenary. It's not just about the money."

Her hair fluttered around her shoulders as she shook her head, and her signature scent floated through the enclosed space. "Don't get me wrong. The fact that there are other motivating factors is good. Money's a good motivator. Answer me this, would you be considering the position if I weren't here?"

He reached across the console and drew a finger along her jawline. "Yes. But I'm also motivated *because* you're here."

"Good." She sucked in a breath and looked as if she stared over the side of a cliff.

"What's wrong, babe?"

"Move in with me," she blurted out.

What? His eyes flared, but he didn't shift away. "That's a big step, for both of us. I planned to rent. Are you sure moving in would be a good idea?"

"Sure. I mean, yes. After all, you're willing to make a cross-country move. Whether it's for me or for any other reason, it's time I stepped up to the plate. I want to be engaged in this relationship."

His eyebrows went up. "Is that a proposal?"

"Uh, that might have been a poor choice of words." Her eyes flashed in panic. "I meant … committed."

His mouth puckered.

"I mean involved … Oh, hell, you know what I mean."

Adam held back a grin. It was funny to see Poppy this flustered.

"Crap," she muttered and bowed her head.

He decided to put her out of her bumbling misery. Lifting her chin, he swooped in for a kiss, effectively silencing her foolishness.

"Why?" Their noses touched, and their breaths mingled.

"What do you mean, why?" She sounded confused.

"Tell me more. Why do you want me to move in?"

She released a huge sigh. "Well, it's fast becoming clear to me that you're one of the few people in my life I can rely on."

"What else?"

"You mean besides the fact I think I'm falling in love with you?"

His heart bloomed at her admission. "We're moving along rather quickly. It seems out of character for you." He leaned his forehead against hers.

"I know. And I didn't plan any of it. It's unbelievable." She beamed at him. "I'm flying blind here, but if you're willing to take my hand,"—her fingers wove through his—"we can fly together."

With every fiber of his being, he wanted to bind himself to this woman. Since she seemed to be willing, he couldn't deny himself the opportunity to live with her. "It'll probably take some months before I move. Smitty is pushing me to start by the end of summer, but I want to give my partners plenty of time to replace me, so it may be later."

"I'll wait. I'll visit you in Ohio. I'm determined to make it work."

"Well, since I think I'm falling in love with *you*, then, yes." He cupped her face. "I'll move in."

"Excellent. As Sophie would say, 'we'll be livin' in sin.'"

"Must be the red hair."

"Must be."

Chapter Twenty-Five

October

"Hey, sweetie, I need to stop by the storage unit on the way home from work, so I'll probably be home around seven." I deleted Adam's voicemail; he left it around five and it was now ten past seven.

The scent of tomatoes and garlic from the lasagna take-out filled the kitchen and made my stomach grumble as I laid place settings and poured Chianti for the two of us. Adam's voicemail made the guilt I'd been wrestling with for the past two months rear its head again. In August, Adam made the move out to California. However, my cute two-bedroom townhouse couldn't accommodate all his paraphernalia, even though I'd done a fair amount of purging before his arrival. Most of his stuff was jam-packed into a dimly lit, 10 ×10 storage unit. Boxes filled with books and dishes, couches, chairs, and a dining room table stacked up along the walls with skinny alleys between. I'd discouraged Adam from getting rid of anything, just in case things went south and he ended up getting his own place. But knowing most of his worldly goods were crammed into that sad little room continued to eat at me, which is why I'd spent the morning looking at larger places.

The front door opened and closed; a sound I absolutely loved to hear. The first week after Adam moved in, it had been disconcerting; however, his presence in my life brought such joy, I couldn't imagine going back to living without him.

"Yum, whatever you're cooking smells fantastic." Adam wandered into the kitchen, looking tired but adorable in a white dress shirt and loosened red tie.

"It's lasagna, take-out. Sorry, I didn't have time to make dinner tonight. What did you have to get at the storage unit?"

"A Dan Brown book one of the nurses wanted to borrow," he said as he washed his hands. "I had to dig through three boxes before I found it, which is why I'm later than expected."

I frowned as I scooped a square of lasagna onto each of our plates. "I wanted to talk about that."

"What about it?" He slid into his usual seat and spread the napkin on his lap as I doled out salad.

"Well, I was on Realtor.com today, and there were a few places I think we should check out."

The glass of wine paused halfway to his mouth. "You want to sell your place?"

I gave a half-shrug. "Sell or maybe rent."

The glass made a sharp clink on the table as Adam returned it without taking a drink. "Why?"

"I thought we should get a bigger place so you could move your stuff out of storage."

"It's fine. Don't worry about it." He stabbed at his salad.

"It's not fine when you have to spend twenty minutes digging through a stack of boxes for a book. Listen, there was a place that sounded good. It had three bedrooms and a study with built-in bookshelves. Perfect for all your books. Hold on a sec, let me get the iPad and you can see it." I rose.

Adam grabbed my wrist and stayed me. "Just a minute."

I returned to my seat and my eyebrows quirked up. "It can wait until after dinner if you prefer."

"Why do you want to move?"

"I told you. So we can move your stuff out of storage. You know I feel guilty as hell that half your life is sitting in that dungeon of a room."

"We've been over this. I don't mind; it's not a big deal. I'm fine with the way things are, and I don't think we should buy a house together until we're willing to make a commitment."

"We have made a commitment. We're living together."

"That's not what I mean, and you know it."

"Okay, fine. Then let's get married." I crossed my arms and set my mouth in a determined line.

"This isn't a joking matter, Poppy." Adam knit his brows as he picked up his glass.

My brain must have short-circuited, because his dismissal goaded me into saying, "Who said I'm joking? I've just made a proposal. I believe I deserve an answer."

Wine shot out of Adam's mouth.

"Damn it." I wiped my face and blotted at the stains on my cream blouse with my napkin. "I'll never be able to get the stains out of this."

"Shit, sorry." He used his own napkin to wipe the table.

Silence descended as we cleaned up the mess and pretended to ignore the 2,000-pound elephant in the room.

"I'm going up to change," I mumbled, hot-footing it out of the kitchen and up to the bedroom, castigating myself as I went. *Where the hell did that come from?* It's not as though we hadn't talked about marriage, but more as something in the distant future, not two months after living together. *Did I want to marry Adam?* The question rolled around in my mind as I changed out of the blouse. The months of traveling back and forth, catching each other for a night here and there, had worn thin, and I'd quickly grown to love having him home every night. Especially after coming in late from an event; it was so nice to climb into a warm bed and have his arms curl up around me. The mind-blowing sex was a nice perk, too.

His support during my mother's ongoing fight with cancer was matchless and provided emotional relief on so many levels. I don't know how we … how *I* could have done without him. His medical knowledge alone blew me away, and I know she wouldn't be receiving the same quality of care had it not been for Adam's intervention on her behalf a couple of times.

Additionally, he'd made the ultimate sacrifice, moving out here to California. Was I proposing because of the guilt? Or was my subconscious telling me something on a deeper level? Like that Adam could be my swan.

When I returned, all remnants of Adam's spit-take had been cleared away, and a fresh square of lasagna sat on my plate.

"Will the stains come out of your shirt?"

"No, I threw it out." I cut into the pasta and kept my eyes studiously downward, unable to meet his gaze.

"I'll buy you a new one."

"Don't worry about it." I bit into the cheese-and-sauce-covered noodles.

"I believe you asked me a question."

I swallowed. "Forget it."

"What if I don't want to forget it?"

My cheeks burned, and I remained mute.

"Poppy, did you mean it?" he pressed, and finally I looked up to meet his probing gaze.

Notions tumbled around my head, but my mouth spoke without conscious thought. "I think maybe I did."

"Then my answer is yes." He drew his hand out from his lap and placed a small, black box at my elbow.

A tremor of excitement sizzled through my body as I sucked in a breath. "Adam?"

"Go ahead, open it."

With shaky hands, I reached out. The soft velvet crushed beneath my fingers as the lid opened with a pop. Inside laid an antique, platinum, Art Deco-style engagement ring. It had a round, mine cut diamond in the center surrounded by scrollwork inlaid with tiny diamond baguettes.

"It was my grandmother's," he said hesitantly. "Do you like it?"

I pulled the ring out of its bed to get a closer look at the intricate design. "It's beautiful," I breathed.

"I asked Mom to give it to me before I left Ohio."

"Before you left? I don't understand." My gaze flew to his face.

"Just in case. I figured I'd be ready, should the time arise."

"Did it arise sooner than you'd anticipated?"

"A little." His eyes crinkled merrily in the corners. "I was going to wait until Christmas to pop the question. But as usual, you surprised me and beat me to it."

"Oh, Adam." His face wavered as tears formed.

"We don't seem to do things the orthodox way, do we? I thought I'd take you out to a fancy restaurant, maybe the theater, and have champagne chilling to celebrate."

I sniffed and dabbed at my tears. "I guess I keep screwing it up, don't I?"

"Not at all. I'm thrilled." He laughed. Getting out of his chair, he came around and knelt before me, plucking the ring from my hand. "Poppy Sidwell Reagan, love of my life, will you marry me?"

"Yes," I said simply.

He slid the beautiful antique ring on, and our lips met to seal the deal. "It looks beautiful on your hand."

To my delight, the ring fit perfectly; its warmth encircled my finger as though it had been made for me. "I guess this means we're engaged."

"I believe so." He smiled right back at me, and his eyes danced.

"Are we crazy for doing this?"

"Oh, my little planner, I bet this is blowing your mind."

"It kind of is." My orderly, planned life seemed to be moving forward at the speed of a Boeing 747.

"Think of it this way—we've known each other for almost a year."

I guess when he put it that way, things weren't moving as fast as I'd originally thought. "That's right. Next week it'll be a year since we met in Hawaii. I can't believe it."

His hand caressed my cheek. "So much has happened."

"Yes, it has. I don't know what I would have done without you these past months." My mind flew back to our weekend in Denver when I almost screwed it up for good. "Oh, Adam, thank you for not giving up on me."

"Never, my love. I'd never give up on you," he said fiercely, pulling me into his embrace.

More from This Author
(From Heart of Design by Ellen Butler)

"Sophia Hartland, put that tray down and come with me right now!" Poppy hopped from one foot to another, her face agitated.

"But Hannah said they need more shrimp." I tried to carry the heavy-laden tray past her.

"Oh, bother Hannah!" Poppy grabbed the tray out of my hands and shoved it into the hands of a passing waiter, hired for the night. "Pedro, take these out to the main buffet table and replace the empty."

The surprised Pedro nodded and headed back out into the throng of party guests.

"Here, put some of this on." Poppy handed me a tube of lip gloss from her pocket. She reached behind my head, and, undoing the alligator clip, allowed the heavy, dark tresses to fall down my back. She ruffled the locks with her fingers.

"What are you doing?" I stood with an opened tube of gloss in my right hand and tried ineffectually to grab with my left the clip Poppy had removed from my hair and attached to her pants. "I need that! It gets too hot with my hair down."

She grabbed me by the shoulders, and, with a hearty shake, got my full attention. "Sophie! Ian O'Connor wants to meet you!" Her hazel-green eyes bore into me.

"Okay. Who's Ian O'Connor and why does he want to meet me?"

"What! Are you kidding? Do you live in a hole? Ian O'Connor! You know, Eeeaann Oh-Coonnneerr." She said it like I was deaf and could read her lips if she spoke nice and slow.

I shook my head, completely lost.

"He's one of the hunks on the hottest new cop show this year, *LA Heat.* It was a mid-season replacement in the spring, and it's been picked up for a full season this fall. He's so smokin' hot, women throw their bras at him. You know, he plays Ryder McKay."

"Nope." I shook my head. "Sorry. Not one of the shows I watch. Why does he want to meet me?"

"He said he liked the painting in the front hall and asked who did it. I was pseudo-stalking him, and thus in hearing distance, so I cozied up and explained all the credit went to you, my best friend and interior designer," Poppy said in a rush. "And he said he'd like to meet you sometime. And I said, 'well she's here tonight' and if he was serious I could introduce you two." She bounced up and down like a rabbit and squealed, "And he said, 'sure.'"

I rolled my eyes, always the cynic. "Poppy, he probably happened to mention it in passing, and then when you attacked, he was just being nice. This guy has likely made a beeline to another part of the house by now to get away from you, crazy stalker woman. We'll be lucky if he didn't already bolt from the party."

I loved Poppy dearly. She was my best friend in LA, and as the owner of Poppy's Party Planning, she gave me jobs that helped supplement my income when times were slow, and I was between design contracts. I met my intelligent, crimson-haired friend at a party six years ago, early in her career. This job was for a director's birthday party, and Poppy had come up with the idea of going old Hollywood and asked for my help with the party décor. I decided nothing screamed old Hollywood like art deco and created an entire theme around it. Unfortunately, Poppy had a quirky tendency to fall in and out of love with TV and movie actors as often as she changed her socks. I feared Ian O'Connor was her latest fixation.

"Please tell me we aren't doing 2a.m. drive-bys with this Ian fellow."

"Sophie!" she exclaimed. "You have it all wrong. Ian's not my latest crush. Seriously, he wants to meet you. Do you have one of your business cards?"

I always carried business cards with me, especially to Poppy's Hollywood parties. I hoped to break into the A-listers and dreamed of becoming the "it" designer. So far, my business saw mild success, but I had yet to work on a big director's or actor's home.

Pulling a card out of my pocket, I fluttered it in front of her face. "Okay, stalker lady, if this guy is still around, take me to him."

"Here. Use this on your nose. It's shiny." Poppy handed me a small compact and to please her, I powdered my straight nose, wiped a black glob of mascara from beneath my blue-eyed lashes, and slicked on strawberry-flavored lip gloss. My dark hair was ruffled, giving me a slight bedhead look.

"Have you got a comb? My hair is a mess."

"It looks good. You know, sexy messy, like one of those Victoria's Secret models."

I rolled my eyes again. I was about as far from a Victoria's Secret model as you could get. My wavy hair fell just above my bra line when it was down, which was rarely. I was about five seven and currently wore a size eight, which was thin for me. However, in LA, a size eight was pretty much comparable to a rhinoceros when a majority of the women prancing around wore a size two. Poppy, her patience finally at an end, snapped the compact shut, grabbed my hand, and dragged me into the party mob to search for the elusive Ian.

Ian apparently wasn't that elusive; Poppy ran him to the ground at the bar. All I could see was a head of dark, wavy hair and an incredible set of broad shoulders. His back was to us, and he was engaged in a conversation with a sylph-like creature barely wearing a white dress.

I jerked back from Poppy's grasping hand. "I don't think now is a good time. He's busy talking with someone. Maybe I'll meet him later tonight."

"C'mon. Don't be a chicken. Mr. O'Connor. Ian, yoohoo." Poppy waved a hand, her bracelets jingling merrily.

Ian turned and caught Poppy's eye. She crooked her black polished finger, and, much to my surprise, he disengaged himself from the sylph and strolled our way.

Taking a gander at Ian from the front was even better than seeing him from the back. He was one of the many "beautiful people" inhabiting the LA-Hollywood scene. I couldn't see the color of his eyes in the gloom, but the face was well worth looking at. A chiseled jaw and strong cheekbones flexed as he took a drink from the dark beer bottle and licked his lips. He clearly worked out on a regular basis, because his pectorals were perfectly formed and part of a tattoo peeked out from beneath the tight blue T-shirt, which clung to a rock-hard bicep. The air pressure surrounding me dropped, and my mouth went arid as his six-foot-plus frame approached.

"Ian O'Connor, meet my good friend Sophia Hartland, designer extraordinaire."

I blushed at Poppy's intro and subtly wiped a sweaty hand on my pants before taking his warm, caressing grip.

"It's lovely to meet you, designer extraordinaire." He spoke with a slight Irish brogue. He held my hand a moment longer than necessary.

Oh, lord, it wasn't enough that the looks made my heart speed up; the accent was going to put me over the edge. I could see why Poppy was crushing on this dude. I cleared my throat. "You, too, Mr. O'Connor. Poppy's a big fan of your show. She was telling me all about it."

"What about Sophia Hartland? Do you watch my show?" He flashed a perfect, white, toothy Hollywood grin.

I shook my head. "No, I don't care for cop shows."

That got a rumbly laugh. "Ouch. You're the quite the foil to an actor's ego."

Oh, geez. I grimaced. Twenty seconds with this guy and I'd insulted him. I was completely thrown off my game and saying whatever popped into my head. Generally, I had more tact. I knew better at these swanky parties. I needed to be all smiles and ingratiating to get more clients. Unfortunately, toad-eating didn't come naturally to me.

"Sorry. What network is it on? I'll set my DVR to record it. I'm sure I'll love it." I glanced around for Poppy to save me from myself.

She must have wandered off or been called away. Suddenly, I was in a crowded room one on one with this handsome Irish thespian, making an utter fool of myself.

"No, no. Don't apologize. Your first answer was best." His chuckling died down.

"Umm … listen, Poppy said you liked the art deco theme I put together. So … um … here's my card." I thrust the little piece of cardstock at him. Yikes, this was so unusual for me. I never lost my cool over a guy, especially an actor. I mean come on, an actor? What was it was about this dude that was making me behave like a stuttering idiot?

"That'd be grand. I just moved into a new place and figure it needs a lady's touch, so I could have a fancy party like this." His Irish accent pulled out the a's and rolled around in a singsong lilt.

I was relieved to be on a topic where I couldn't fail. "Sure. I'd love to see your place and work with you to create a luxurious space that makes you feel comfortable and yet is great for entertaining. If you want to give me a call, we can set up an initial consultation. I can see your home, and we can determine your style."

He smirked. "Not sure I've got a style, luv."

Back on my A-game, I put on my ingratiating business smile. "Oh, everyone has a style. Sometimes it just needs to be developed and refined. Maybe you're right, and a lady's touch is just what you need." I lightly tapped his solid forearm.

A very tall, very thin Barbie doll blonde with long, flat-ironed hair, wearing a strapless red dress and five-inch heels minced up and cooed at us. "Ian, honey, a group of us are gathering in the billiard room to play pool. Come play with us." She pouted. The way she hung on Ian's arm shouted possessive girlfriend, and the glare she sent my way declared, "hands off."

"Who's this?" Barbie simpered.

"Tanqueray, this is Sophia."

Tanqueray? Really? I did a mental head slap.

Tanqueray thrust an empty champagne glass into my hand. "Sophia, why don't you be a sweetheart and get me a refill. Can you bring it to the billiard room?"

"Hold up, Tanqueray. Sophia's an interior designer. She's not the waitress."

Barbie doll eyed my black pants, sturdy black shoes, and tailored white button-down, which clearly identified me as one of the wait staff. Her eyebrow rose in disdain.

I stuck on a honeyed smile. "Actually, I am working tonight. I help Poppy when she's short on staff." I laid the champagne glass on a passing waiter's tray and shifted my gaze back to Tanqueray, speaking directly to her with my faux smile.

"Tanqueray, Tommy the bartender is right behind you," I pointed over her shoulder. "*He* can get you whatever you need."

She made a tsking sound as her jaw dropped. Dismissing her, my eyes locked back to Ian. A muscle twitched at the corner of his mouth, and an eyebrow rose. *Oh crap.* I couldn't tell if he was irritated or amused by my dismissal of his girlfriend. I decided I'd better try to make nice and get the hell out of his presence before producing any further *faux pas.*

"Mr. O'Connor, why don't I put together a tray from the buffet and have it sent to the billiard room? It was nice meeting you." With that, I turned on my heel and strode out of sight.

Ten minutes later Poppy found me in the kitchen banging my head against the pantry door.

"Hey, Soph, what's wrong? Why are you abusing the pantry?"

"I royally screwed that up. This could have been my big chance to get into the Hollywood crowd."

"Uh-oh. What happened?"

"I allowed Ian's girlfriend to get under my skin and I was rude to her, right in front of him. I don't think he was impressed." Clunk, clunk went my head.

"Okay, honey. Stop that. You're going to leave a bruise on your forehead." She pulled me away. "C'mon. It couldn't have been that bad."

I explained our conversation.

"Ugh. Tanqueray? Seriously?" Poppy peered at me.

"Seriously."

"Gee whiz, I would've given Ian more credit than to date a woman named Tanqueray. I mean really, who the hell names their kid after a bottle of gin?" Her throaty laugh lightened my mood.

"It's probably a stage name. She looks like a slasher." Slasher is the title Poppy and I'd given to the hundreds of wannabe model slash actresses who crawled the streets of LA like cockroaches.

"Don't beat yourself up over it. There are other Hollywood schmoozers here. Why don't you take half an hour to do some networking? I'm sure you'll score a new client."

So, I handed out five more cards. Two were to Hollywood spouses, one to the wife of a producer and the other to a director. The rest ended up in the clutches of trophy girlfriends, what Poppy and I called hangers-on, also known as "entourage" to bigwigs, the people actually making the money. I didn't hold high hopes of obtaining an actual client out of anyone except possibly one of the trophy girls.

Poppy sent me home around two in the morning when the party had wound down to about two dozen older guests. All the young starlets and actors gathered their entourages around midnight and moved onto the latest "it" club to see and be seen. The maneuverings of the Hollywood grind made me glad I wasn't trying to become a slasher. There was too much relying on looks, weight, and whether or not you were liked by certain producers and directors. I was content to have my business, good friends, and my dog. Anything else was overrated. Or at least that's what I liked to tell myself.

Praise for *Heart of Design*:

"Loved all the characters in the book: Ian and his Irish accent, Poppy, her mom and the squawking bird ringtone, and the sister Holly. The secondary story line with Holly added intrigue to the book. All in all a must read!"—5 stars, Harps Romance Book Review

"Have you ever read one of those books where you go, 'What the hell was she/he thinking?' Yeah, this isn't one of them. The characters make smart choices, because the drama is generated from actual events, not manufactured from emotional outbursts. Plus, the dialogue and characters were spot on. I will read more of this author in the future."—4 stars, Musings and Ramblings

"Ellen Butler has written a witty, fast-paced romance that was just a pure pleasure to read. I could easily hear Ian's deep Irish brogue as his flirting made Sophie blush all over. It's the mark of a great writer and I look forward to reading more stories like this one."—4 Stars, Reader's Favorite

In the mood for more Crimson Romance?
Check out *Running Interference by Elley Arden* at
CrimsonRomance.com.

Printed in the United States
By Bookmasters